CATWAD

FOUR ME?

IN MEMORY OF MARILYN PELZEL,
WHO I THINK WOULD HAVE LIKED THE BURP JOKE.

THANKS TO KRISTEN LECLERC, MICHAEL PETRANEK, KATIE FITCH,
DAVID SAYLOR, AND DEBRA DORFMAN.

© 2020 Jim Benton

All rights reserved. Published by Graphix, an imprint of Scholastic Inc.,
Publishers since 1920. SCHOLASTIC, GRAPHIX, and associated logos are
trademarks and/or registered trademarks of Scholastic Inc.

ISBN 978-1-338-67089-9

10 9 8 7 6 5 4 3 2 1   20 21 22 23 24

Printed in the U.S.A.   40

First edition, October 2020

Edited by Michael Petranek
Book design by Katie Fitch

FOUR ME?

JiM BeNTON

AN IMPRINT OF

📖 SCHOLASTIC

BEWARE

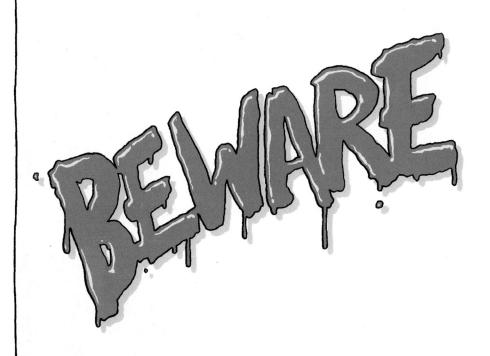

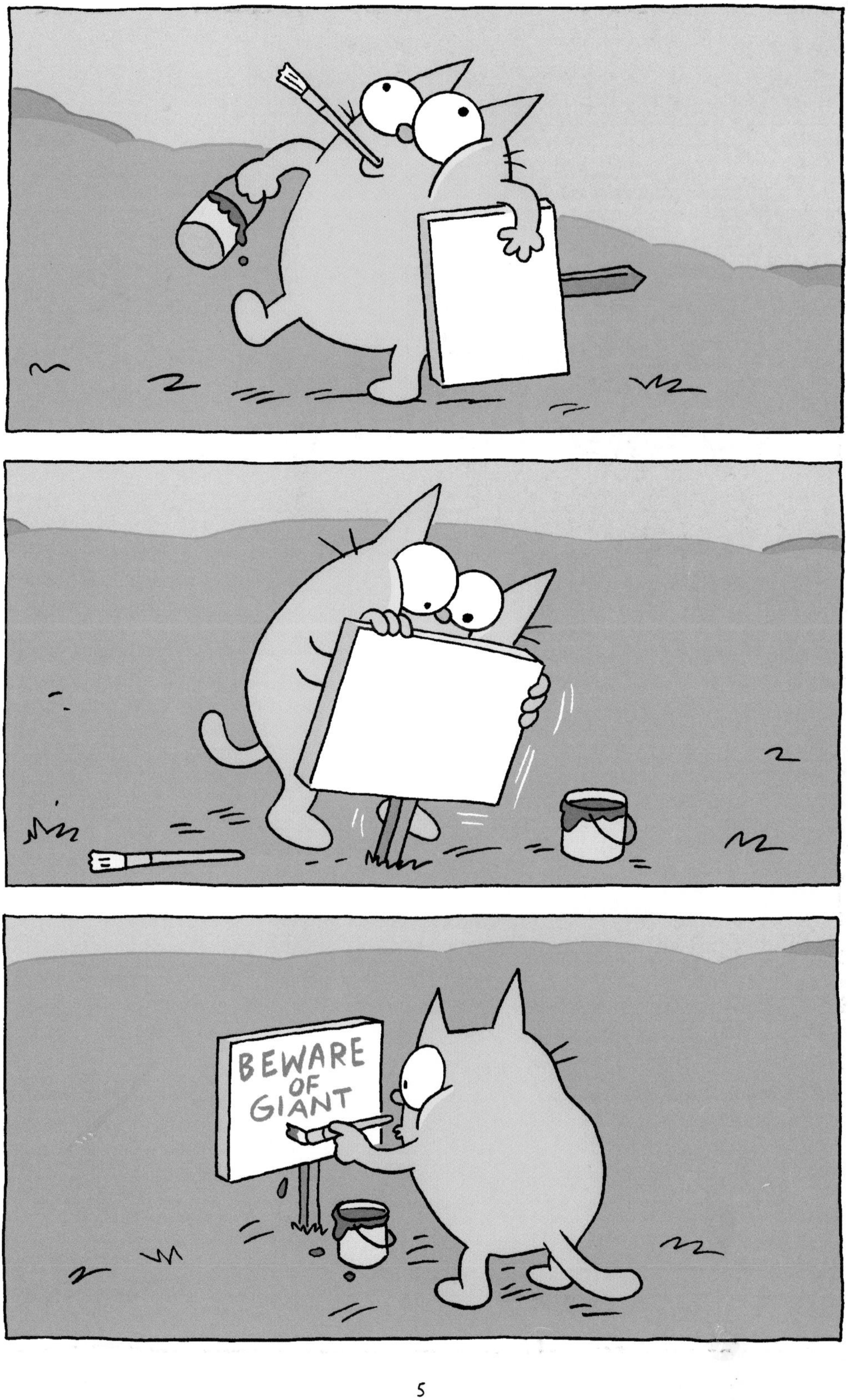
BEWARE
OF
GIANT

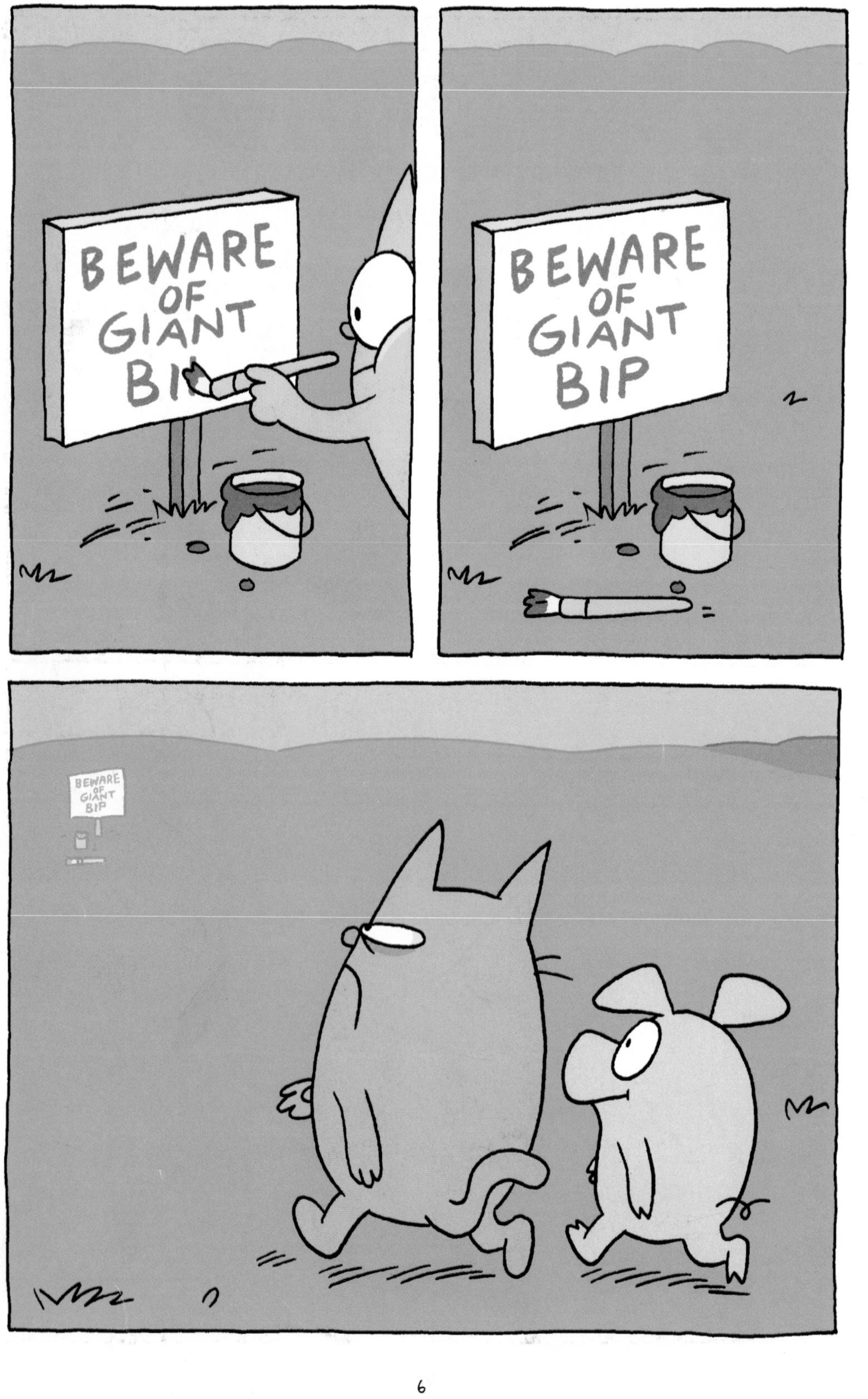
BEWARE OF GIANT BI
BEWARE OF GIANT BIP
BEWARE OF GIANT BIP

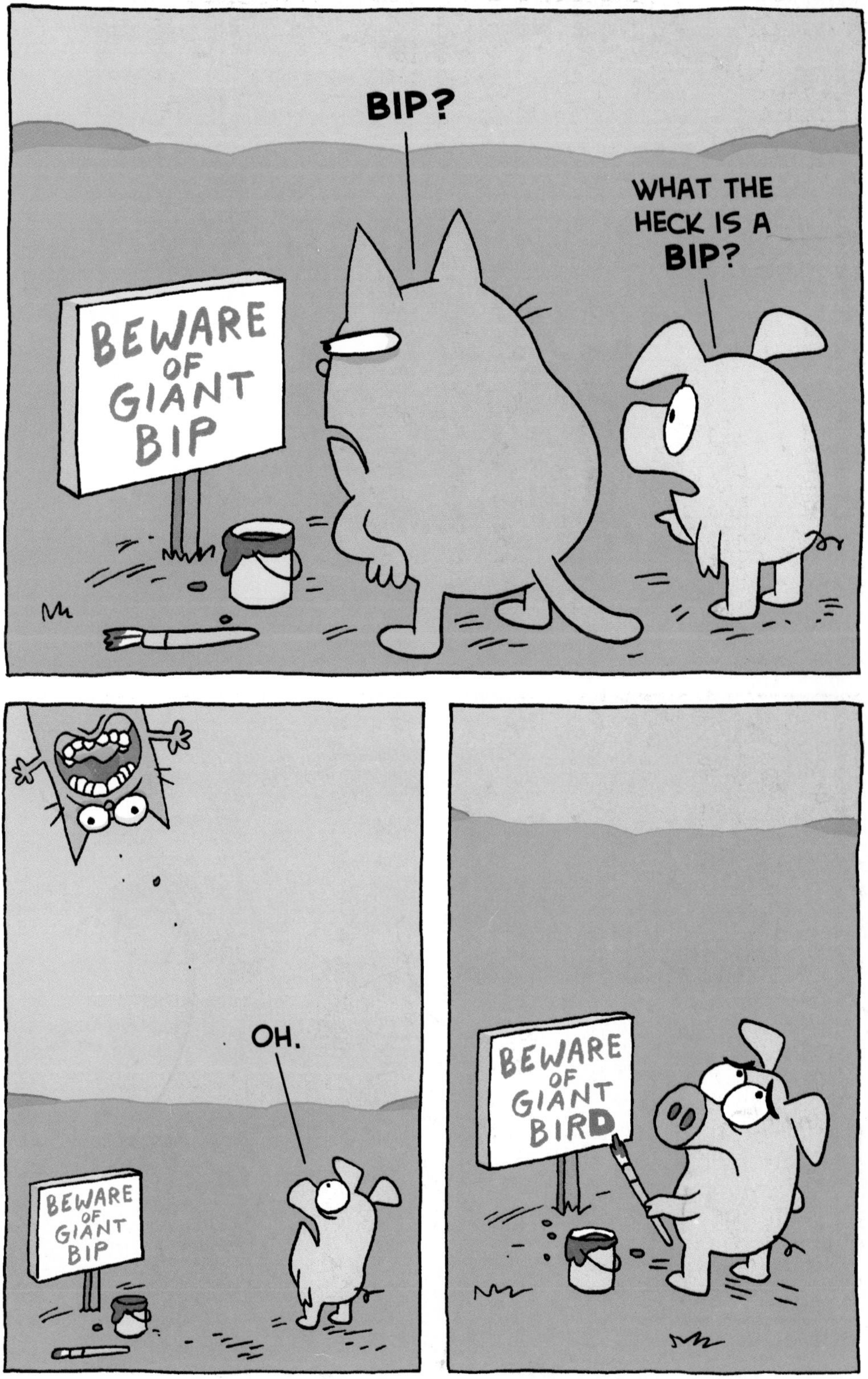
BEWARE OF GIANT BIP
BIP?
WHAT THE HECK IS A BIP?
OH.
BEWARE OF GIANT BIP
BEWARE OF GIANT BIRD

GOLF

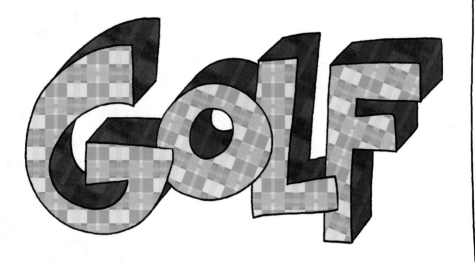

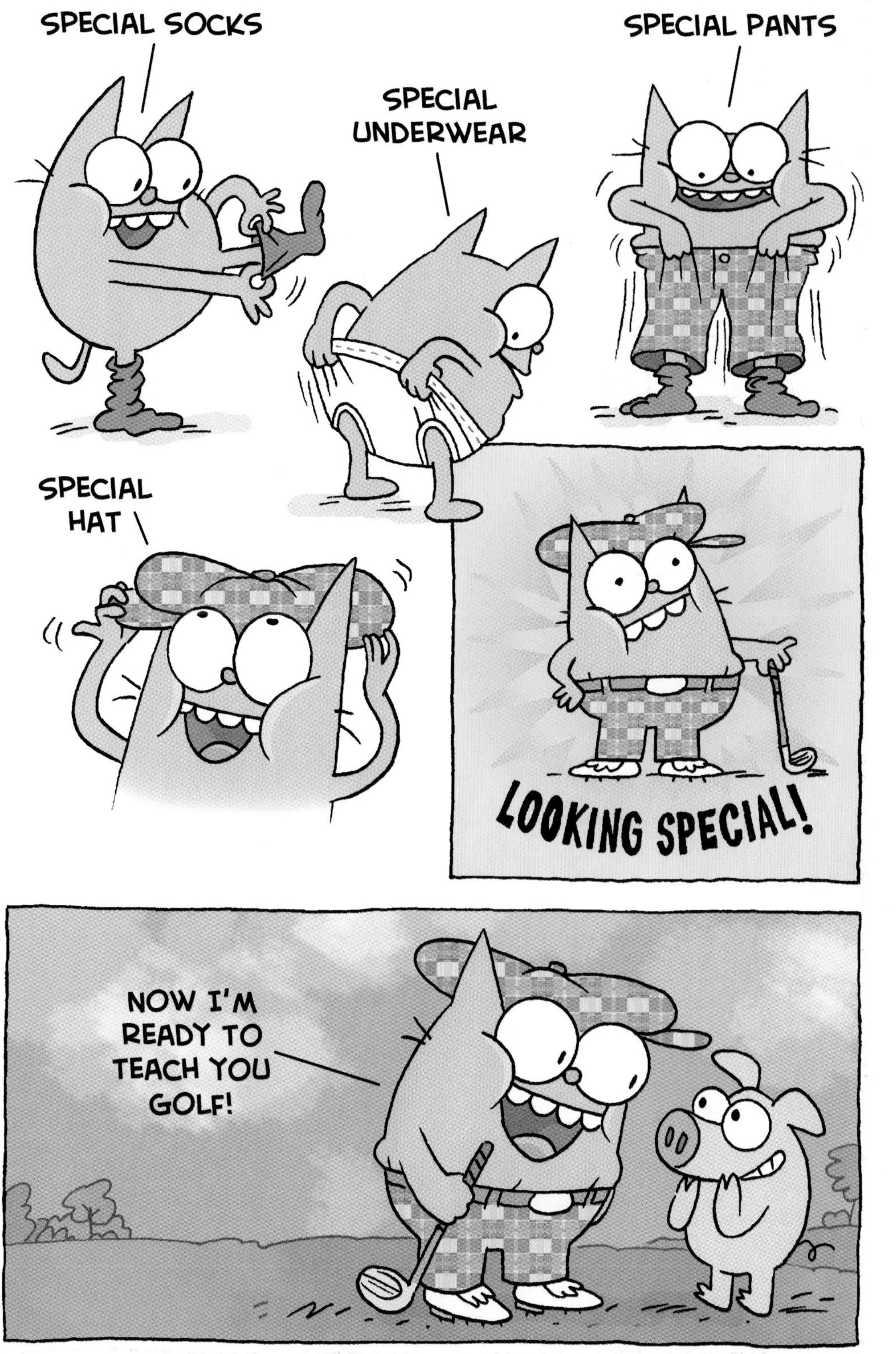
SPECIAL SOCKS
SPECIAL UNDERWEAR
SPECIAL PANTS
SPECIAL HAT
LOOKING SPECIAL!
NOW I'M READY TO TEACH YOU GOLF!

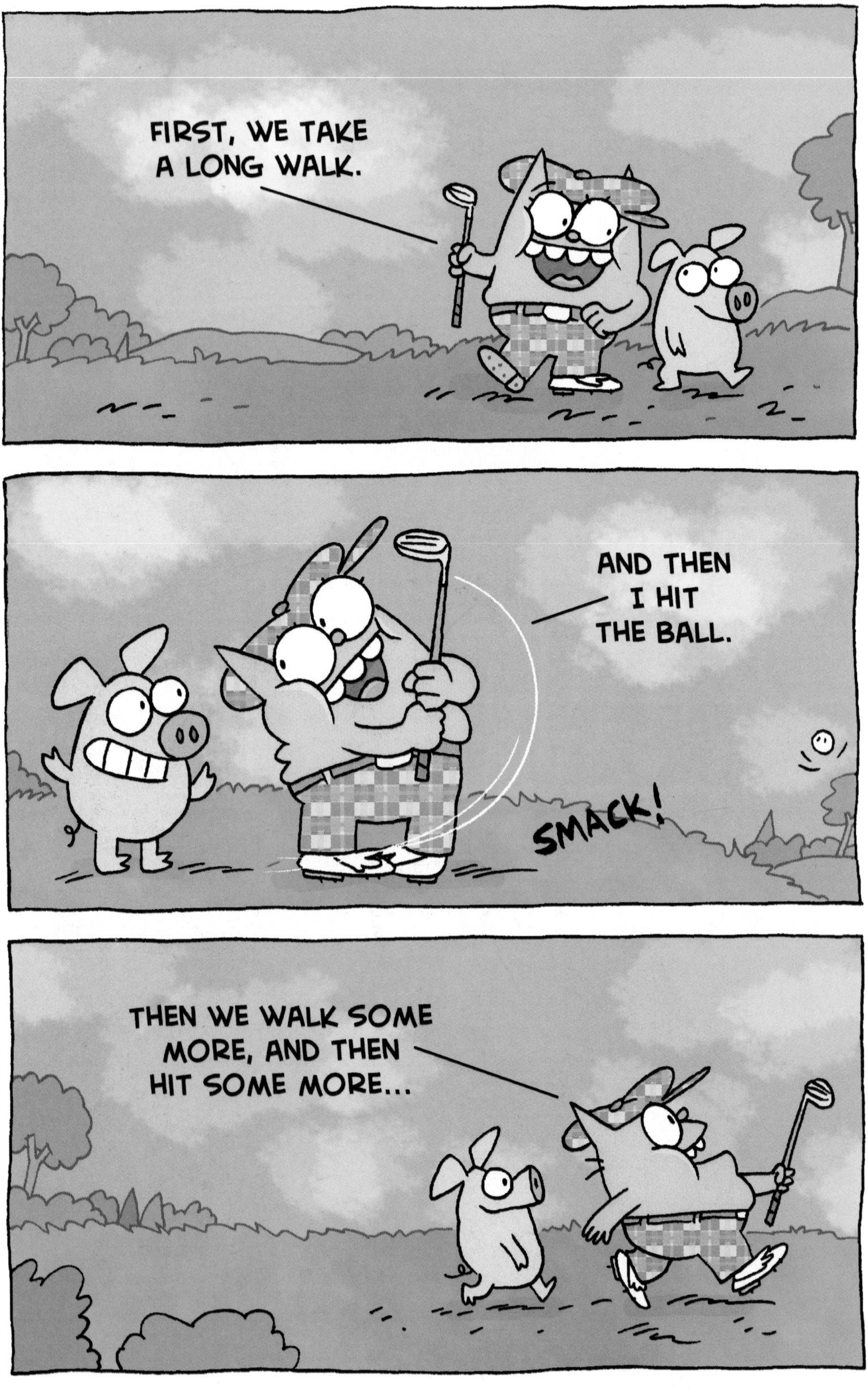
FIRST, WE TAKE A LONG WALK.
AND THEN I HIT THE BALL.
SMACK!
THEN WE WALK SOME MORE, AND THEN HIT SOME MORE...

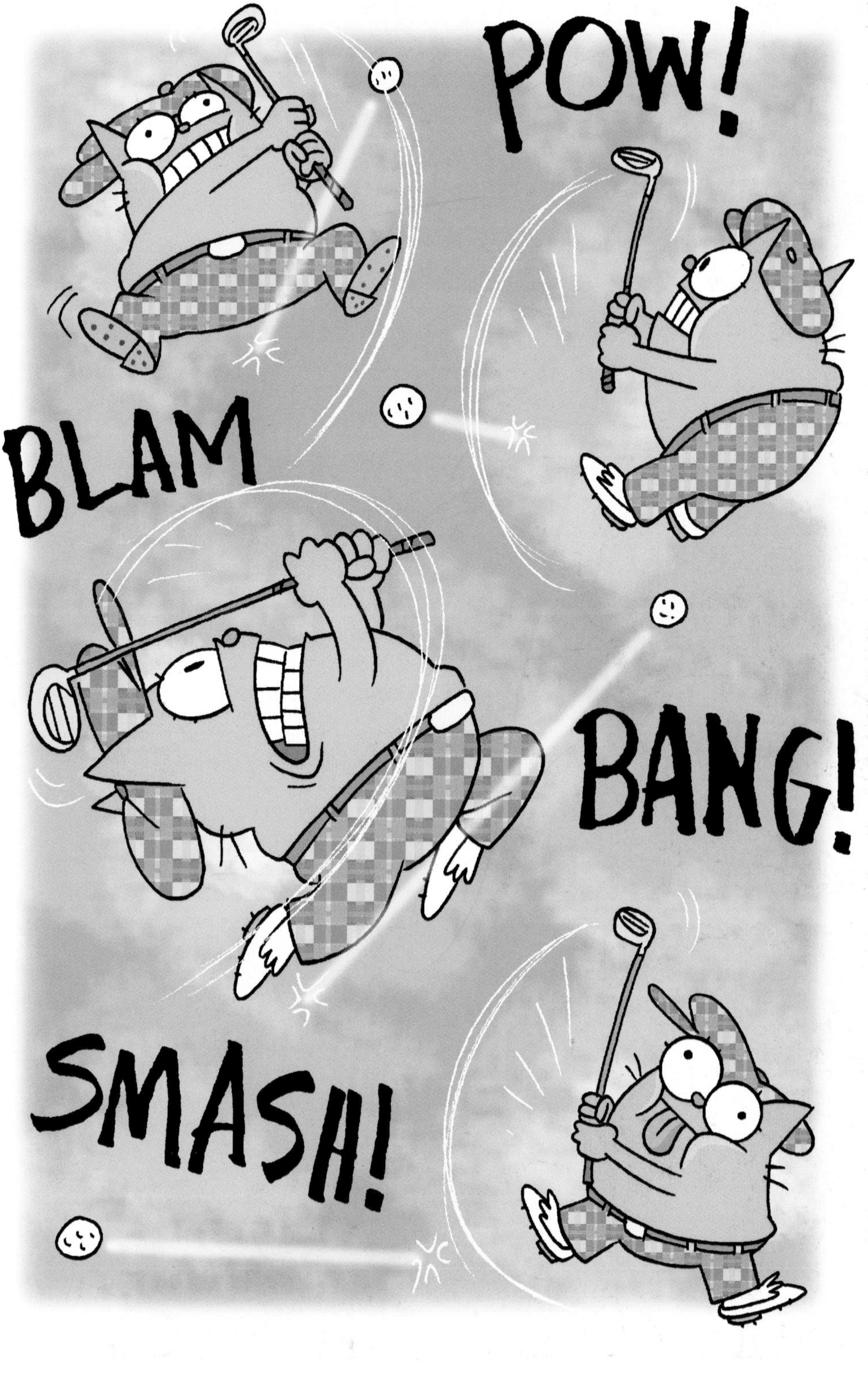
POW!
BLAM
BANG!
SMASH!

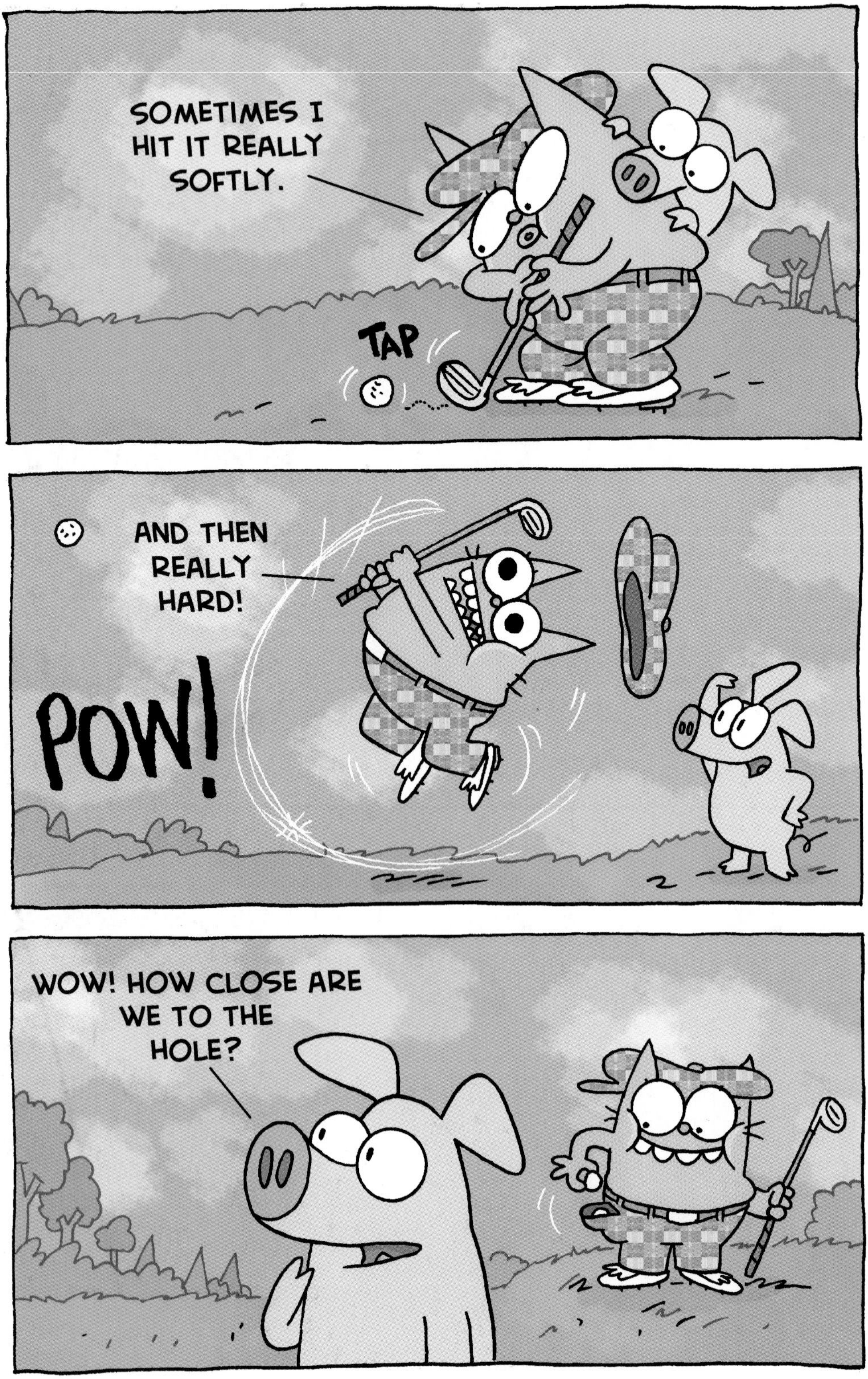
SOMETIMES I HIT IT REALLY SOFTLY.
TAP
AND THEN REALLY HARD!
POW!
WOW! HOW CLOSE ARE WE TO THE HOLE?

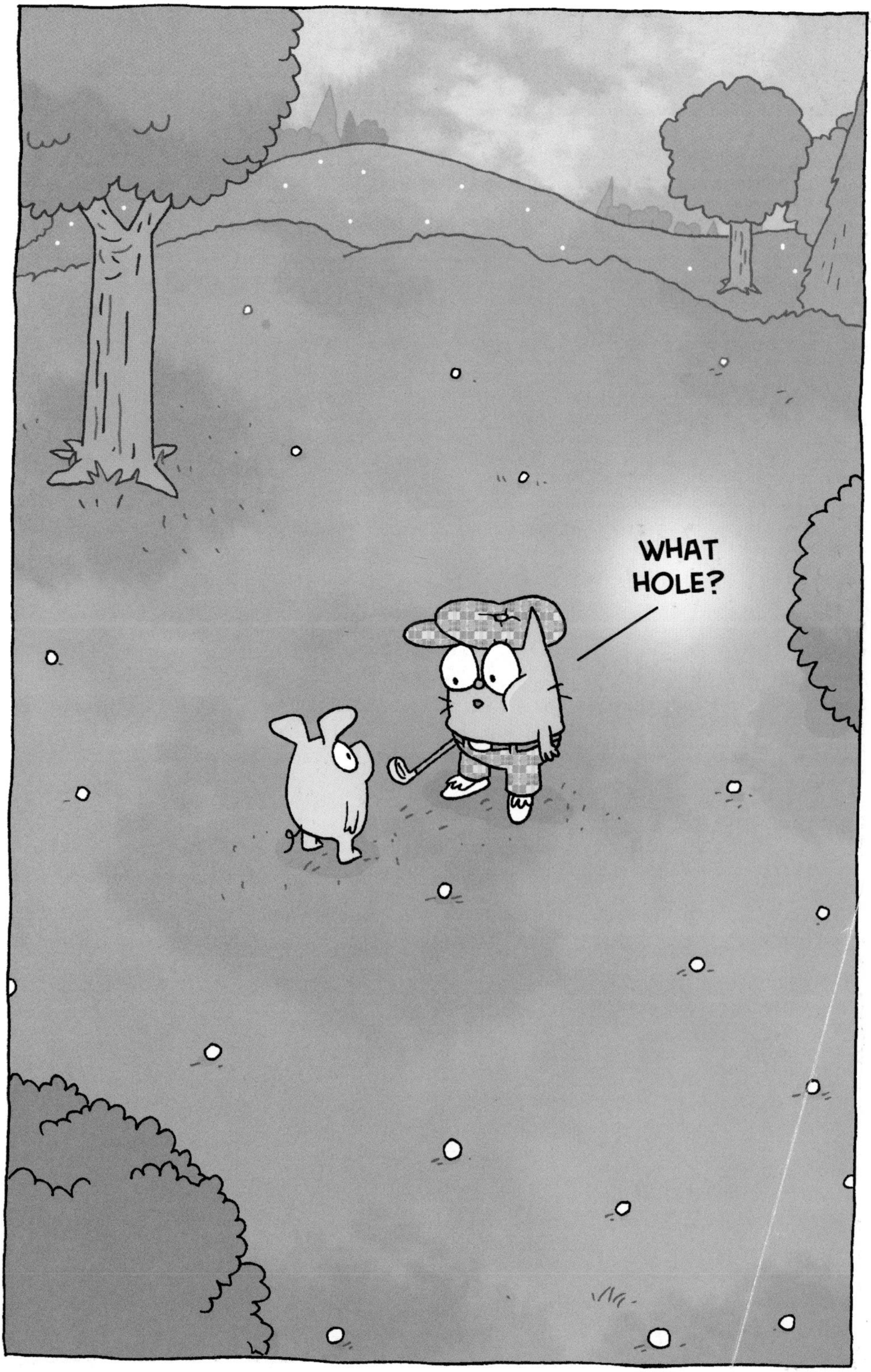
WHAT HOLE?

BLARFOZ

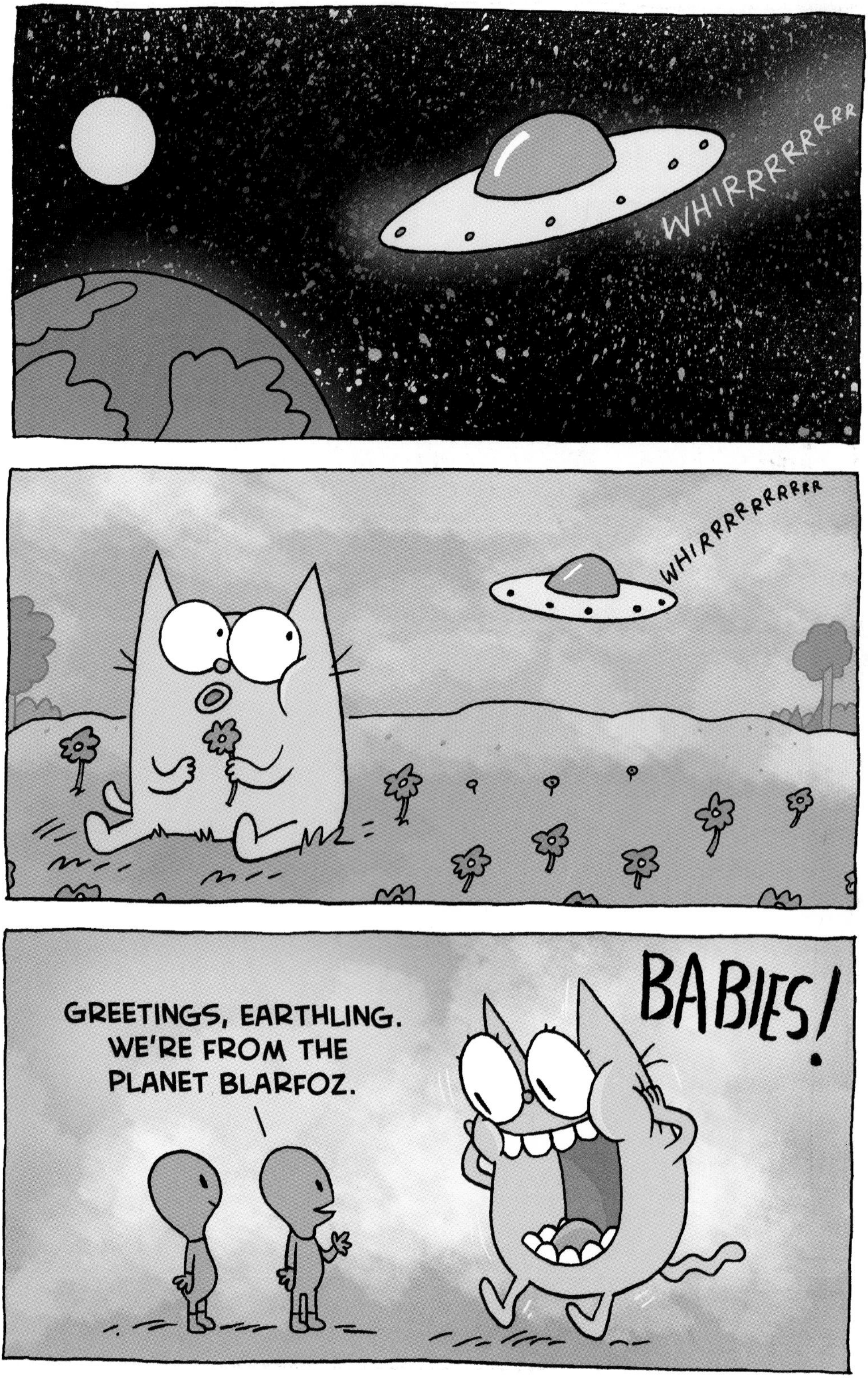
WHIRRRRRRRR
WHIRRRRRRRRRR
GREETINGS, EARTHLING. WE'RE FROM THE PLANET BLARFOZ.
BABIES!

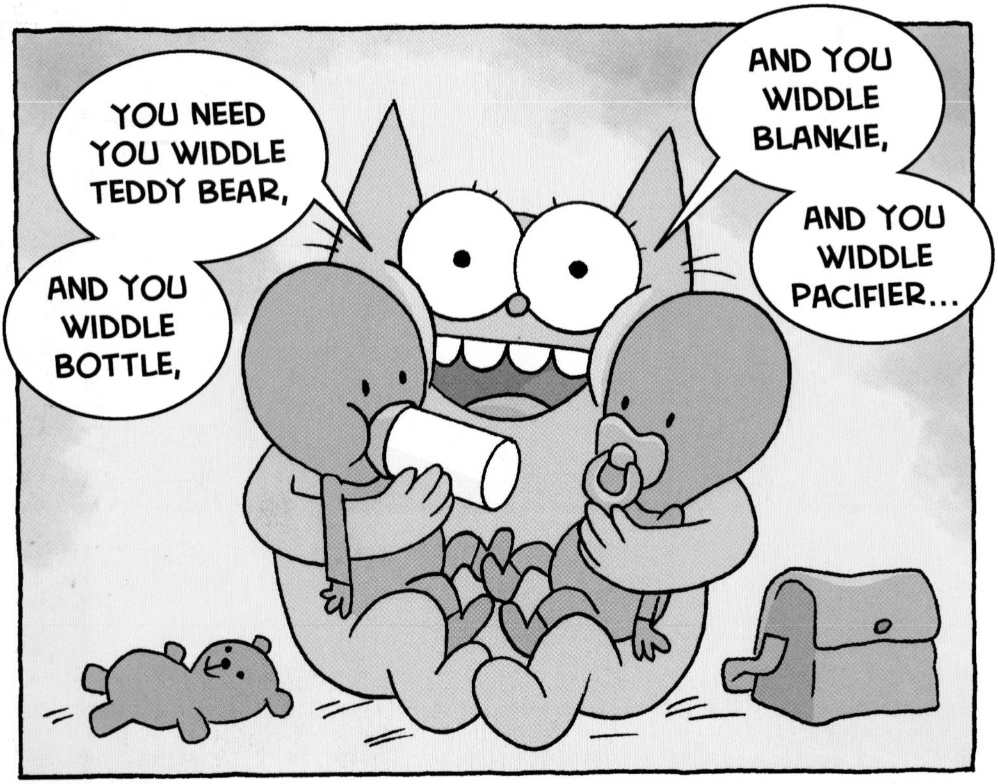
YOU NEED YOU WIDDLE TEDDY BEAR,
AND YOU WIDDLE BOTTLE,
AND YOU WIDDLE BLANKIE,
AND YOU WIDDLE PACIFIER...

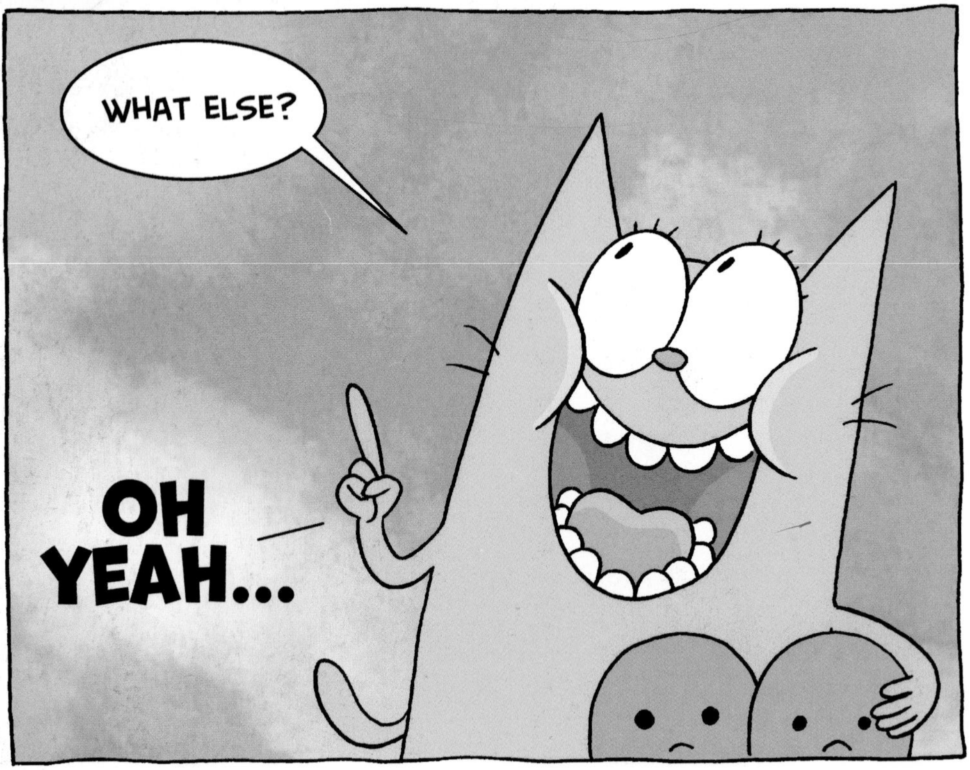
WHAT ELSE?
OH YEAH...

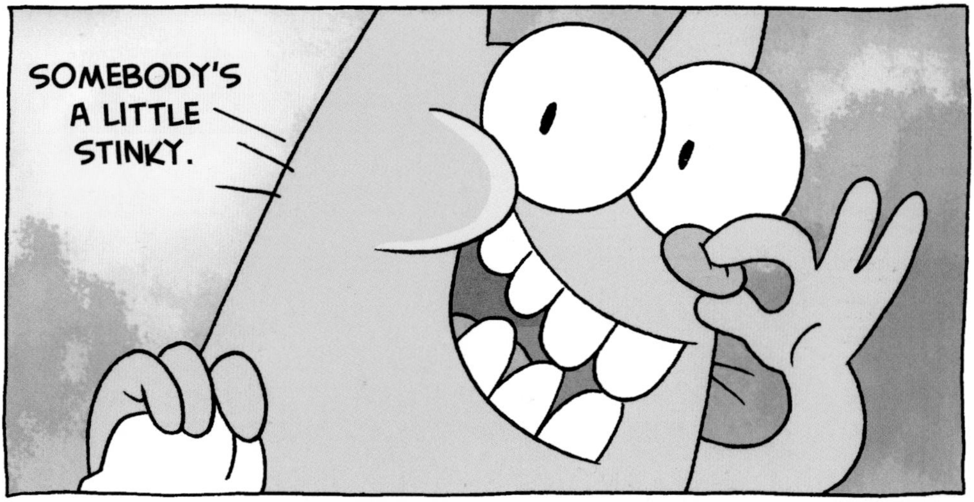
SOMEBODY'S A LITTLE STINKY.

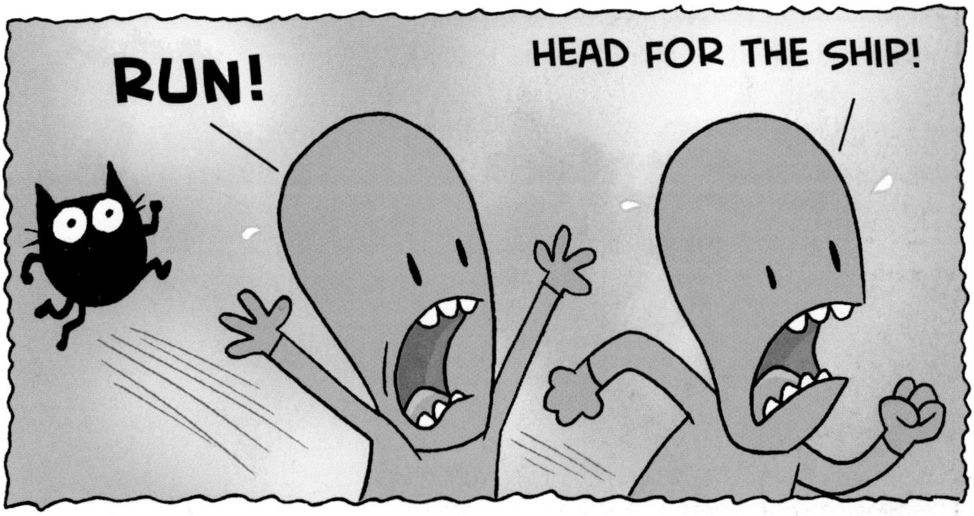
RUN!
HEAD FOR THE SHIP!

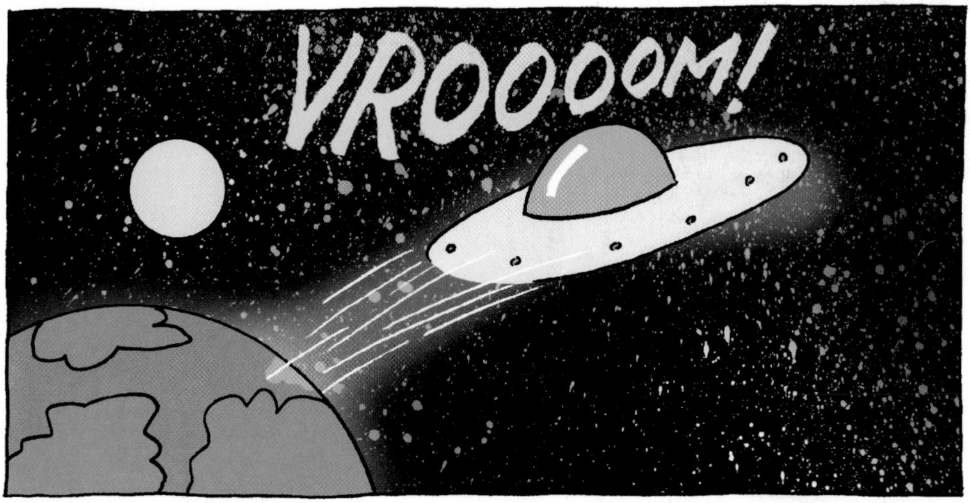
VROOOOM!

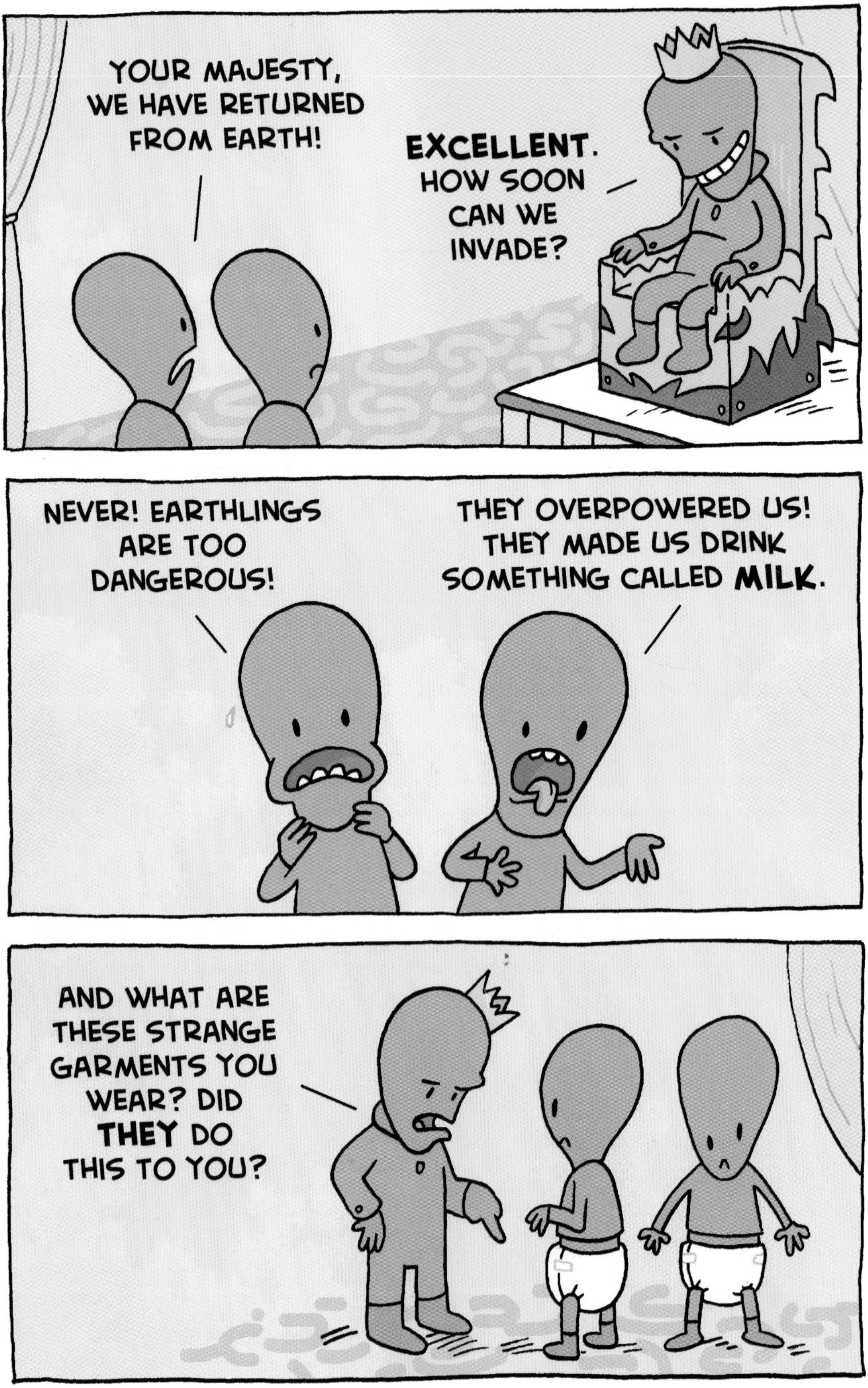
YOUR MAJESTY, WE HAVE RETURNED FROM EARTH!
EXCELLENT. HOW SOON CAN WE INVADE?
NEVER! EARTHLINGS ARE TOO DANGEROUS!
THEY OVERPOWERED US! THEY MADE US DRINK SOMETHING CALLED **MILK**.
AND WHAT ARE THESE STRANGE GARMENTS YOU WEAR? DID **THEY** DO THIS TO YOU?

COULD WE **PLEASE** NOT TALK ABOUT THE DIAPERS?
IT'S PROBABLY THE MAIN REASON WE DON'T WANT TO GO BACK.

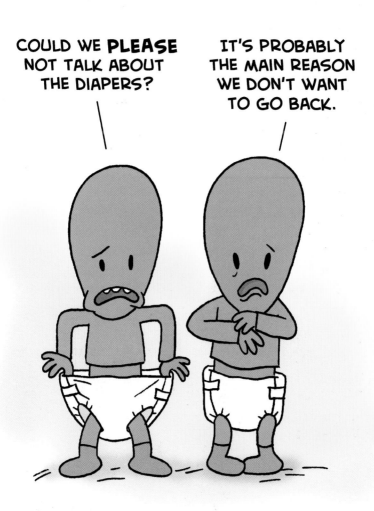

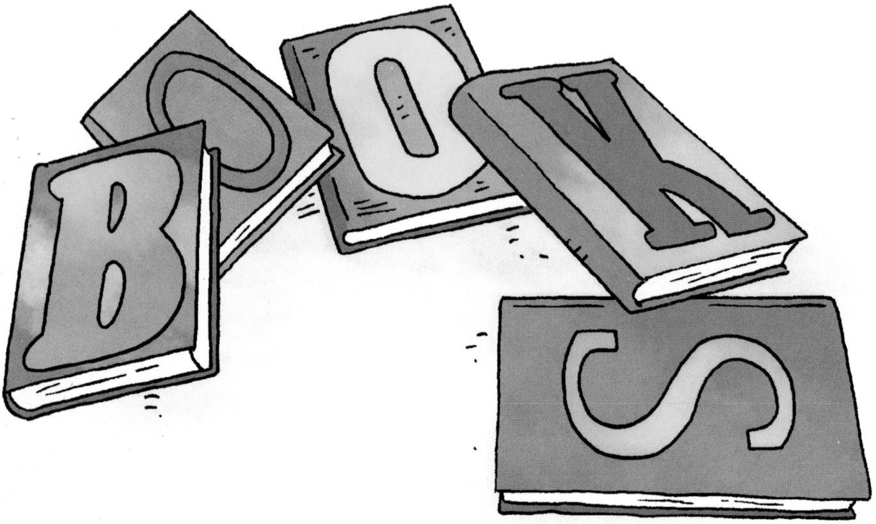
BOOKS

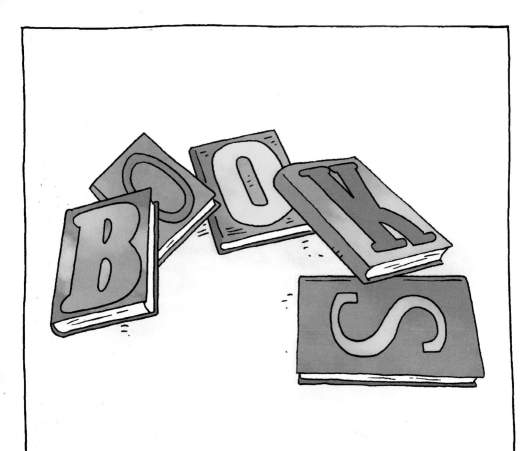

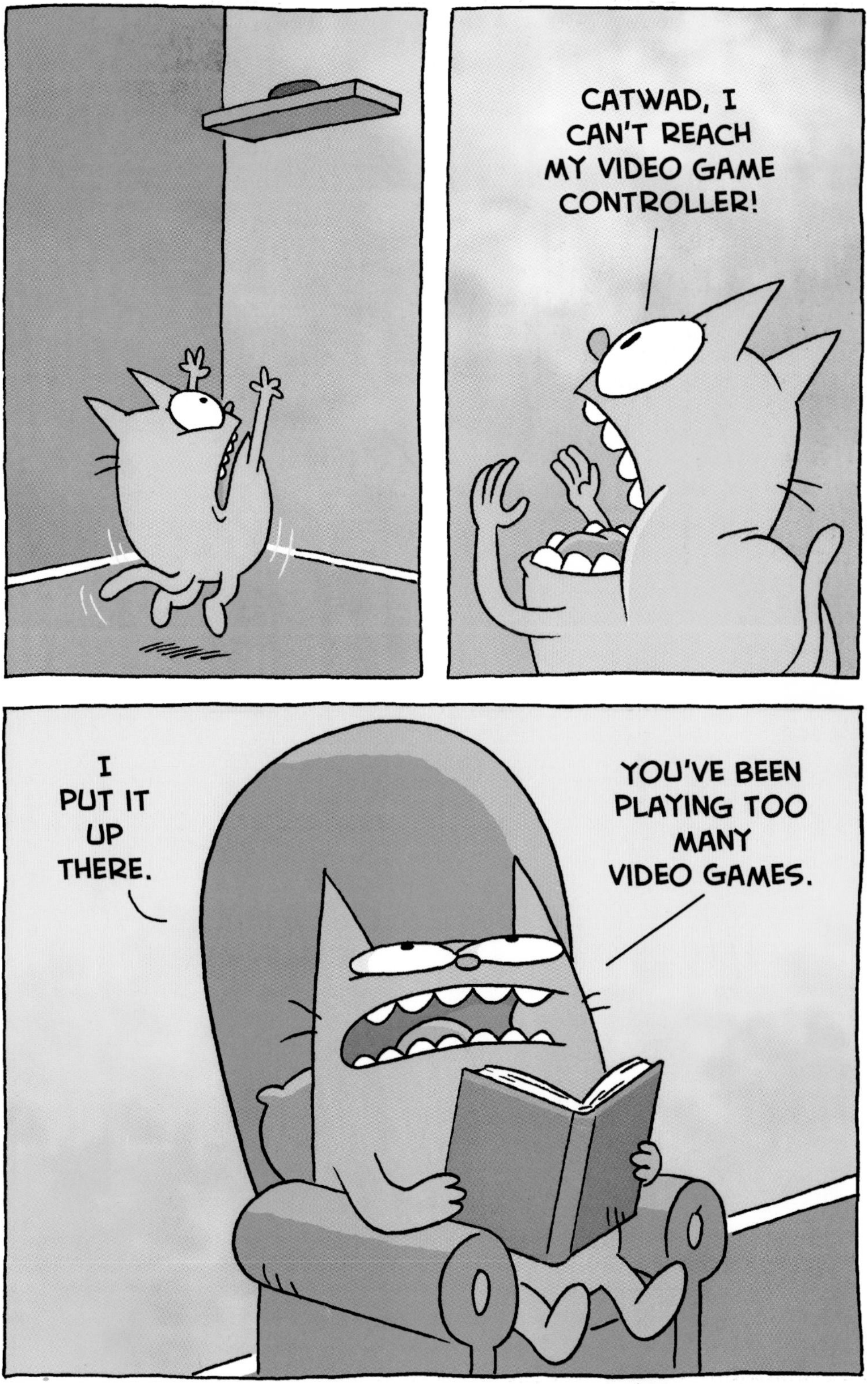
CATWAD, I CAN'T REACH MY VIDEO GAME CONTROLLER!
I PUT IT UP THERE.
YOU'VE BEEN PLAYING TOO MANY VIDEO GAMES.

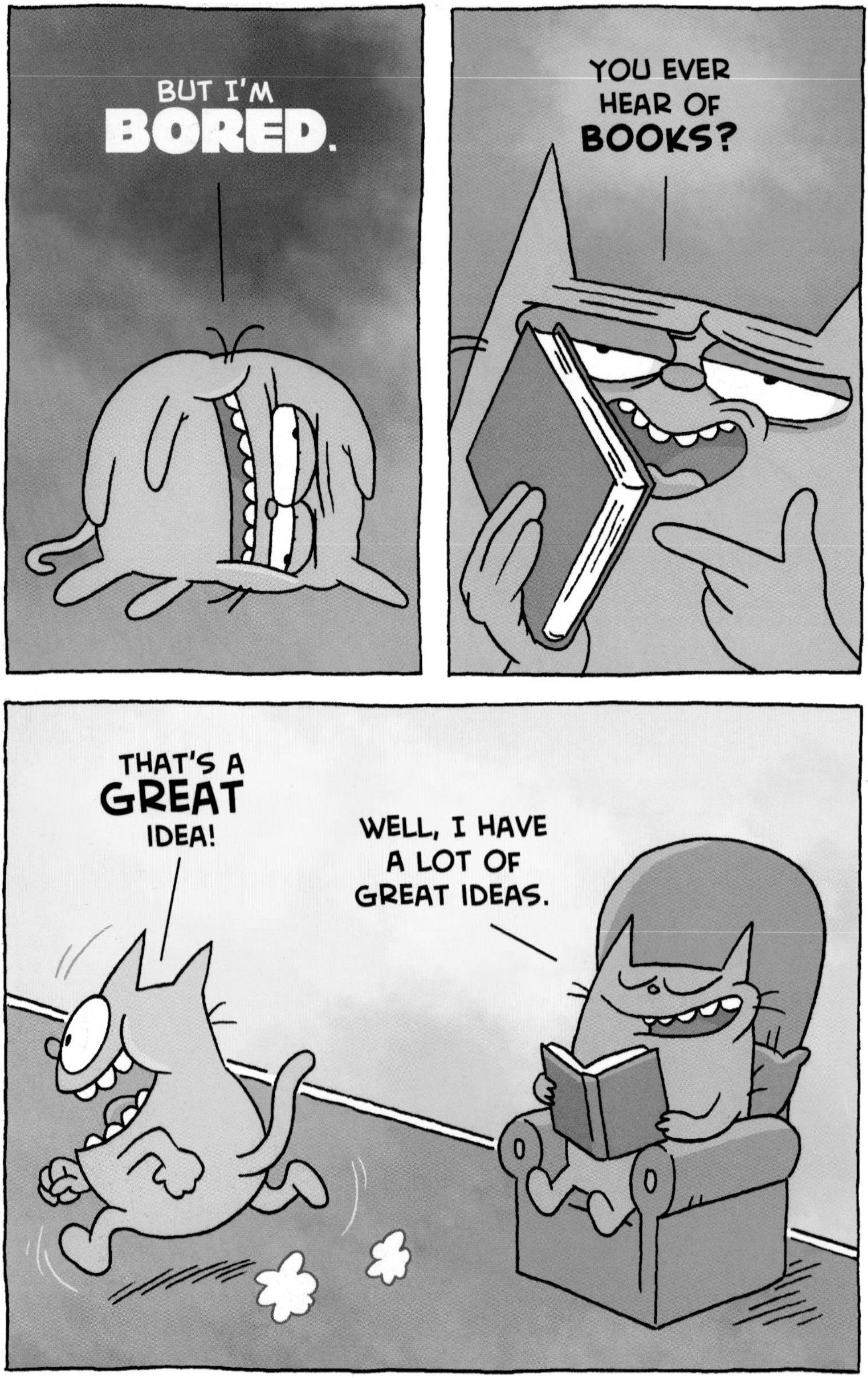
BUT I'M BORED.
YOU EVER HEAR OF BOOKS?
THAT'S A GREAT IDEA!
WELL, I HAVE A LOT OF GREAT IDEAS.

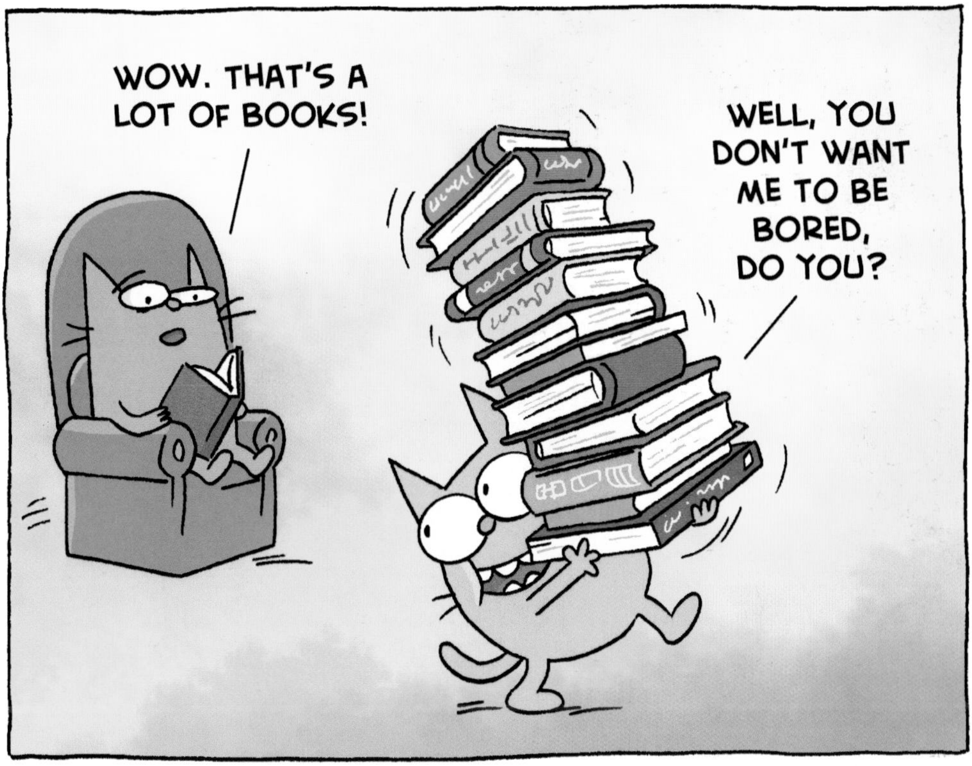
WOW. THAT'S A LOT OF BOOKS!
WELL, YOU DON'T WANT ME TO BE BORED, DO YOU?

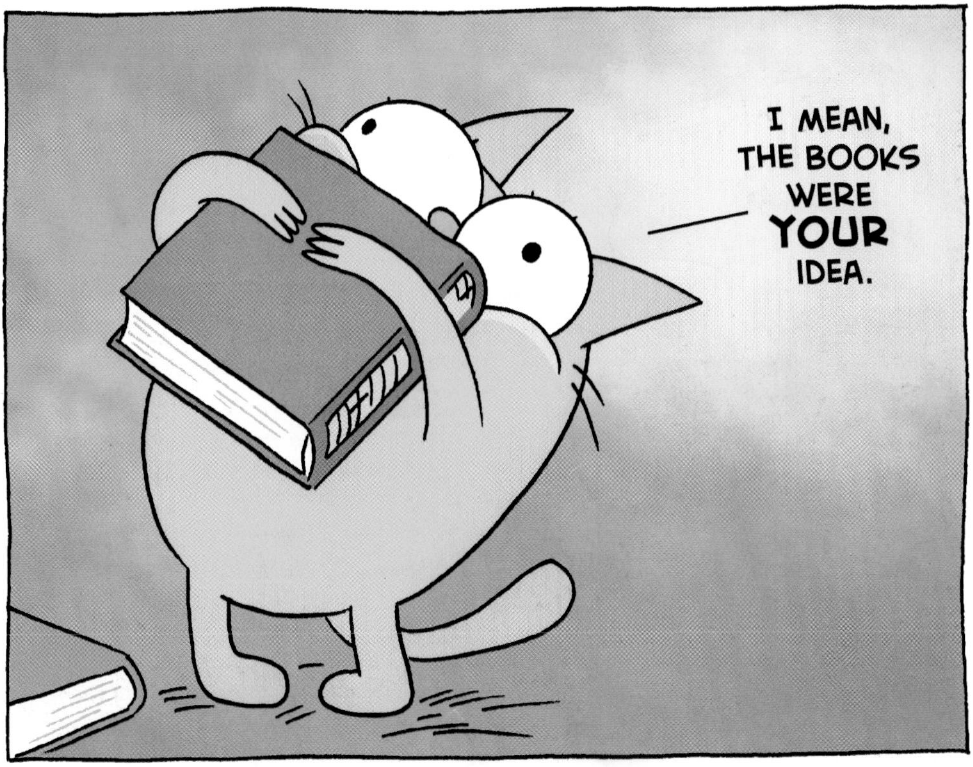
I MEAN, THE BOOKS WERE YOUR IDEA.

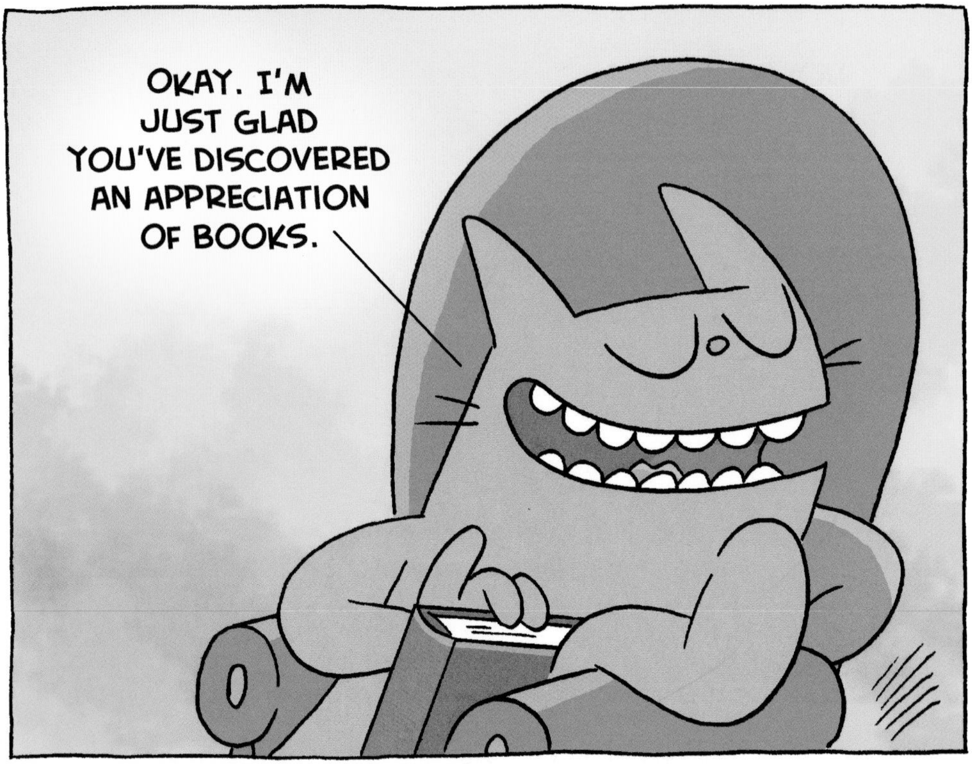
OKAY. I'M JUST GLAD YOU'VE DISCOVERED AN APPRECIATION OF BOOKS.

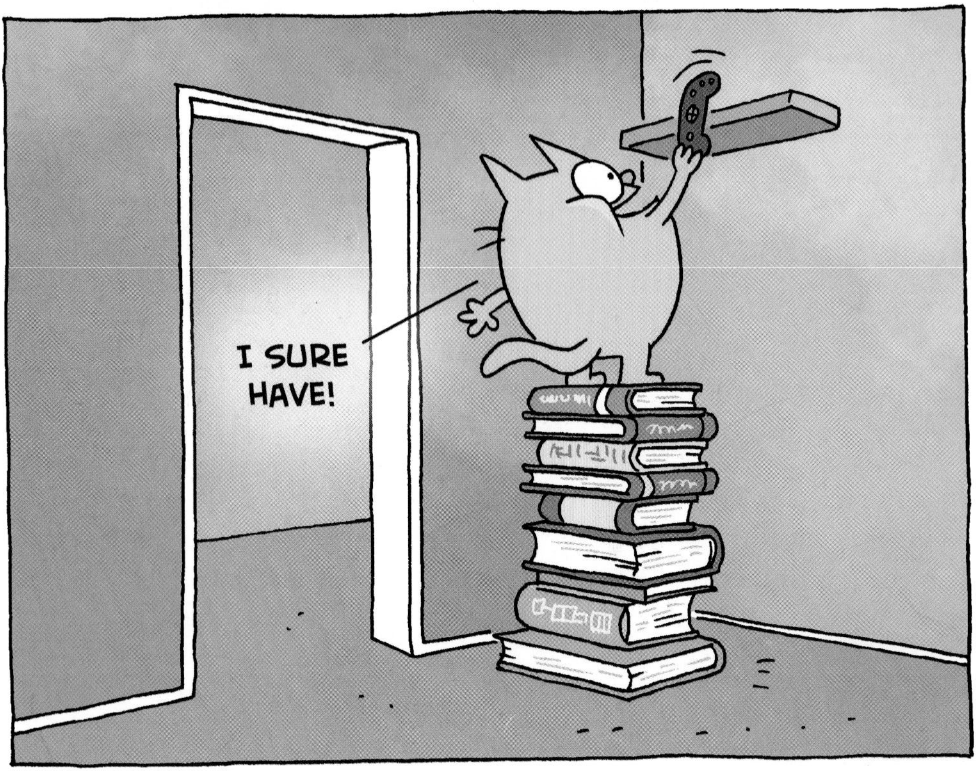
I SURE HAVE!

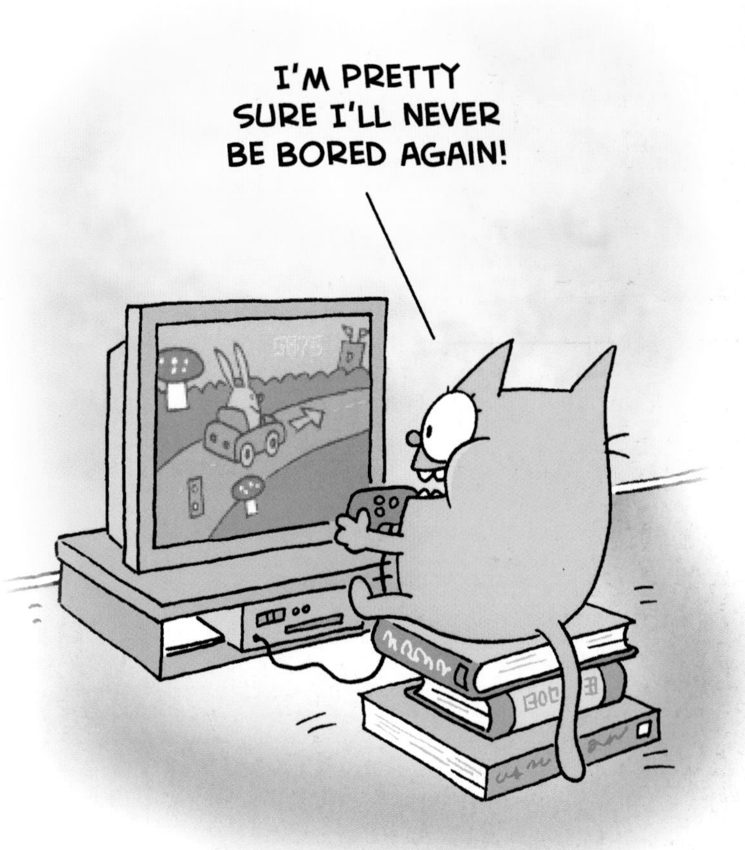
I'M PRETTY SURE I'LL NEVER BE BORED AGAIN!

the new game

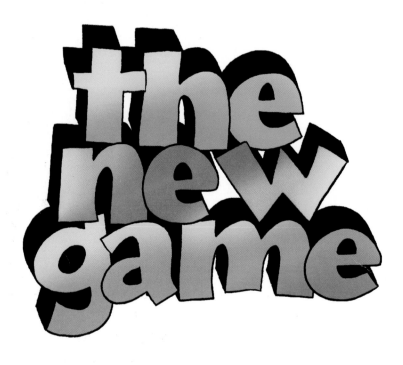

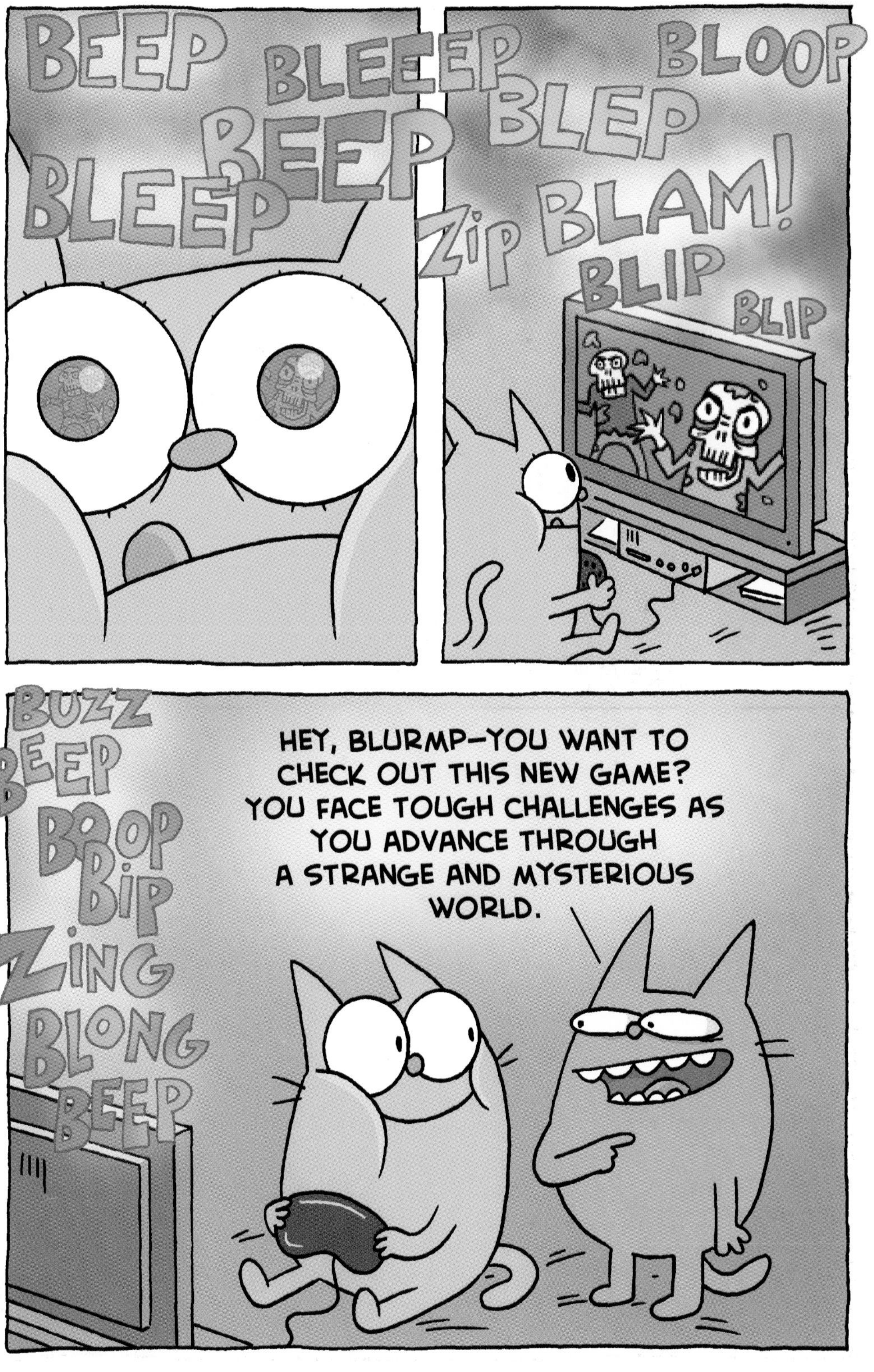
BEEP
BLEEEP
BLOOP
BEEP
BLEP
BLEEP
ZIP
BLAM!
BLIP
BLIP
BUZZ
BEEP
BOOP
BIP
ZING
BLONG
BEEP
HEY, BLURMP—YOU WANT TO CHECK OUT THIS NEW GAME? YOU FACE TOUGH CHALLENGES AS YOU ADVANCE THROUGH A STRANGE AND MYSTERIOUS WORLD.

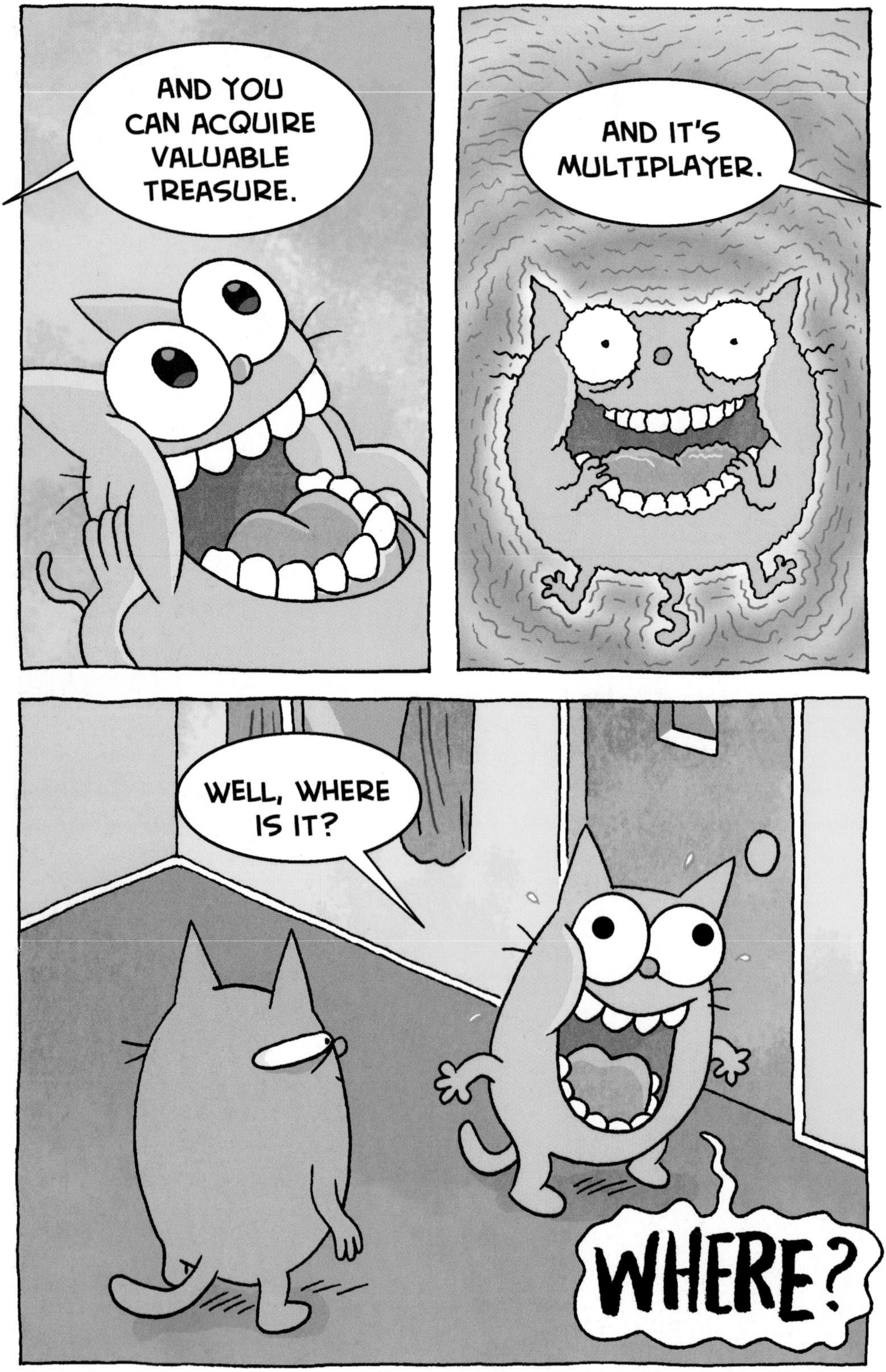
AND YOU CAN ACQUIRE VALUABLE TREASURE.
AND IT'S MULTIPLAYER.
WELL, WHERE IS IT?
WHERE?

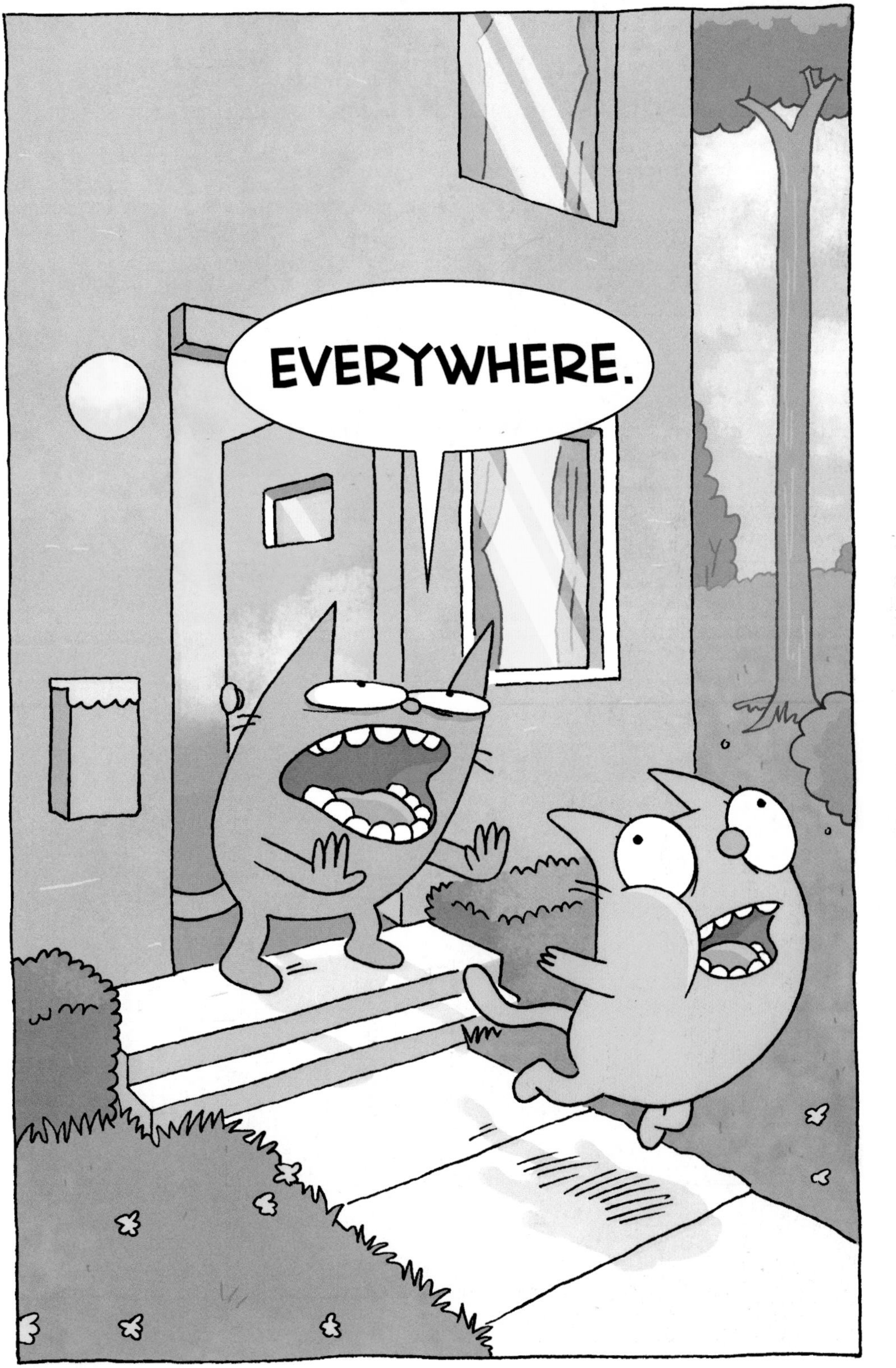
EVERYWHERE.

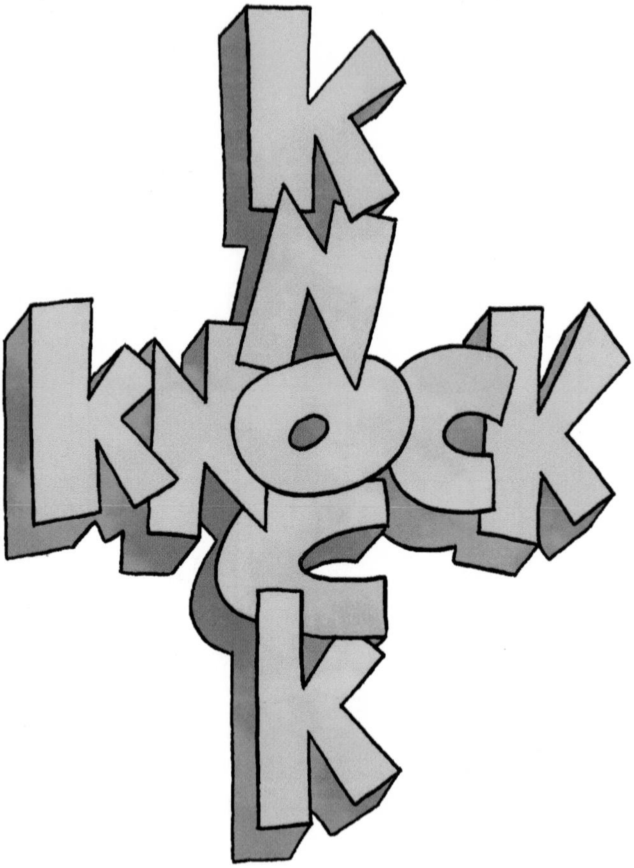
KNOCK
KNOCK

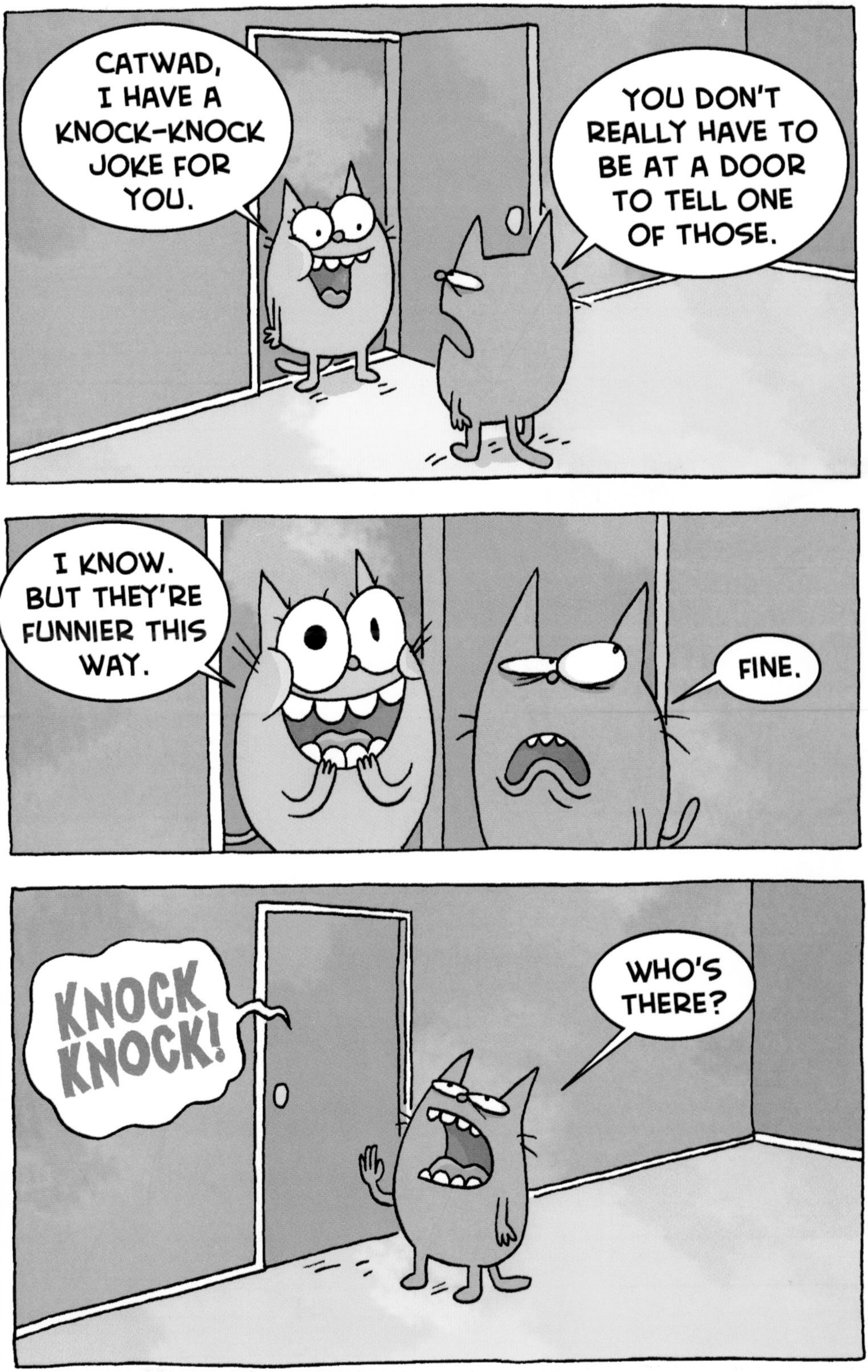
CATWAD, I HAVE A KNOCK-KNOCK JOKE FOR YOU.
YOU DON'T REALLY HAVE TO BE AT A DOOR TO TELL ONE OF THOSE.
I KNOW. BUT THEY'RE FUNNIER THIS WAY.
FINE.
KNOCK KNOCK!
WHO'S THERE?

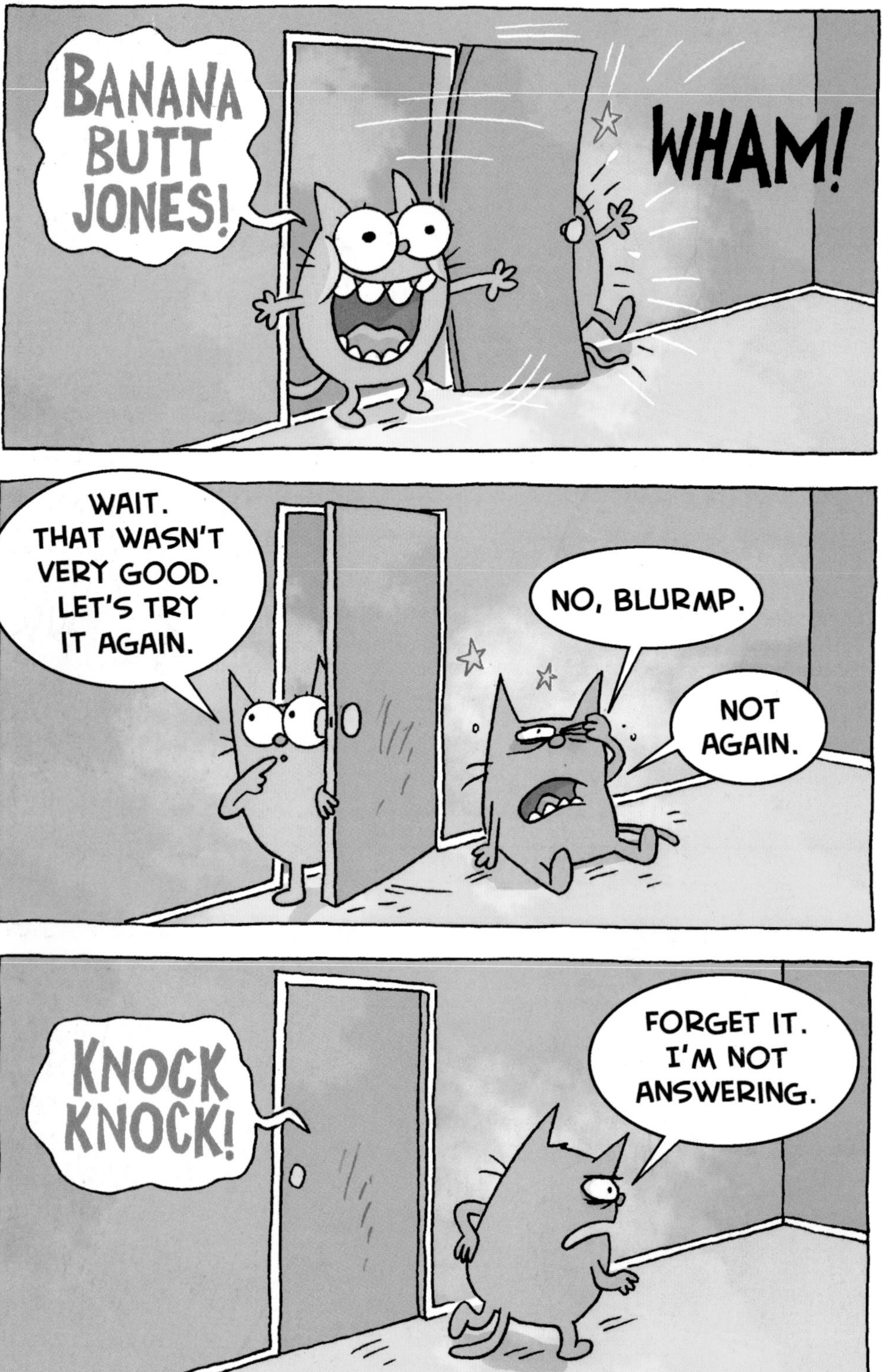
BANANA BUTT JONES!
WHAM!
WAIT. THAT WASN'T VERY GOOD. LET'S TRY IT AGAIN.
NO, BLURMP.
NOT AGAIN.
KNOCK KNOCK!
FORGET IT. I'M NOT ANSWERING.

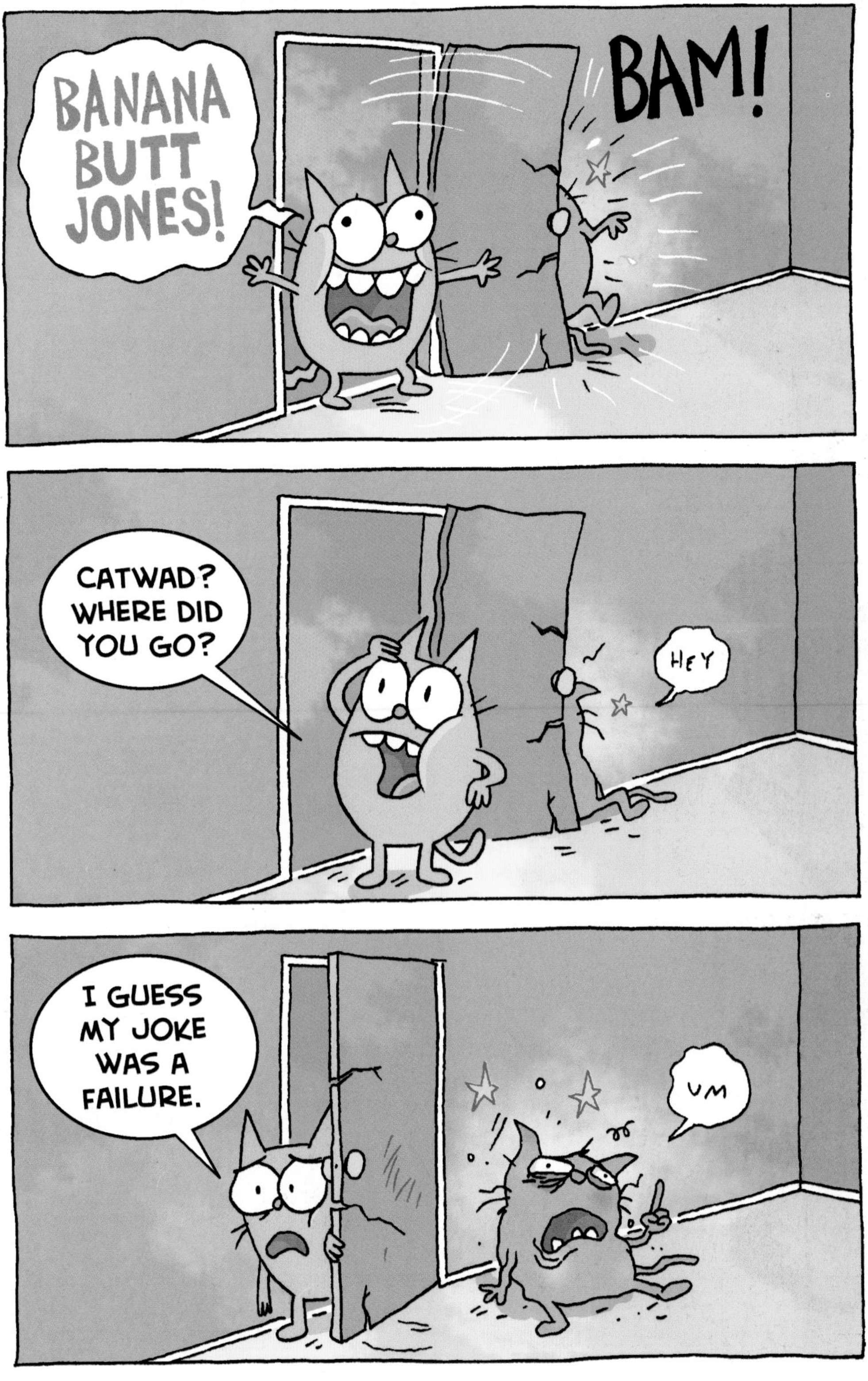
BANANA BUTT JONES!
BAM!
CATWAD? WHERE DID YOU GO?
HEY
I GUESS MY JOKE WAS A FAILURE.
UM

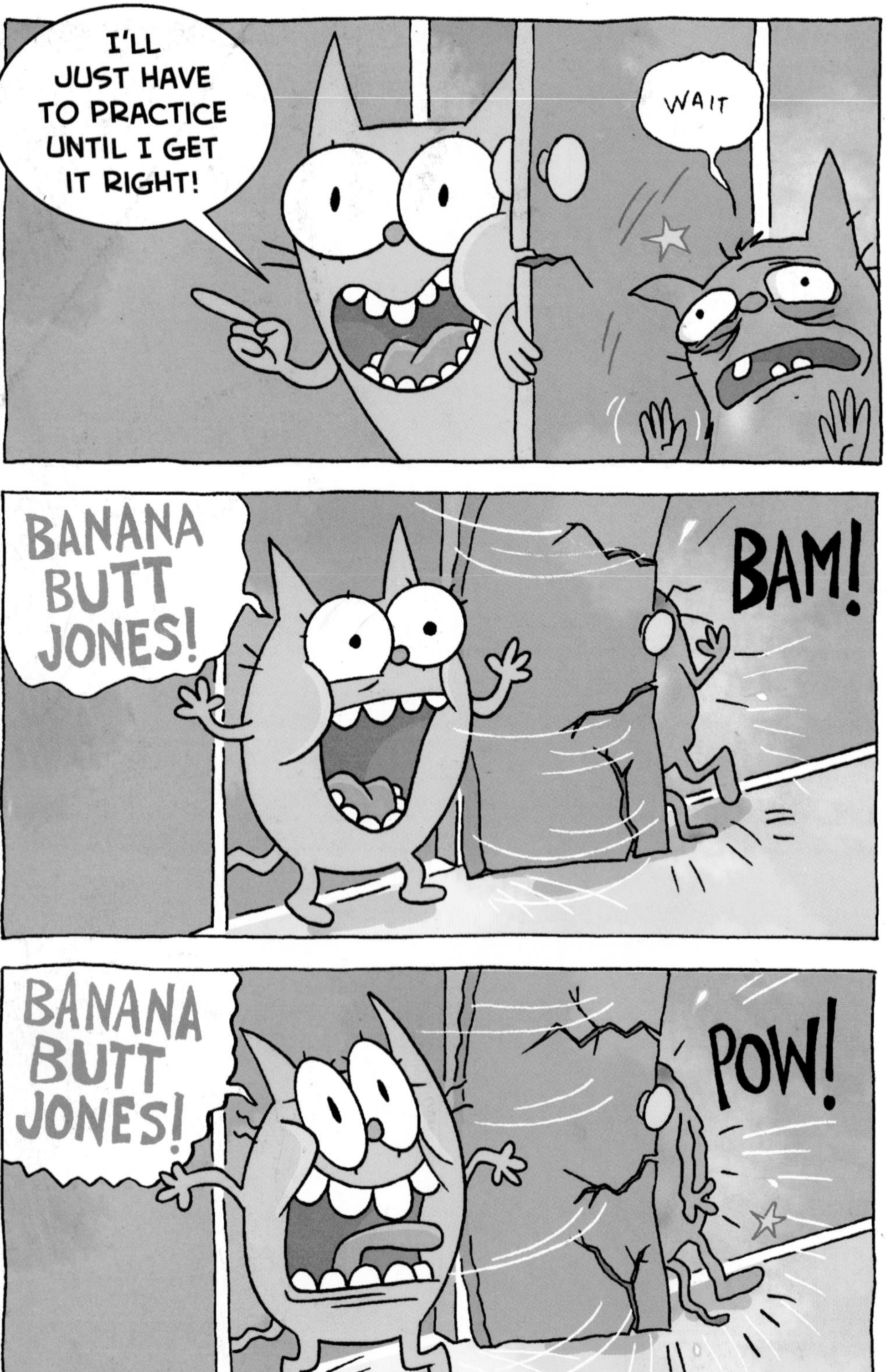
I'LL JUST HAVE TO PRACTICE UNTIL I GET IT RIGHT!
WAIT
BANANA BUTT JONES!
BAM!
BANANA BUTT JONES!
POW!

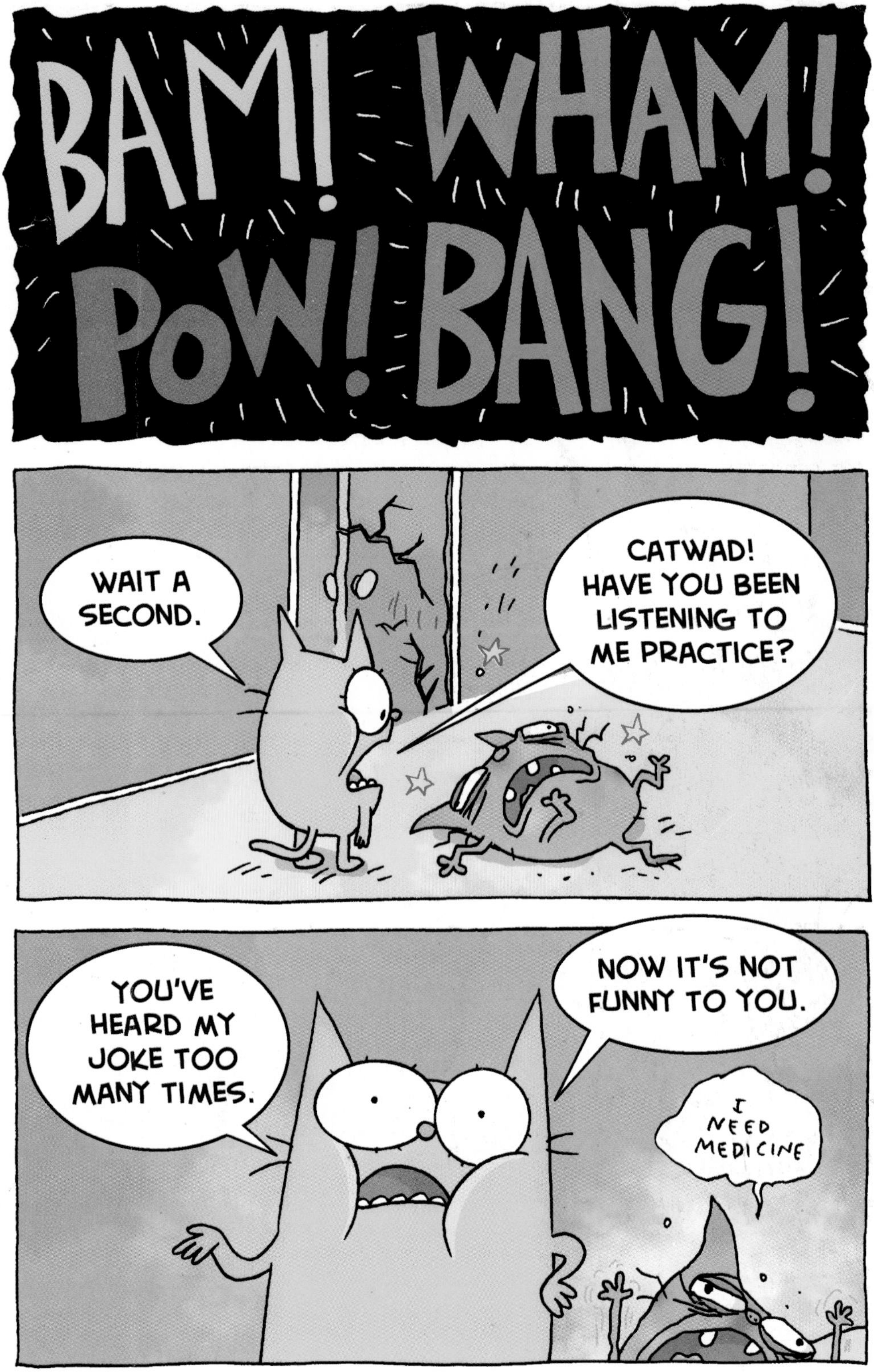
BAM! WHAM!
POW! BANG!
WAIT A SECOND.
CATWAD! HAVE YOU BEEN LISTENING TO ME PRACTICE?
YOU'VE HEARD MY JOKE TOO MANY TIMES.
NOW IT'S NOT FUNNY TO YOU.
I NEED MEDICINE

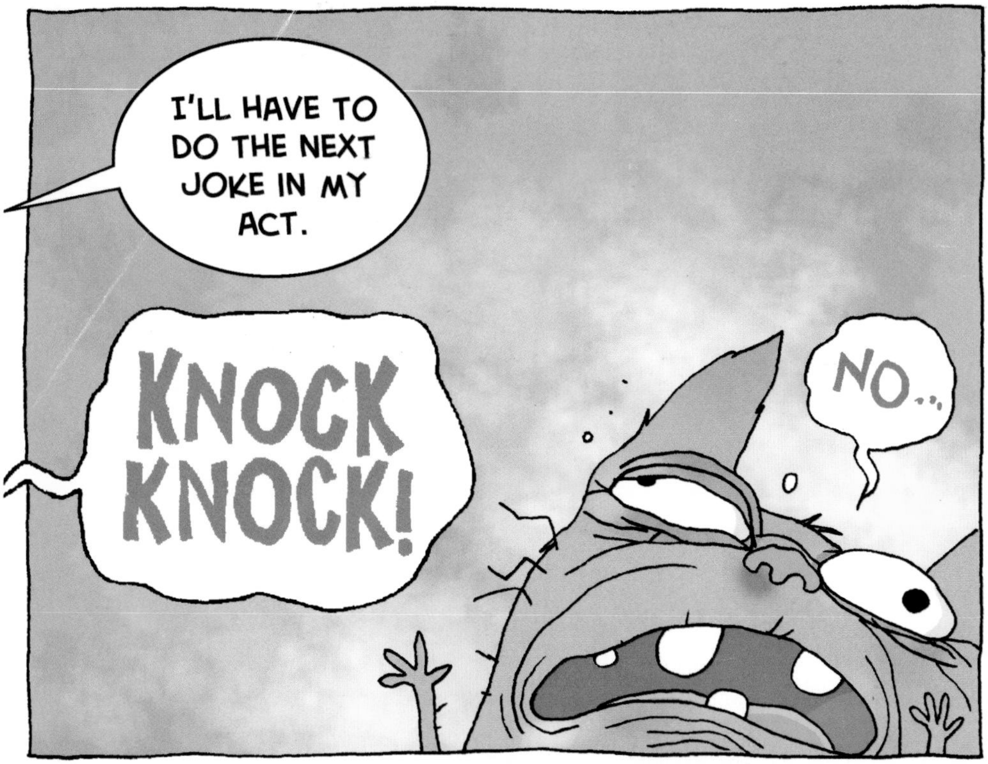
I'LL HAVE TO DO THE NEXT JOKE IN MY ACT.
KNOCK KNOCK!
NO...

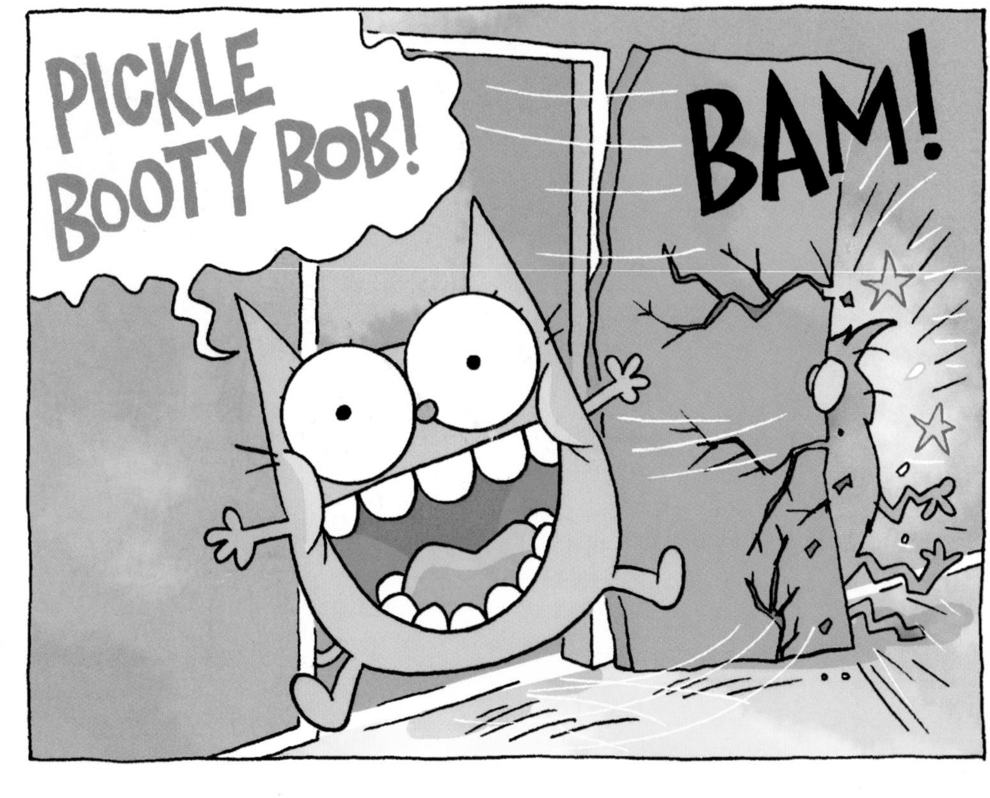
PICKLE BOOTY BOB!
BAM!

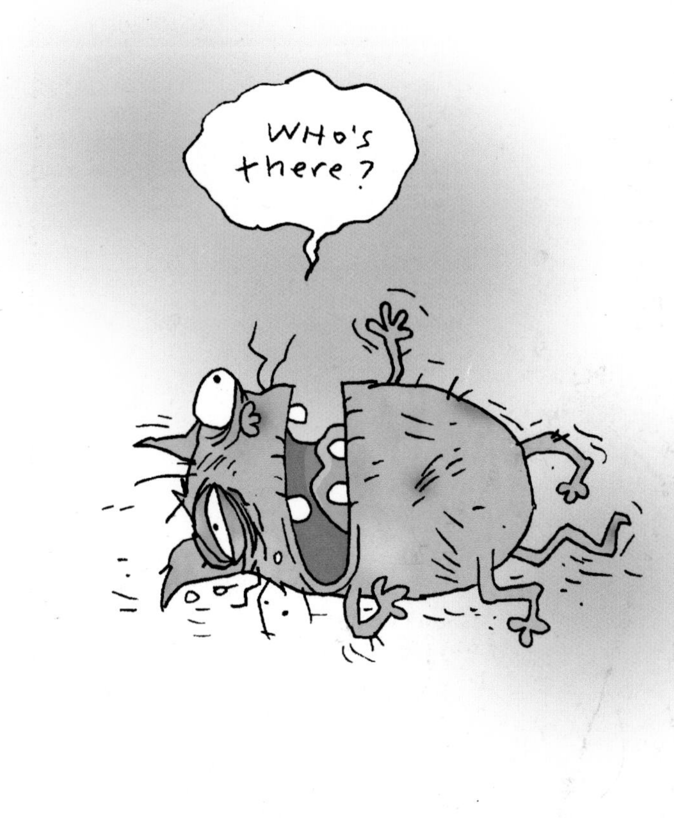
WHO's there?

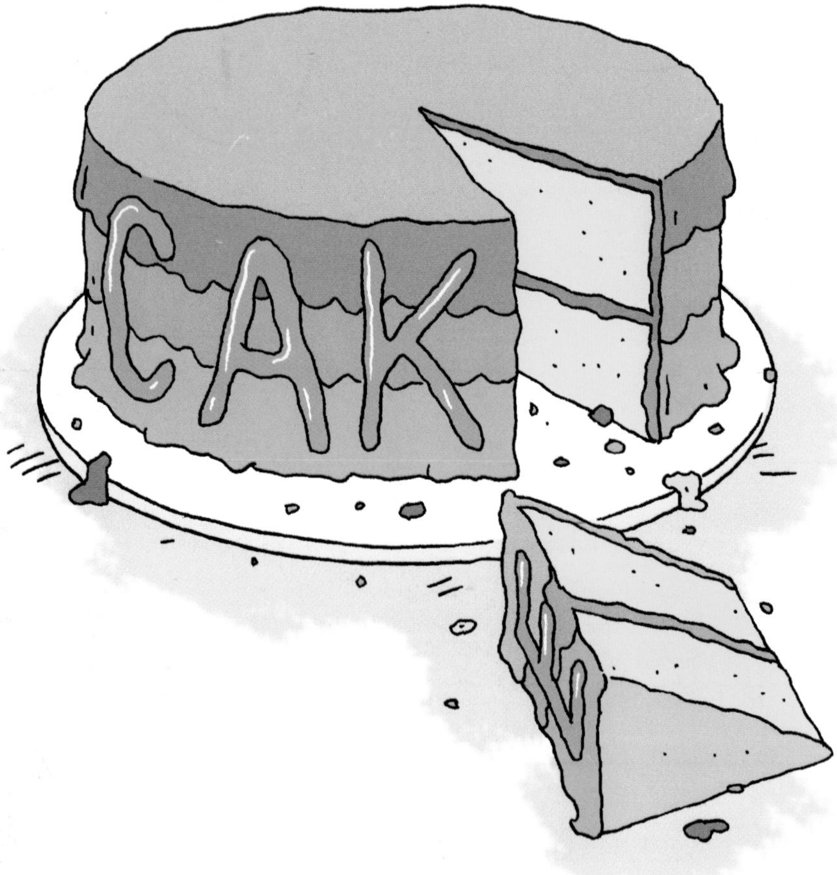
CAK

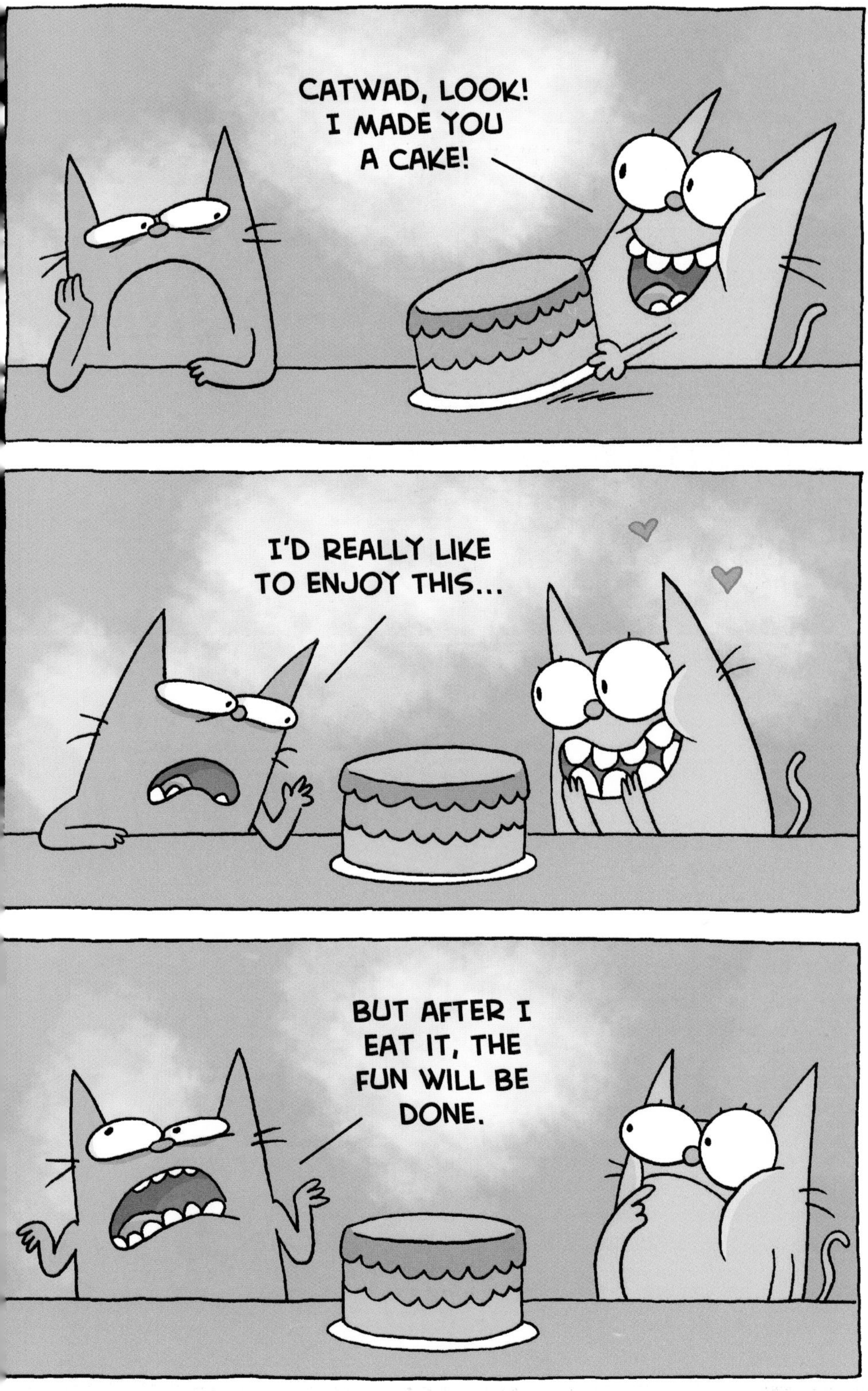
CATWAD, LOOK! I MADE YOU A CAKE!
I'D REALLY LIKE TO ENJOY THIS...
BUT AFTER I EAT IT, THE FUN WILL BE DONE.

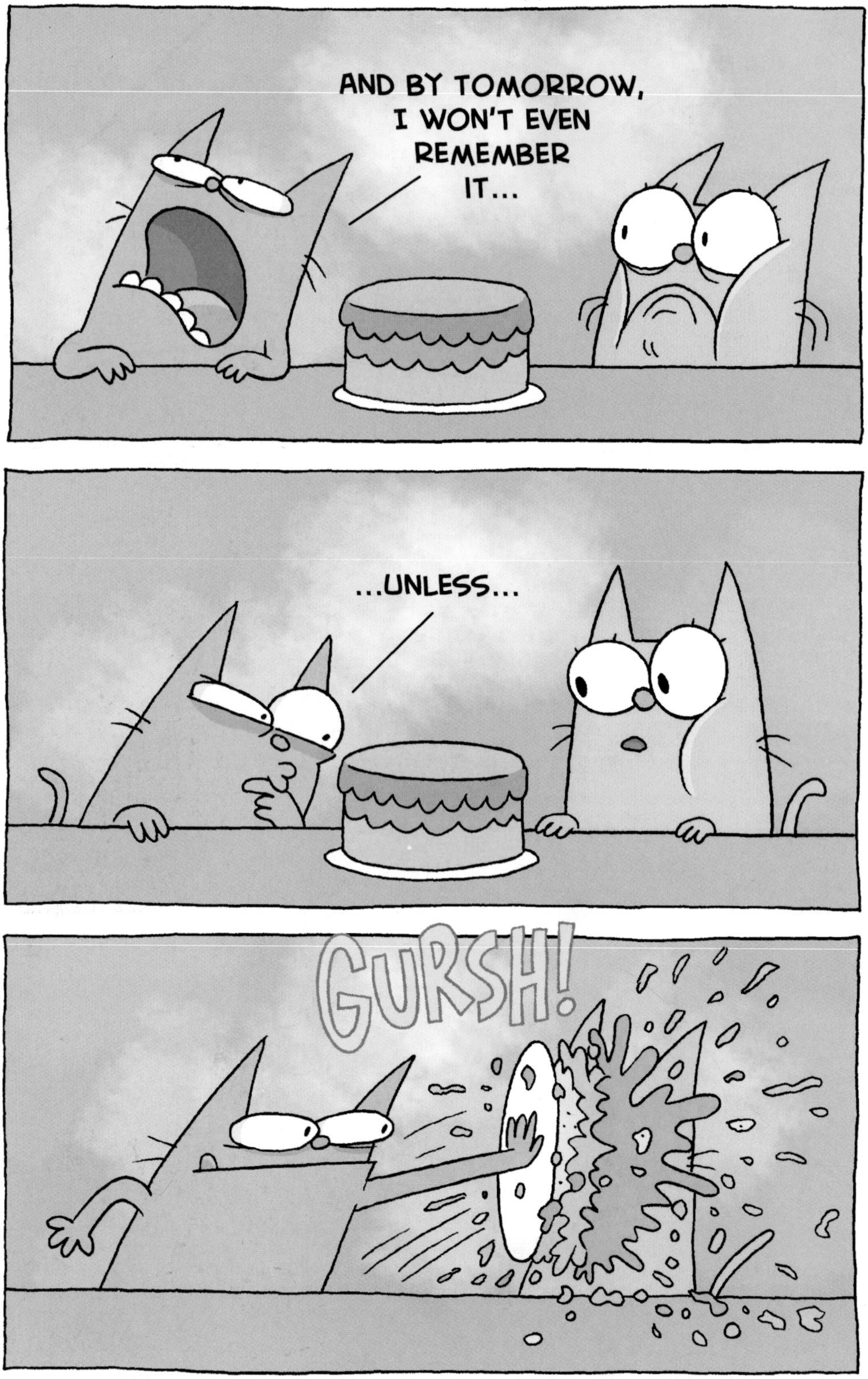
AND BY TOMORROW, I WON'T EVEN REMEMBER IT...
...UNLESS...
GURSH!

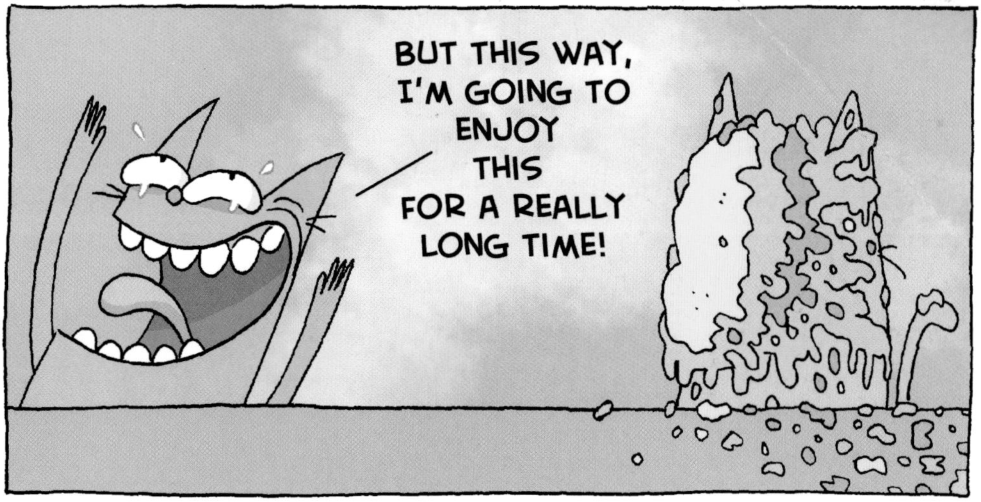
BUT THIS WAY, I'M GOING TO ENJOY THIS FOR A REALLY LONG TIME!

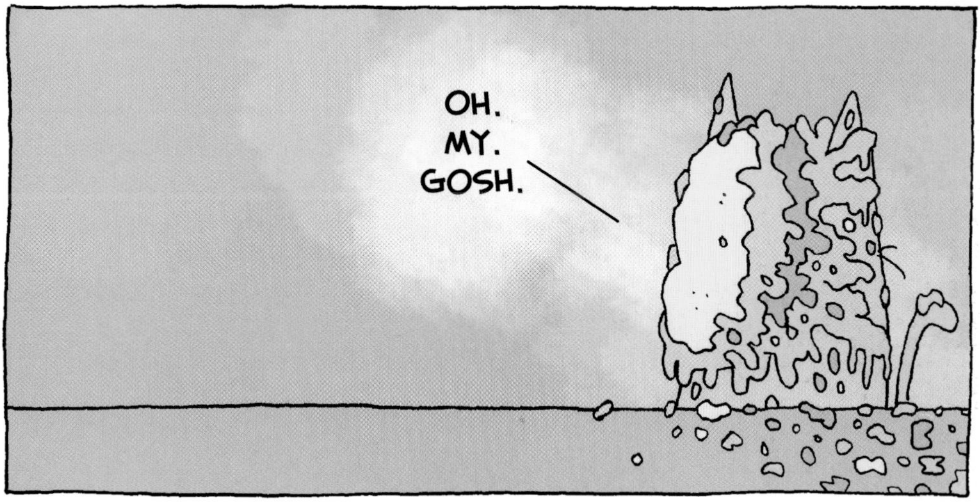
OH. MY. GOSH.

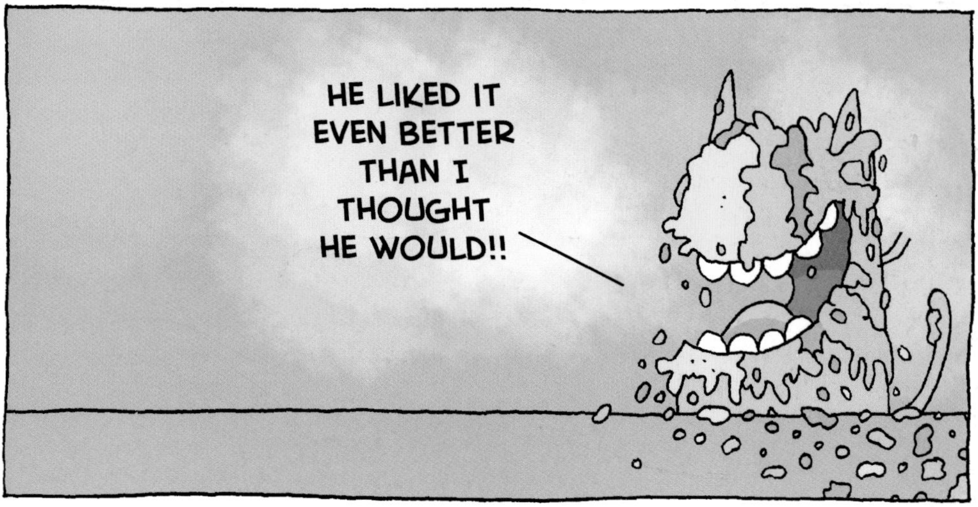
HE LIKED IT EVEN BETTER THAN I THOUGHT HE WOULD!!

RAPUNZEL

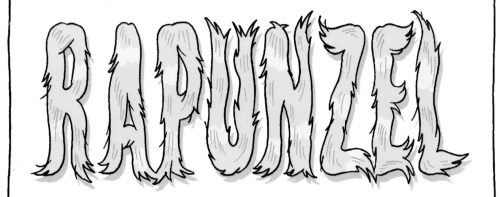

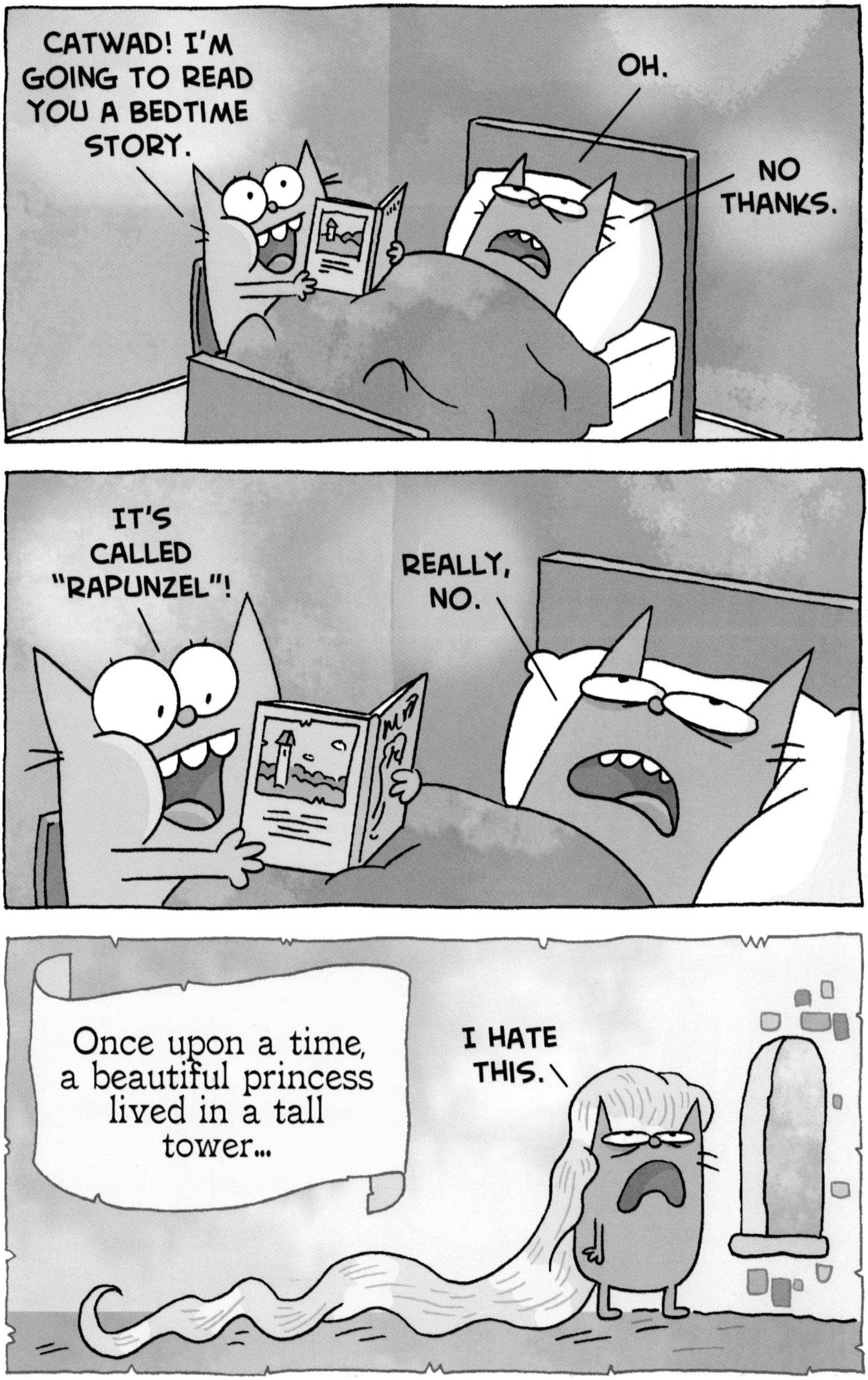
CATWAD! I'M GOING TO READ YOU A BEDTIME STORY.
OH.
NO THANKS.
IT'S CALLED "RAPUNZEL"!
REALLY, NO.
Once upon a time, a beautiful princess lived in a tall tower...
I HATE THIS.

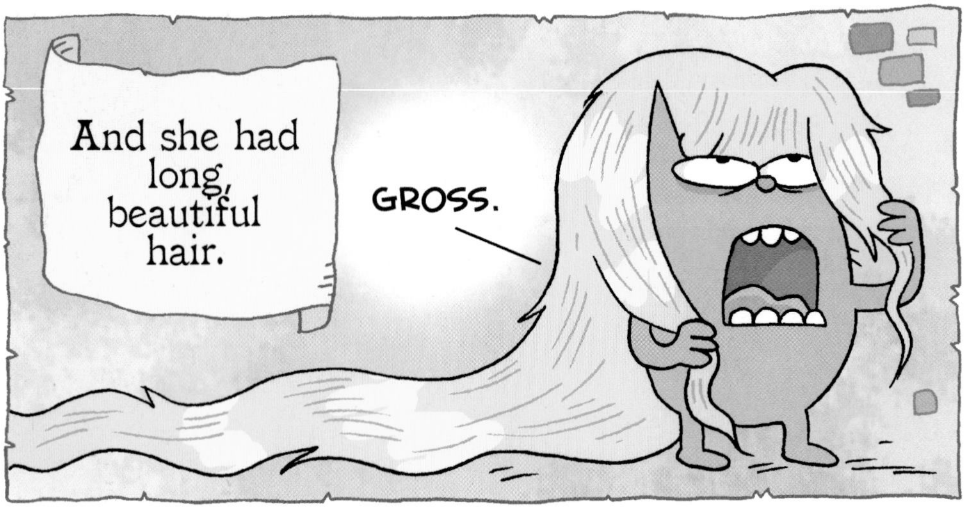
And she had long, beautiful hair.
GROSS.

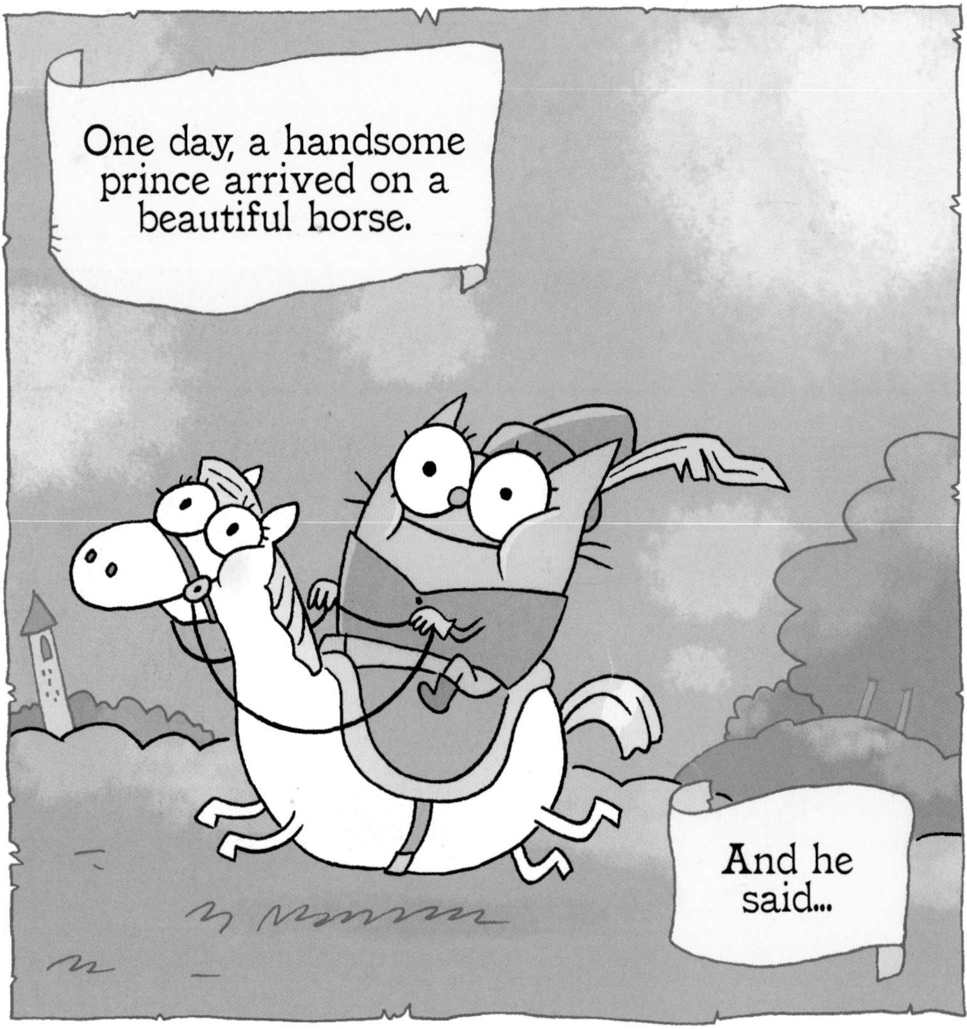
One day, a handsome prince arrived on a beautiful horse.
And he said...

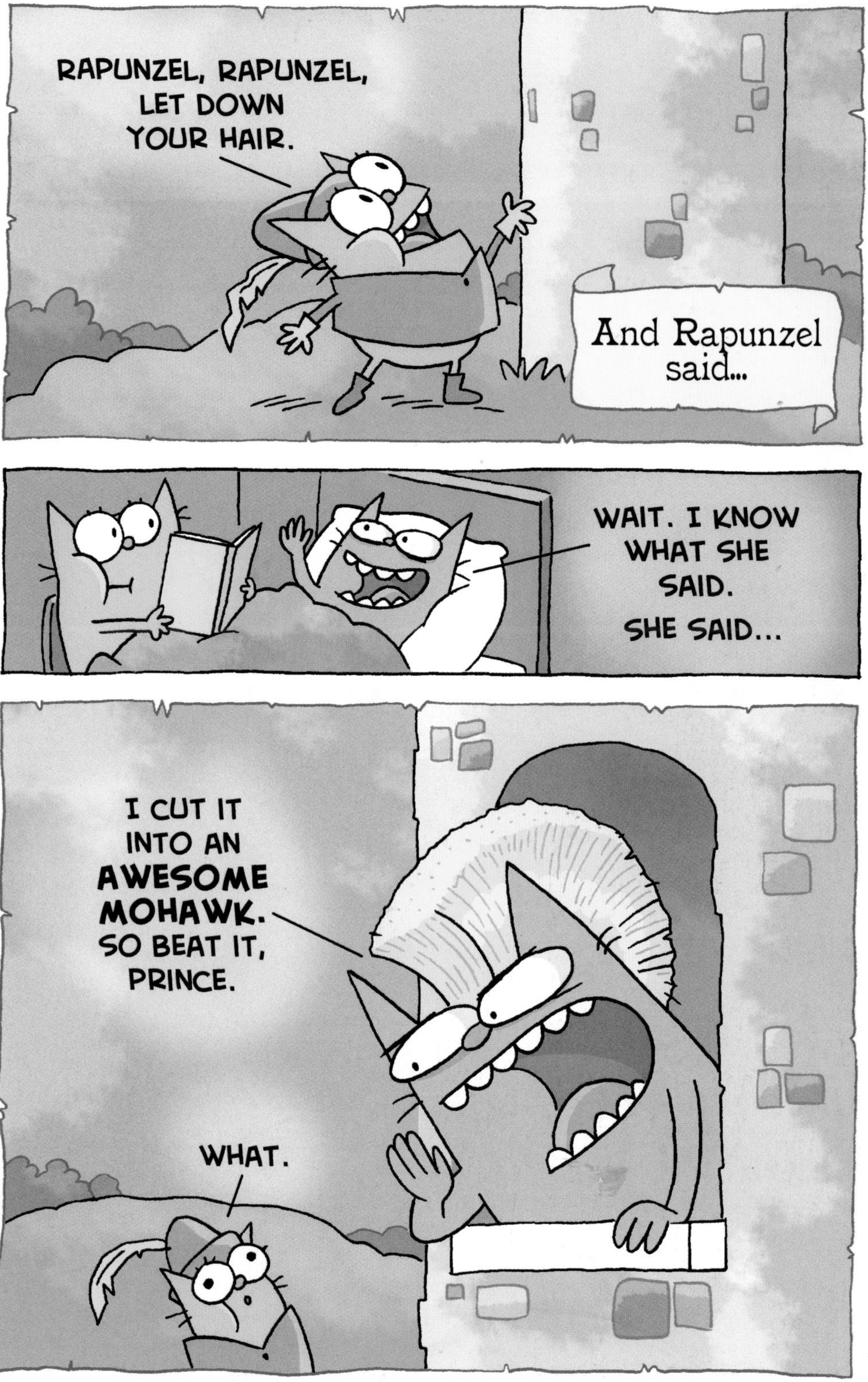
RAPUNZEL, RAPUNZEL, LET DOWN YOUR HAIR.
And Rapunzel said...
WAIT. I KNOW WHAT SHE SAID.
SHE SAID...
I CUT IT INTO AN **AWESOME MOHAWK.** SO BEAT IT, PRINCE.
WHAT.

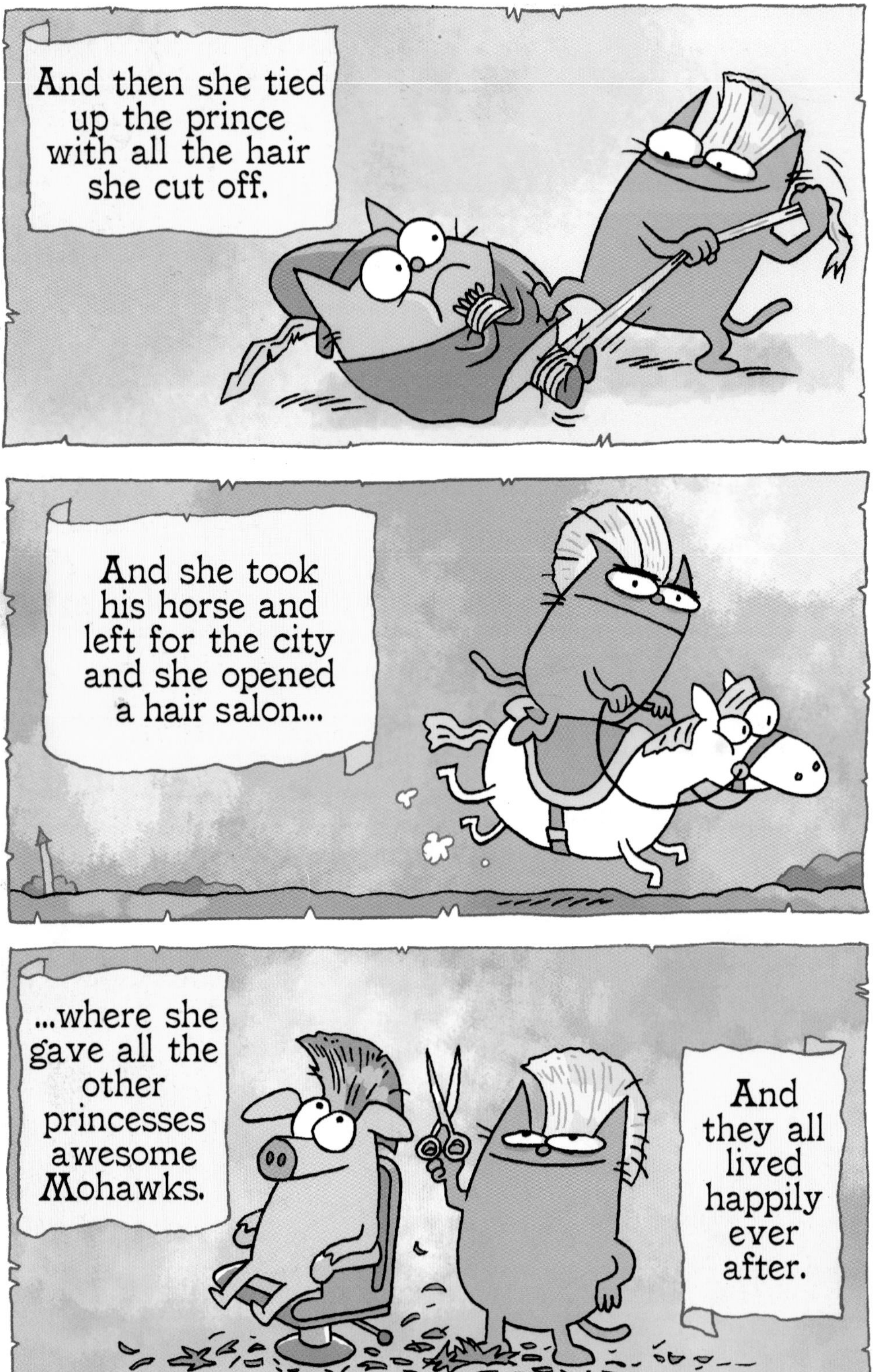
And then she tied up the prince with all the hair she cut off.
And she took his horse and left for the city and she opened a hair salon...
...where she gave all the other princesses awesome Mohawks.
And they all lived happily ever after.

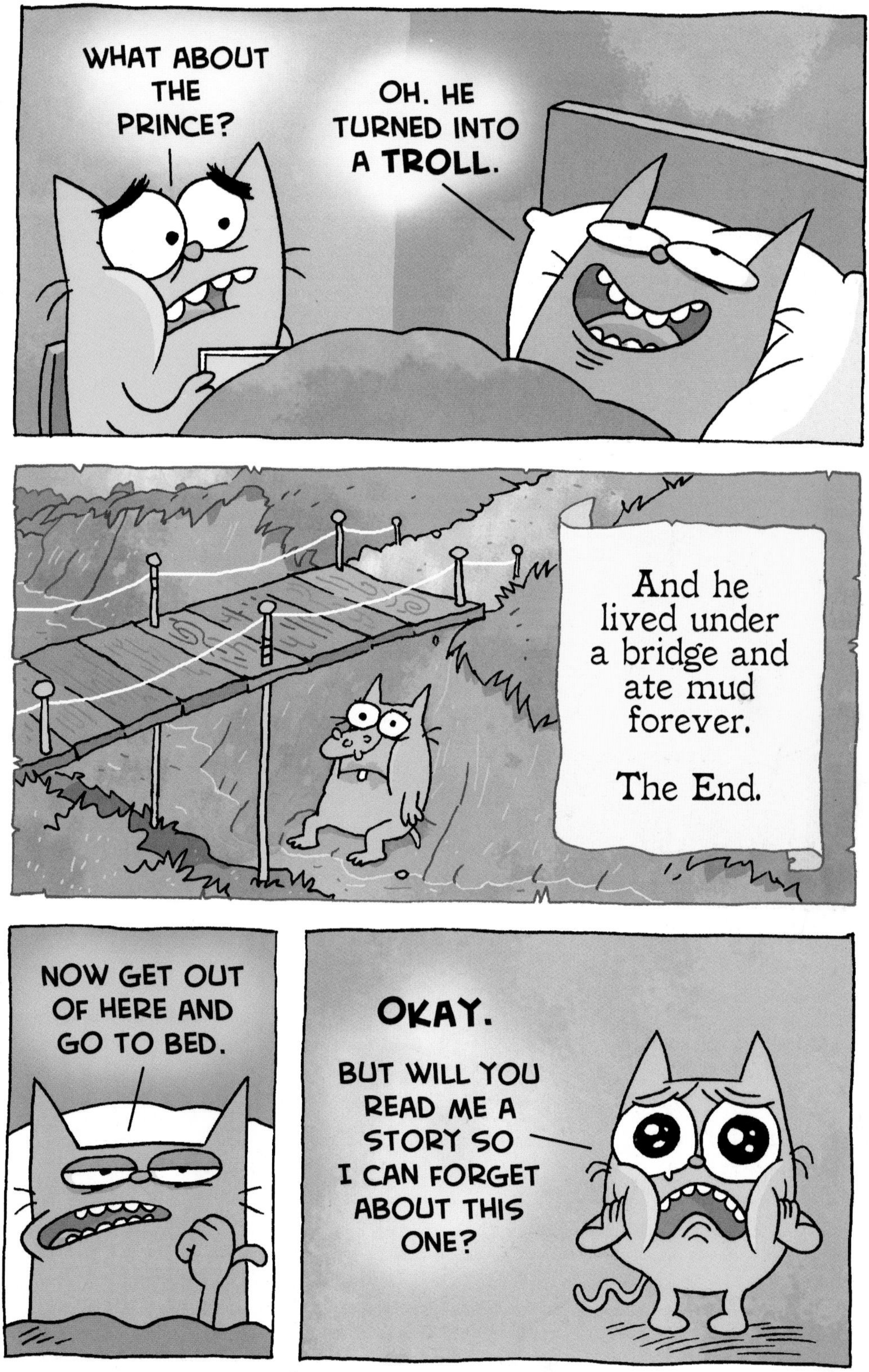
WHAT ABOUT THE PRINCE?
OH. HE TURNED INTO A **TROLL**.
And he lived under a bridge and ate mud forever.
The End.
NOW GET OUT OF HERE AND GO TO BED.
OKAY.
BUT WILL YOU READ ME A STORY SO I CAN FORGET ABOUT THIS ONE?

The DRAGON

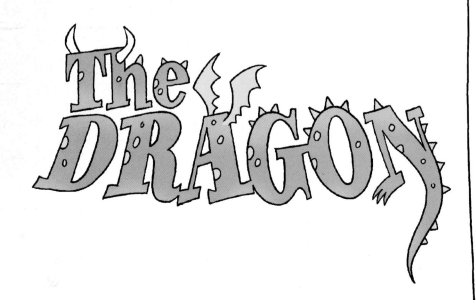

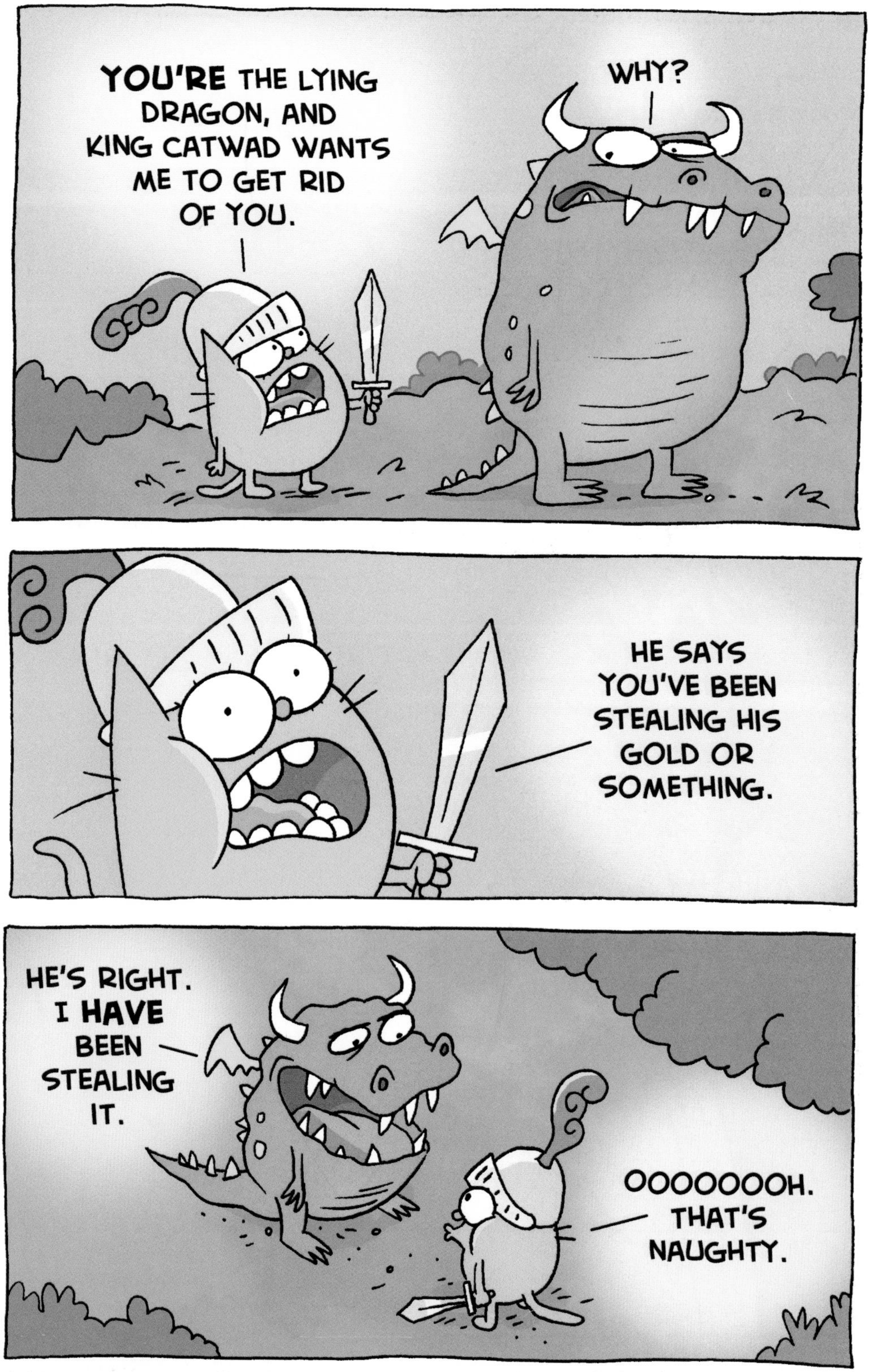
YOU'RE THE LYING DRAGON, AND KING CATWAD WANTS ME TO GET RID OF YOU.
WHY?
HE SAYS YOU'VE BEEN STEALING HIS GOLD OR SOMETHING.
HE'S RIGHT. I HAVE BEEN STEALING IT.
OOOOOOOH. THAT'S NAUGHTY.

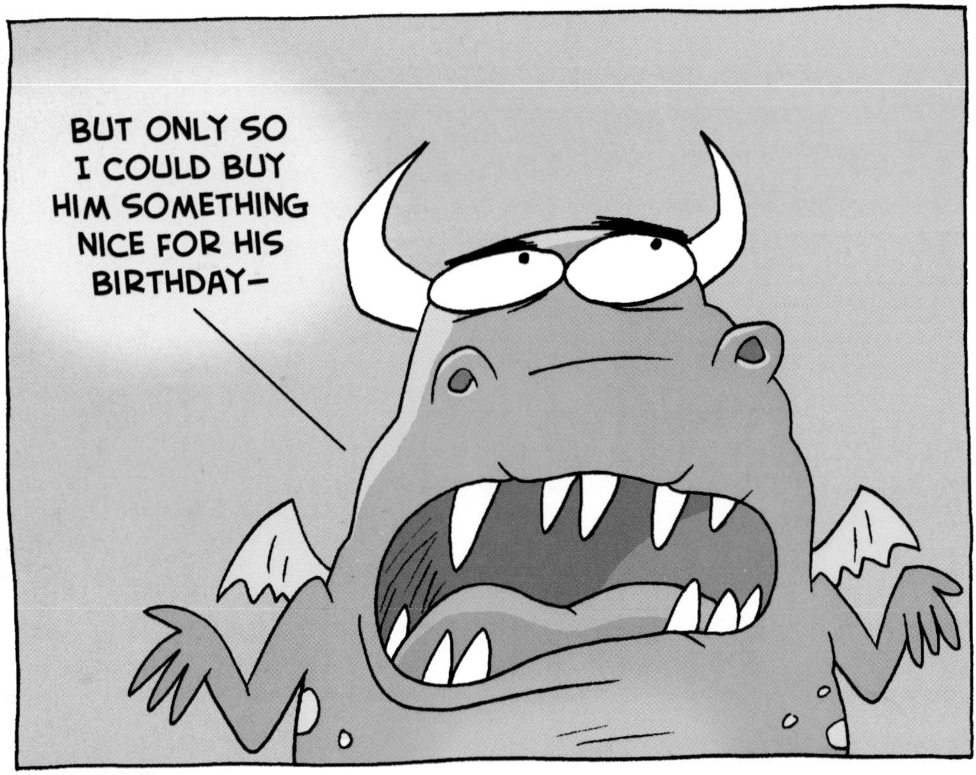
BUT ONLY SO I COULD BUY HIM SOMETHING NICE FOR HIS BIRTHDAY—

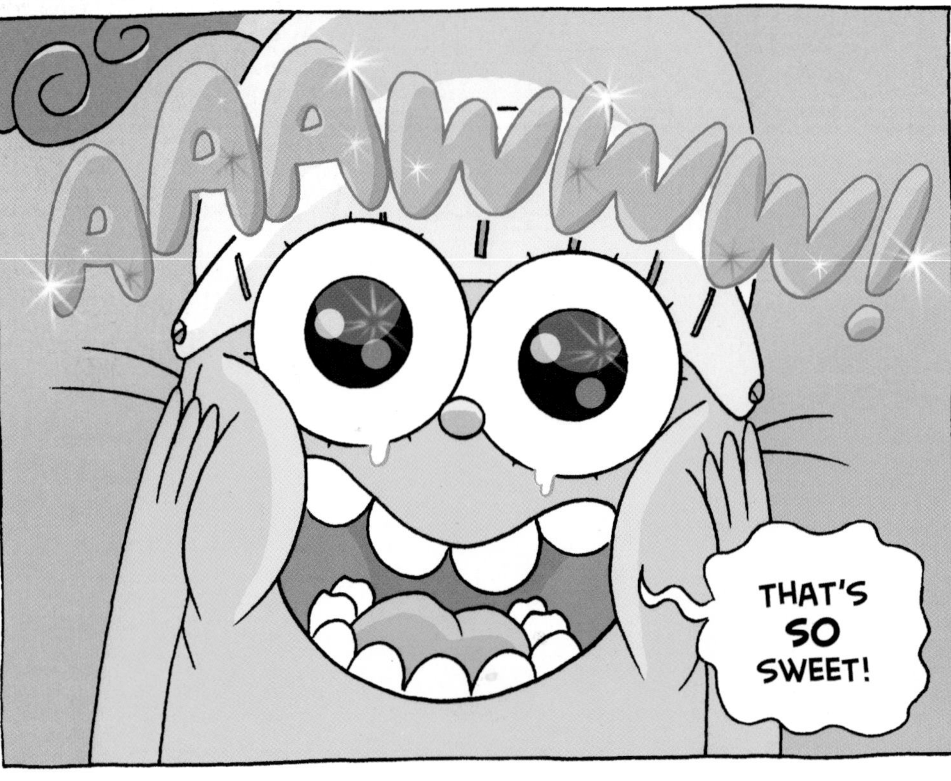
AAAWWW!
THAT'S SO SWEET!

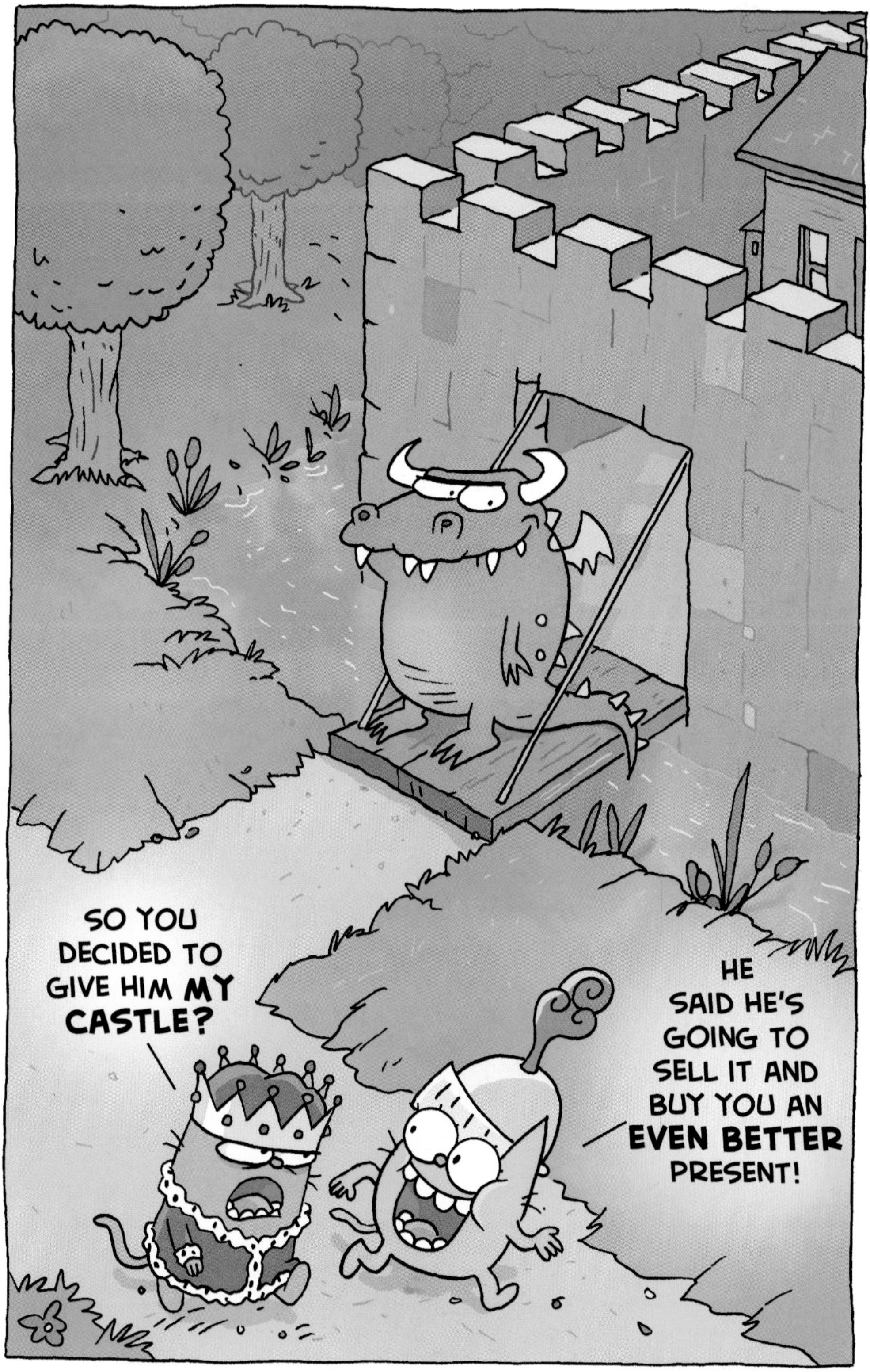
SO YOU DECIDED TO GIVE HIM **MY CASTLE?**
HE SAID HE'S GOING TO SELL IT AND BUY YOU AN **EVEN BETTER** PRESENT!

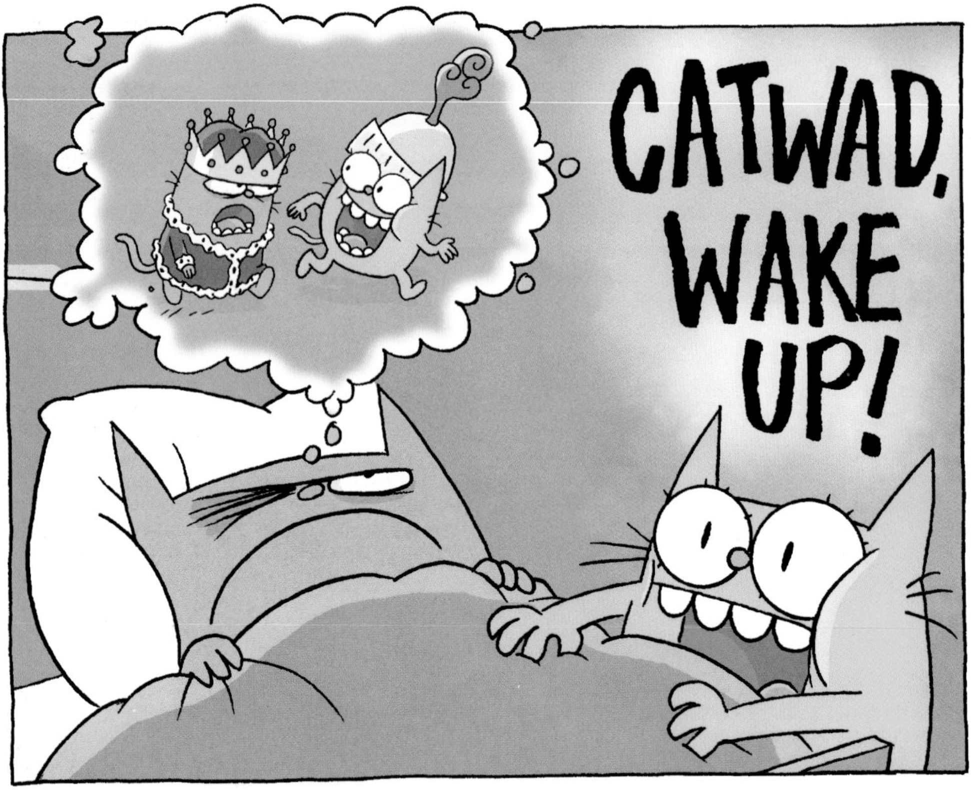
CATWAD, WAKE UP!

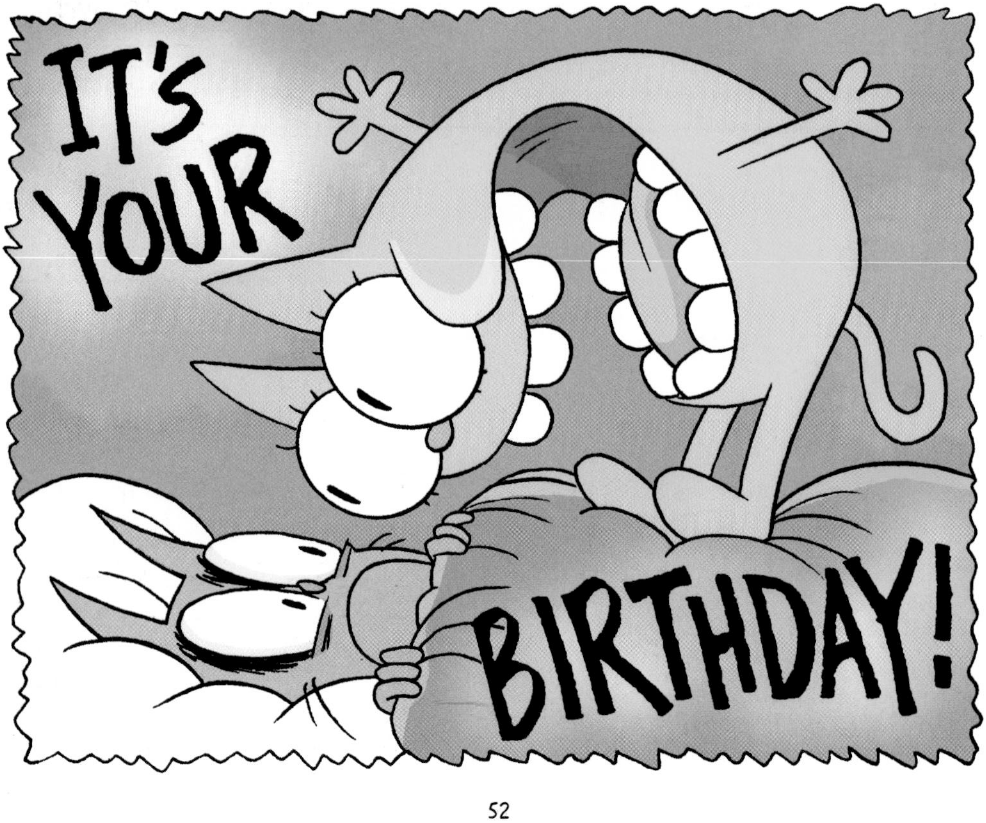
IT'S YOUR BIRTHDAY!

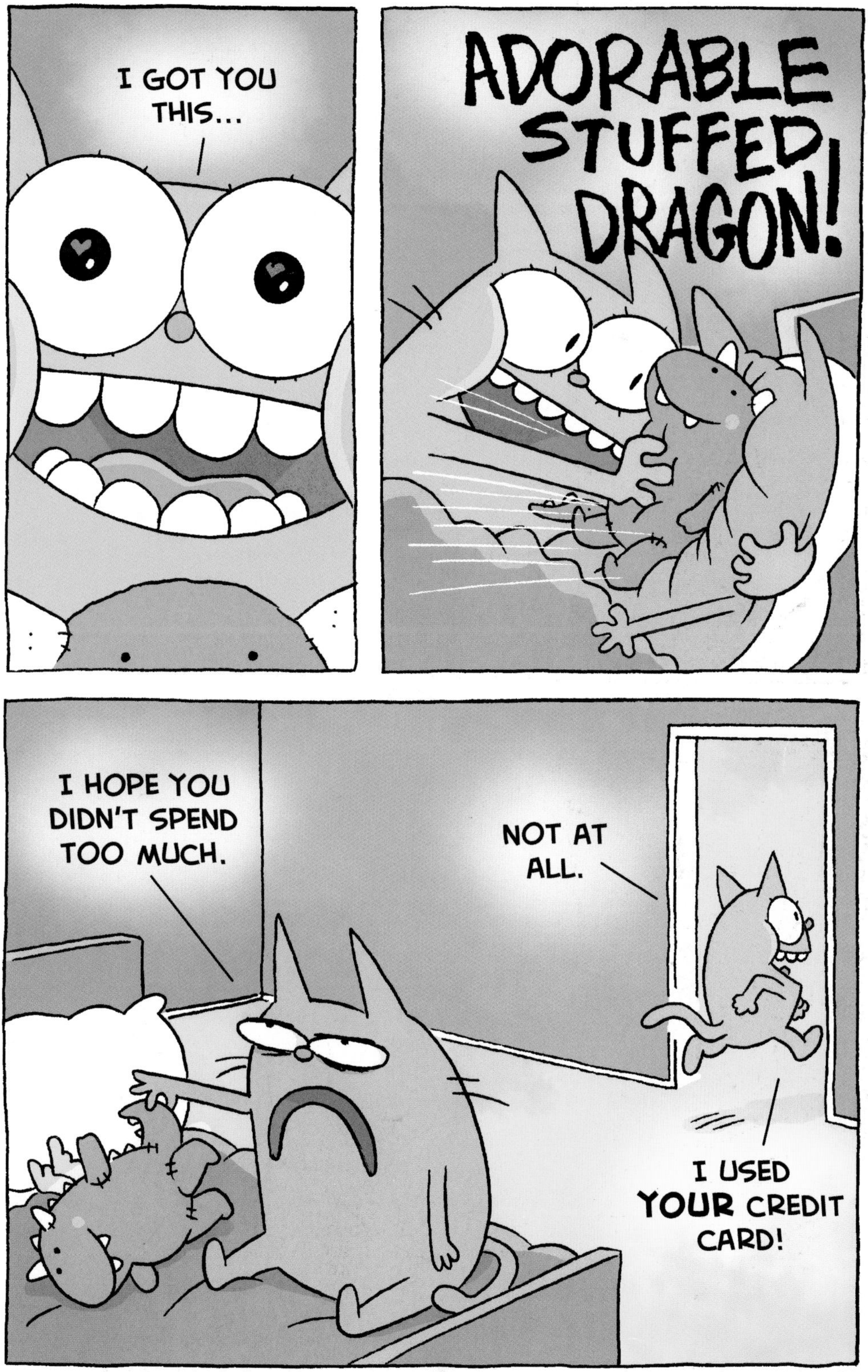

I GOT YOU THIS...
ADORABLE STUFFED DRAGON!
I HOPE YOU DIDN'T SPEND TOO MUCH.
NOT AT ALL.
I USED **YOUR** CREDIT CARD!

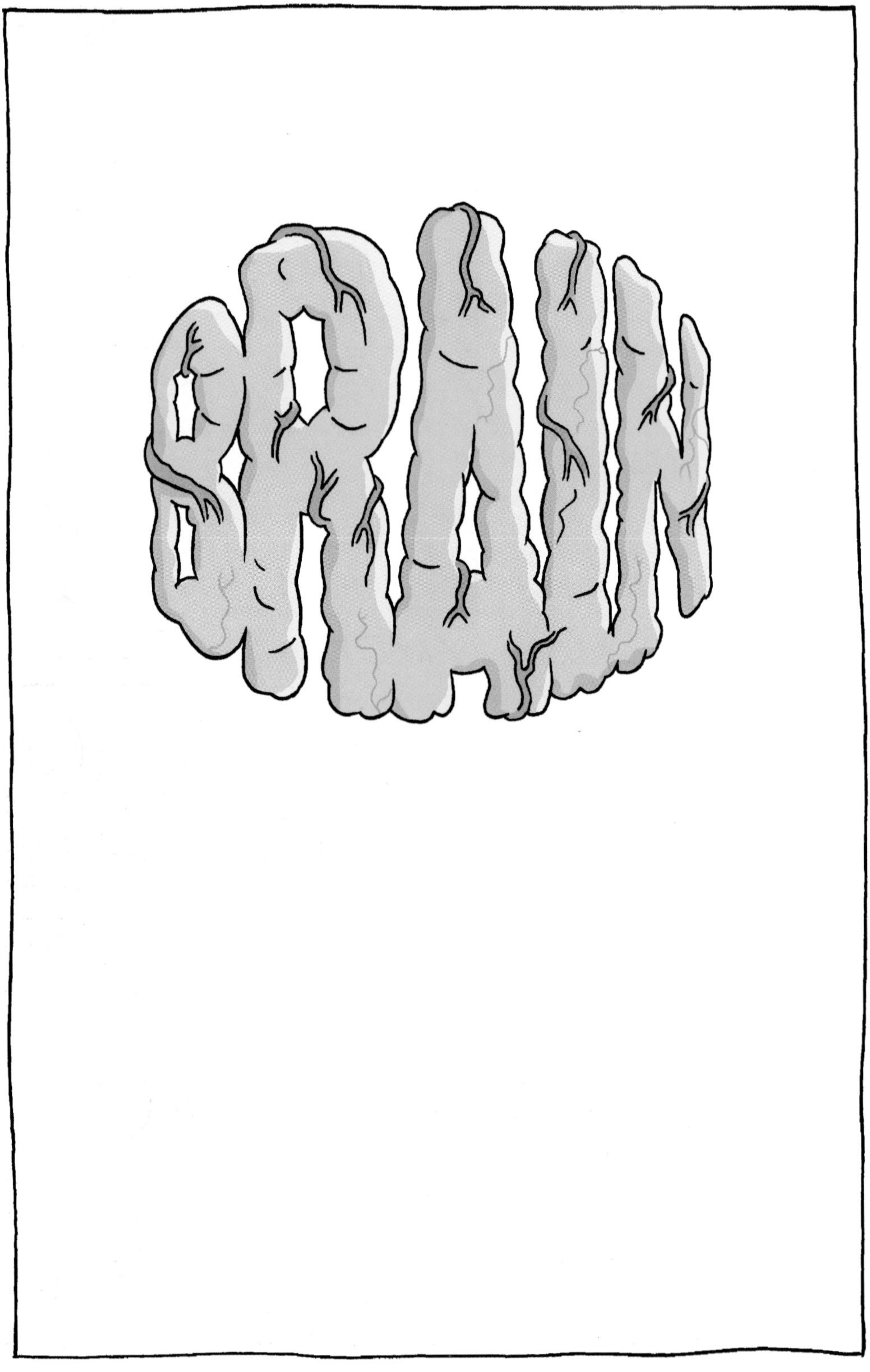
BRAIN

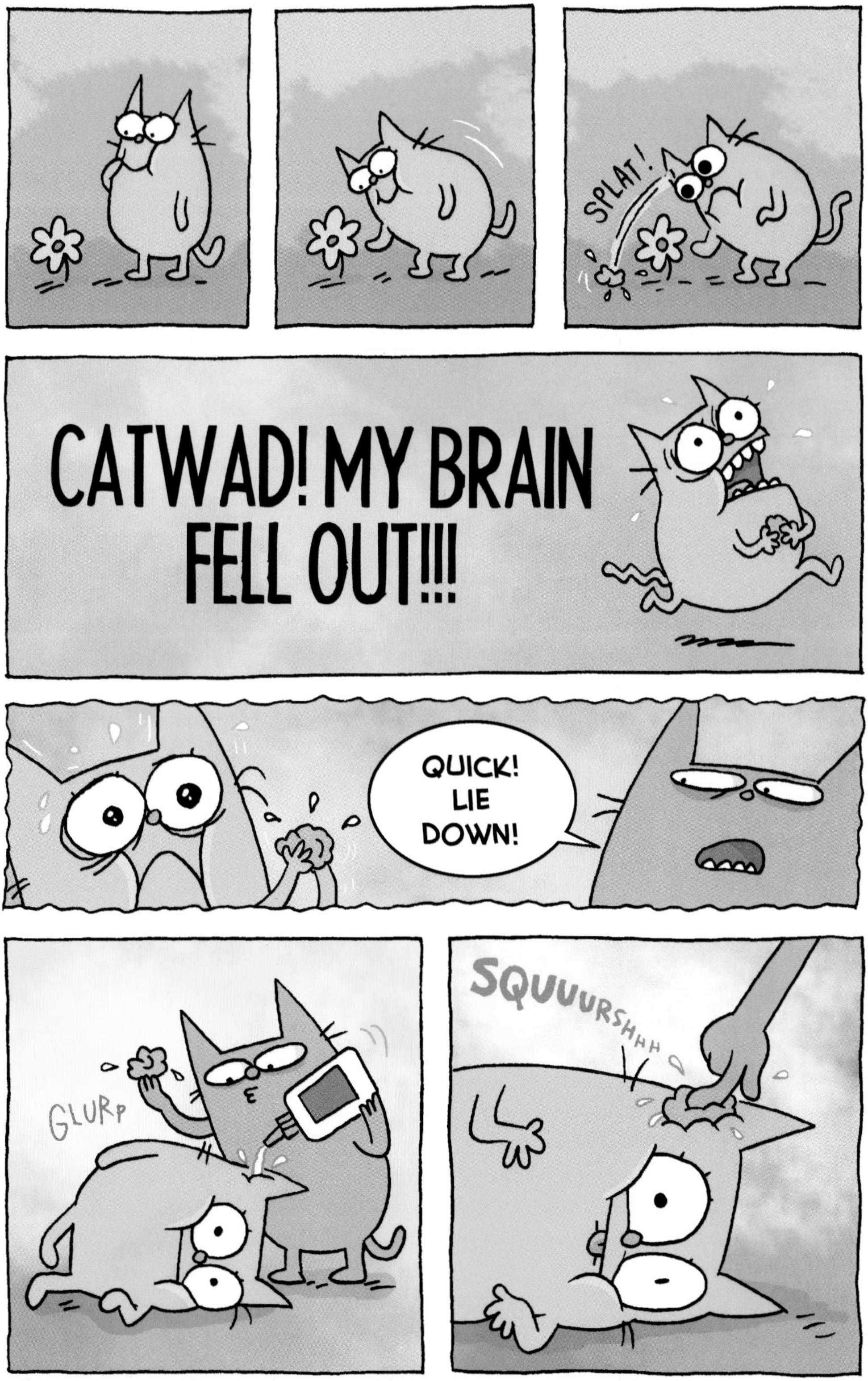
SPLAT!
CATWAD! MY BRAIN FELL OUT!!!
QUICK! LIE DOWN!
GLURP
SQUUURSHHH

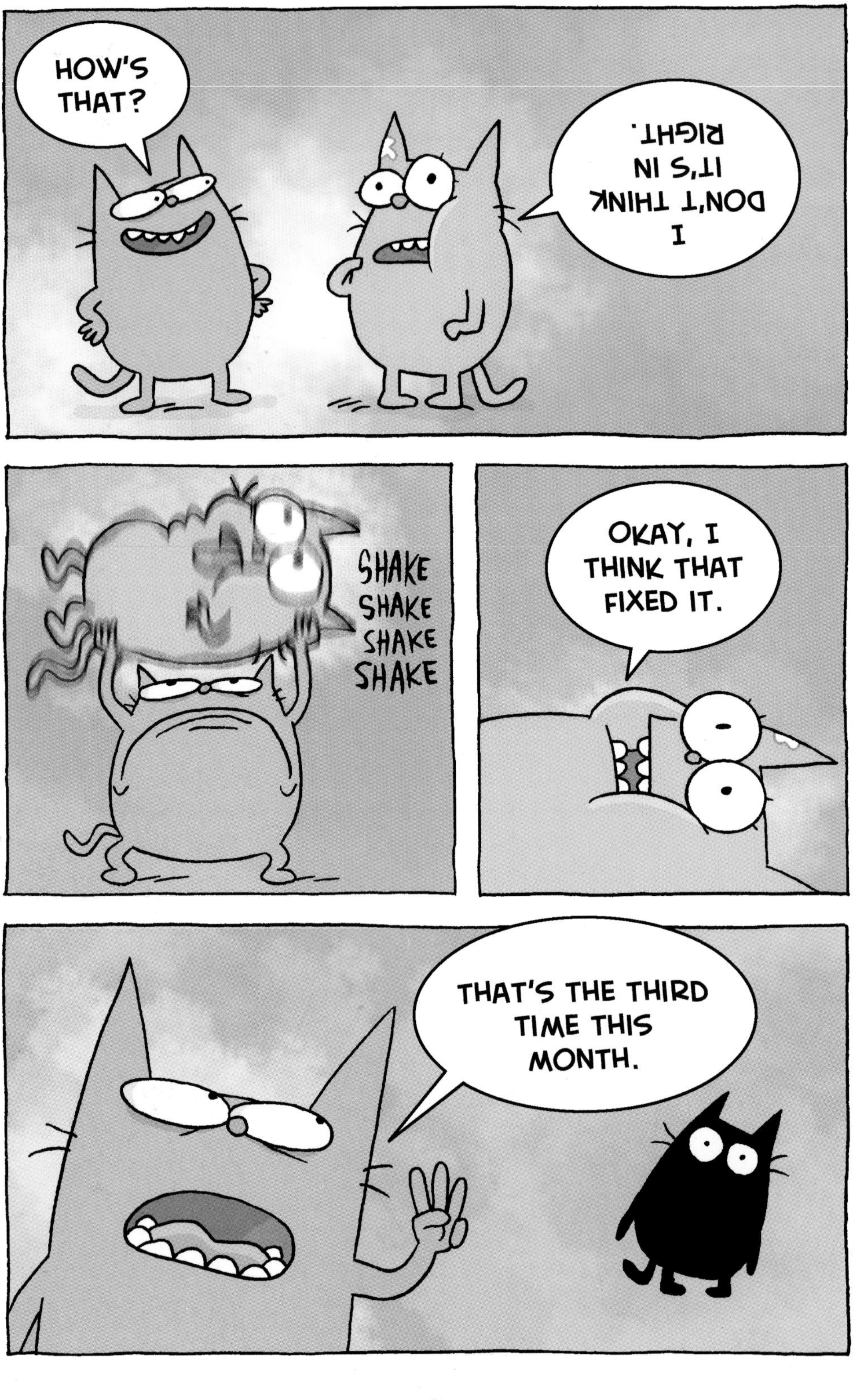
HOW'S THAT?
I DON'T THINK IT'S IN RIGHT.
SHAKE SHAKE SHAKE SHAKE
OKAY, I THINK THAT FIXED IT.
THAT'S THE THIRD TIME THIS MONTH.

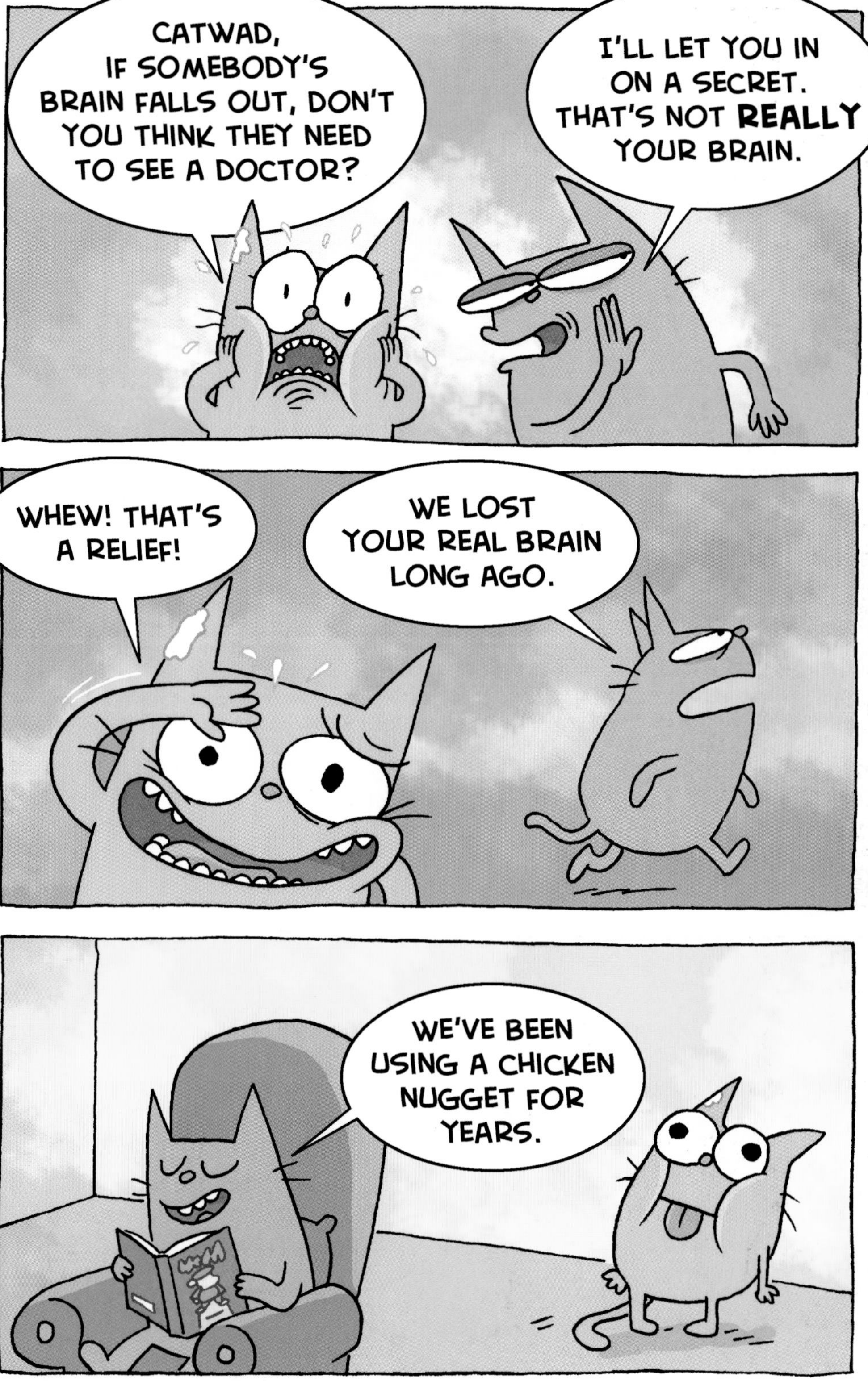
CATWAD, IF SOMEBODY'S BRAIN FALLS OUT, DON'T YOU THINK THEY NEED TO SEE A DOCTOR?
I'LL LET YOU IN ON A SECRET. THAT'S NOT **REALLY** YOUR BRAIN.
WHEW! THAT'S A RELIEF!
WE LOST YOUR REAL BRAIN LONG AGO.
WE'VE BEEN USING A CHICKEN NUGGET FOR YEARS.

MEMORIES

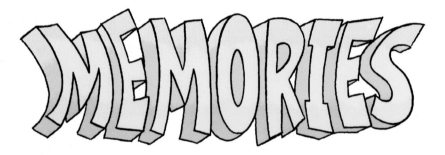

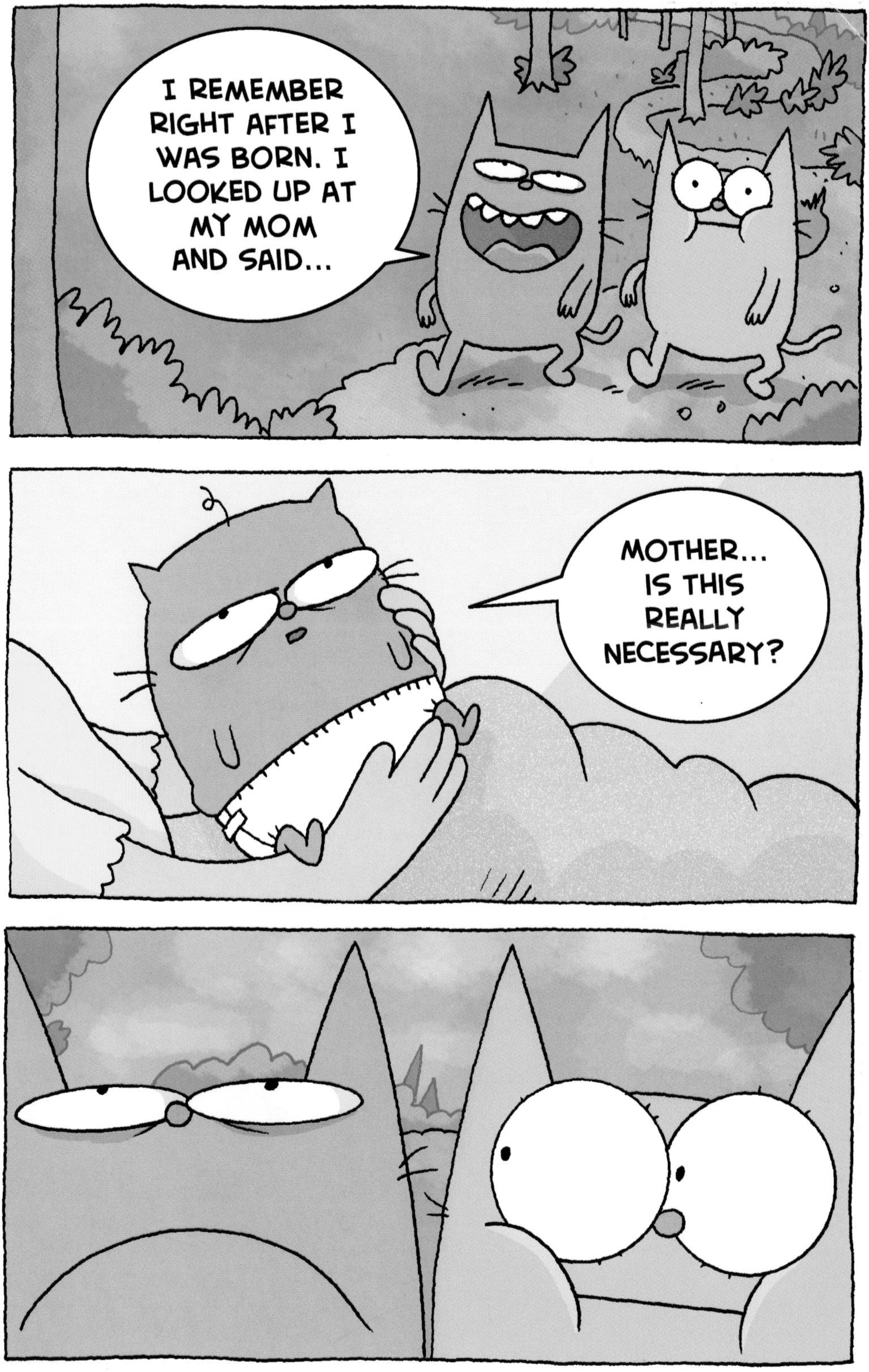
I REMEMBER RIGHT AFTER I WAS BORN. I LOOKED UP AT MY MOM AND SAID...
MOTHER... IS THIS REALLY NECESSARY?

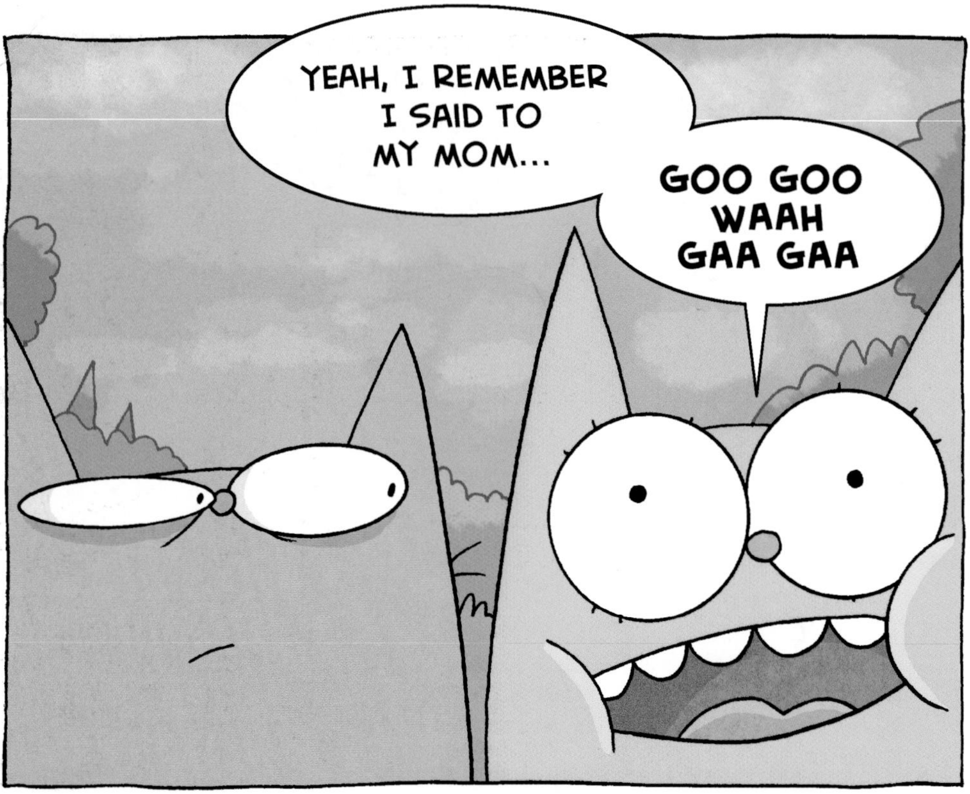
YEAH, I REMEMBER I SAID TO MY MOM...
GOO GOO WAAH GAA GAA

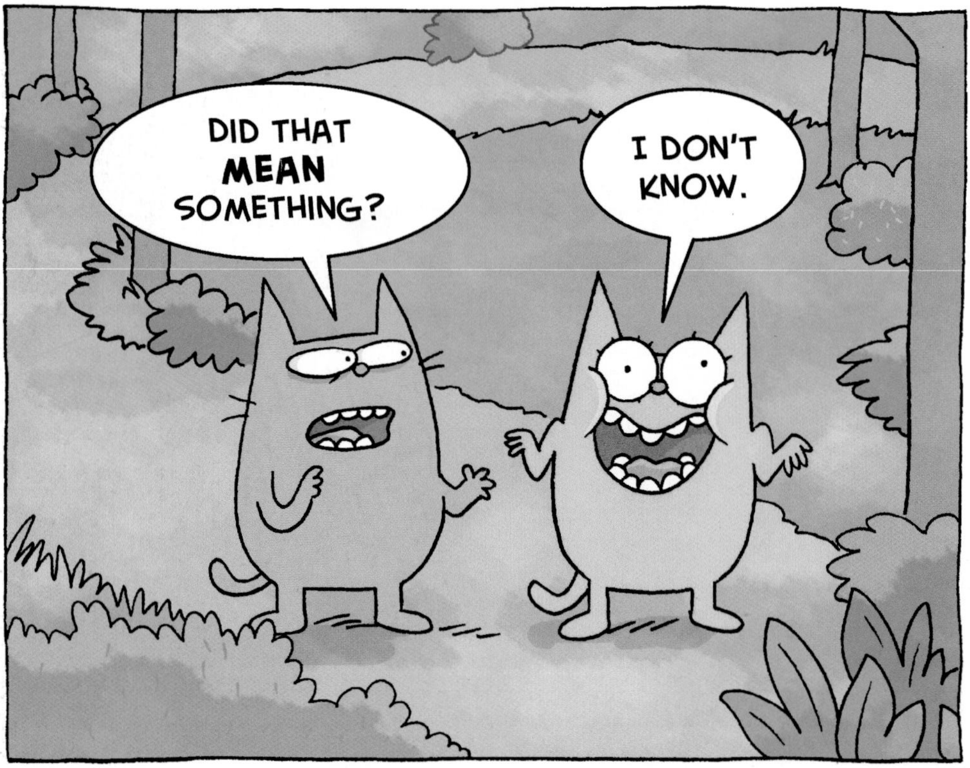
DID THAT **MEAN** SOMETHING?
I DON'T KNOW.

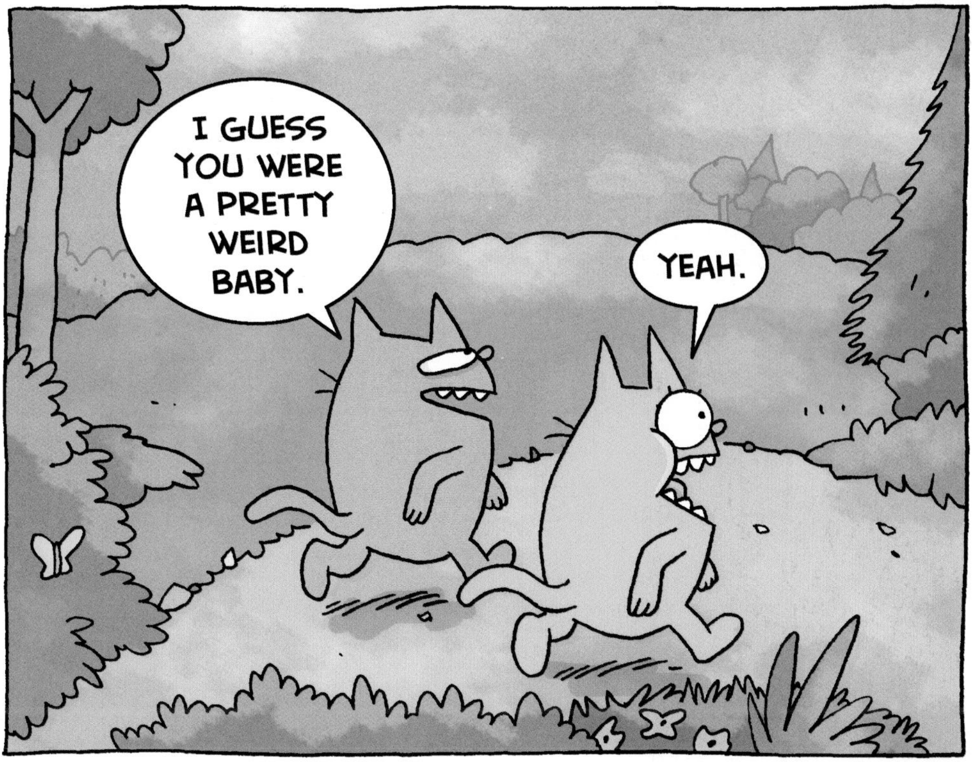
I GUESS YOU WERE A PRETTY WEIRD BABY.
YEAH.

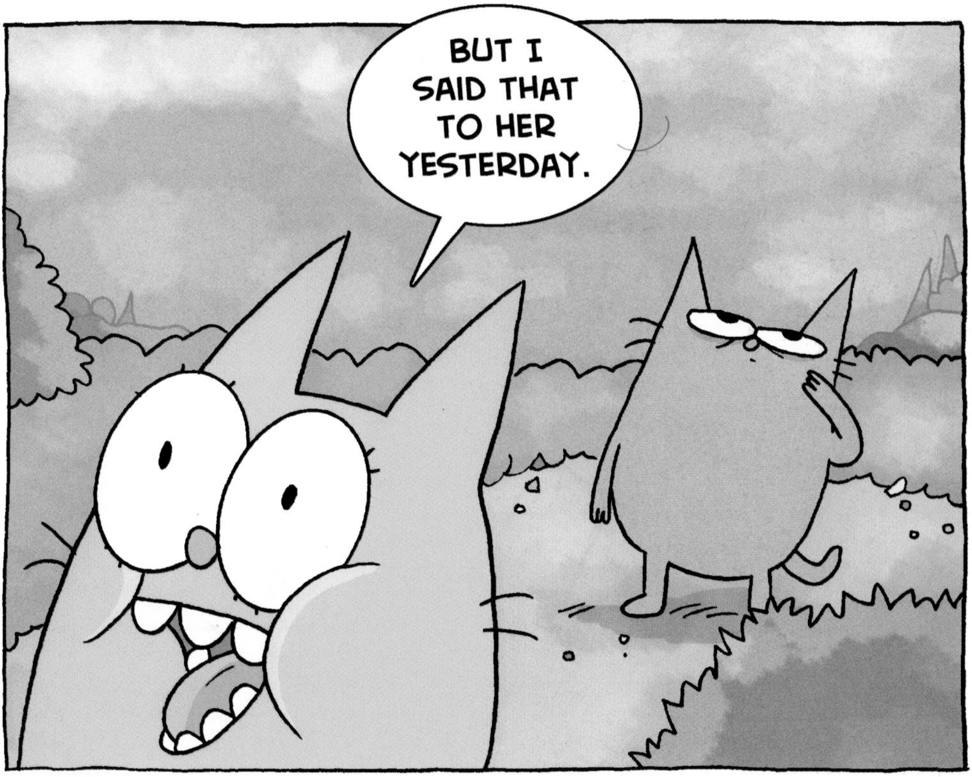
BUT I SAID THAT TO HER YESTERDAY.

NAILED

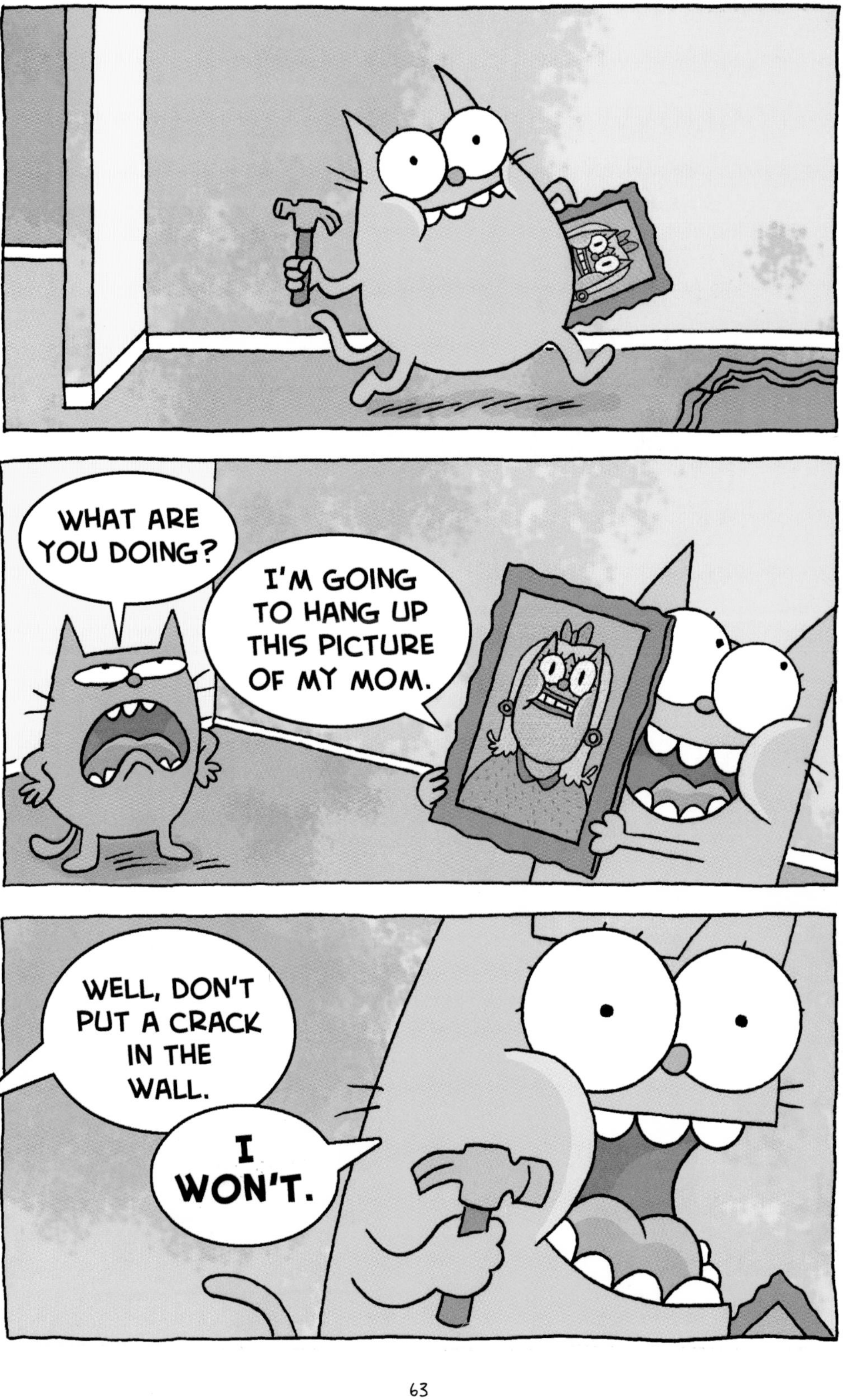
WHAT ARE YOU DOING?
I'M GOING TO HANG UP THIS PICTURE OF MY MOM.
WELL, DON'T PUT A CRACK IN THE WALL.
I WON'T.

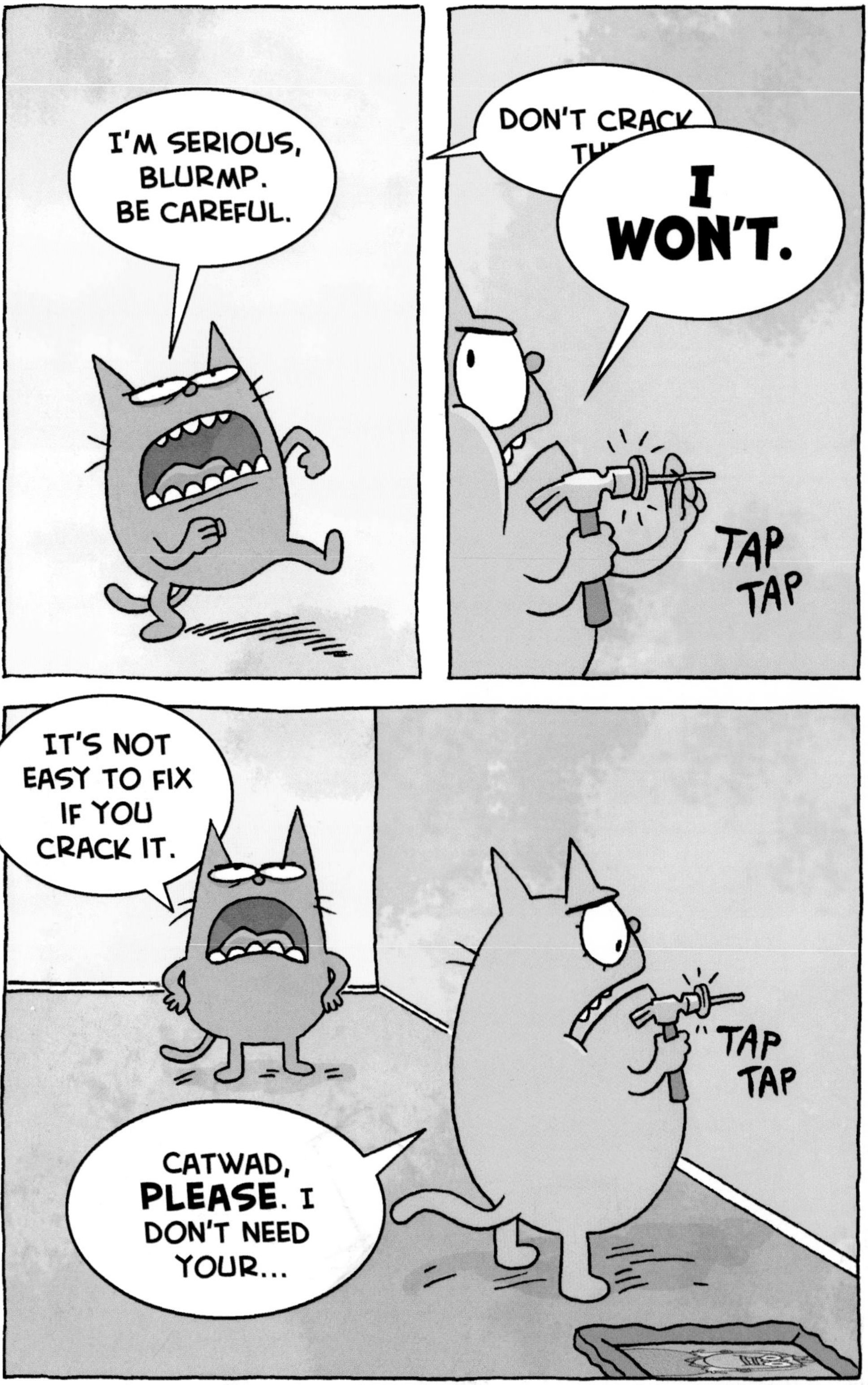
I'M SERIOUS, BLURMP. BE CAREFUL.
DON'T CRACK TH
I WON'T.
TAP TAP
IT'S NOT EASY TO FIX IF YOU CRACK IT.
TAP TAP
CATWAD, PLEASE. I DON'T NEED YOUR...

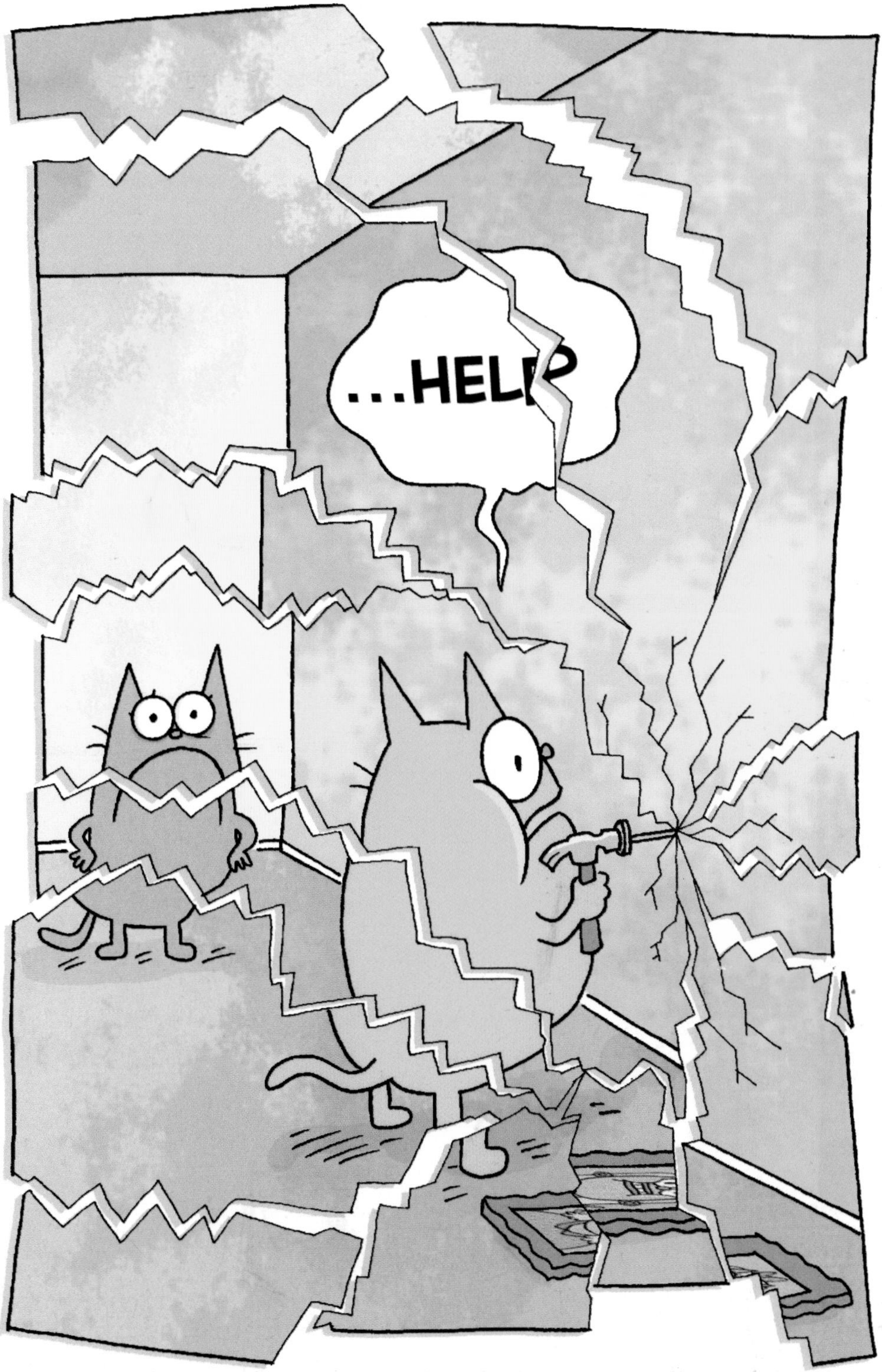
...HELP

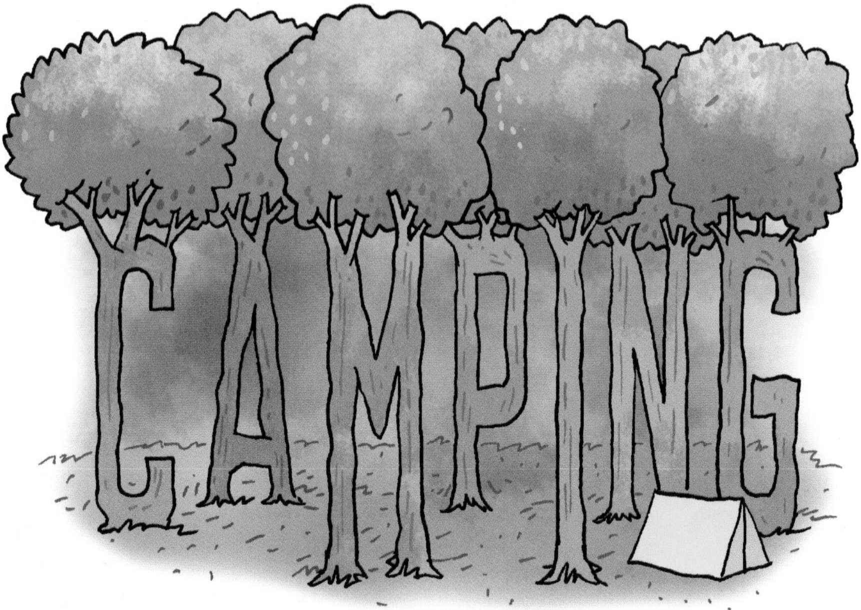
CAMPING

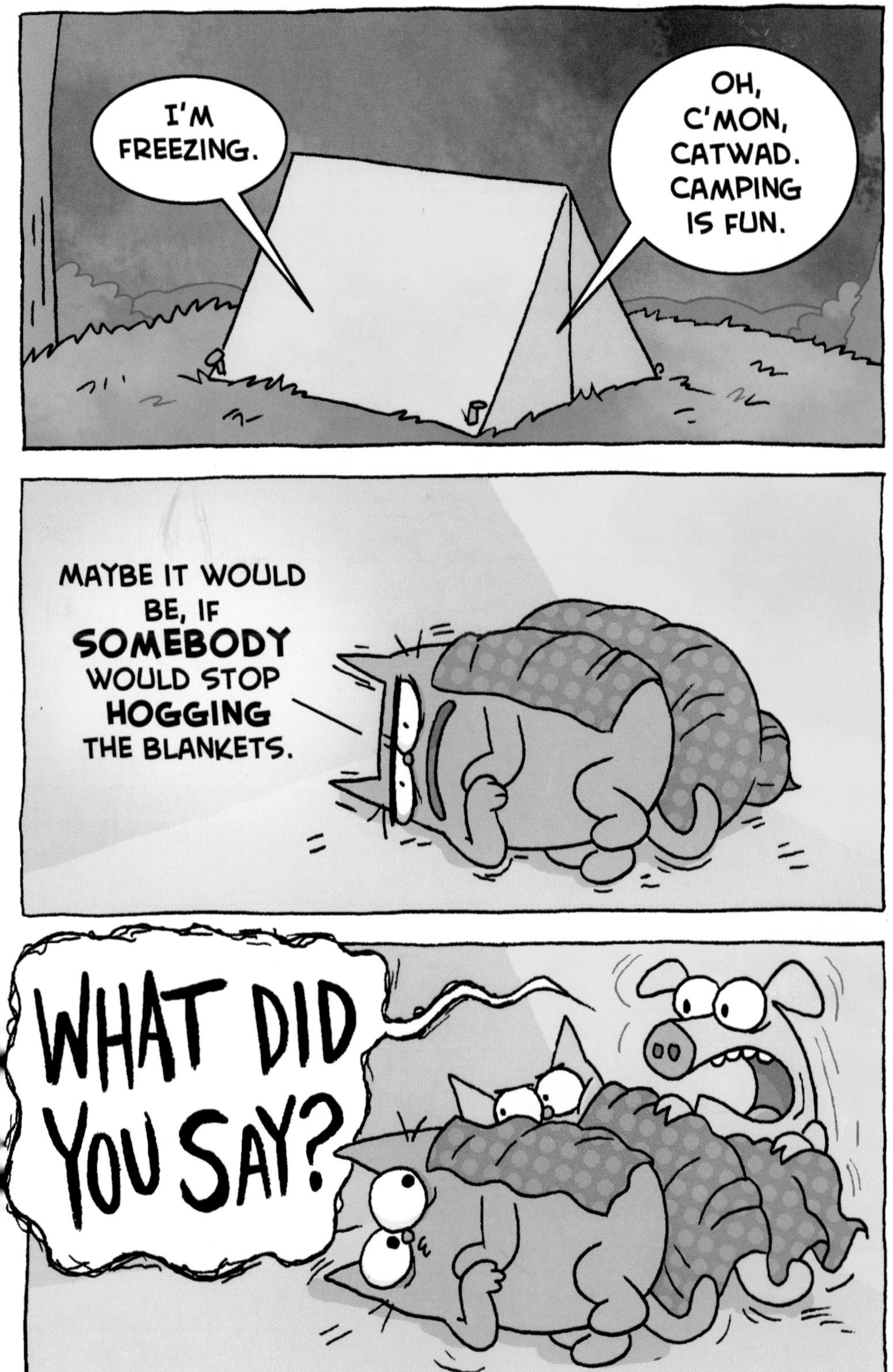
I'M FREEZING.
OH, C'MON, CATWAD. CAMPING IS FUN.
MAYBE IT WOULD BE, IF **SOMEBODY** WOULD STOP **HOGGING** THE BLANKETS.
WHAT DID YOU SAY?

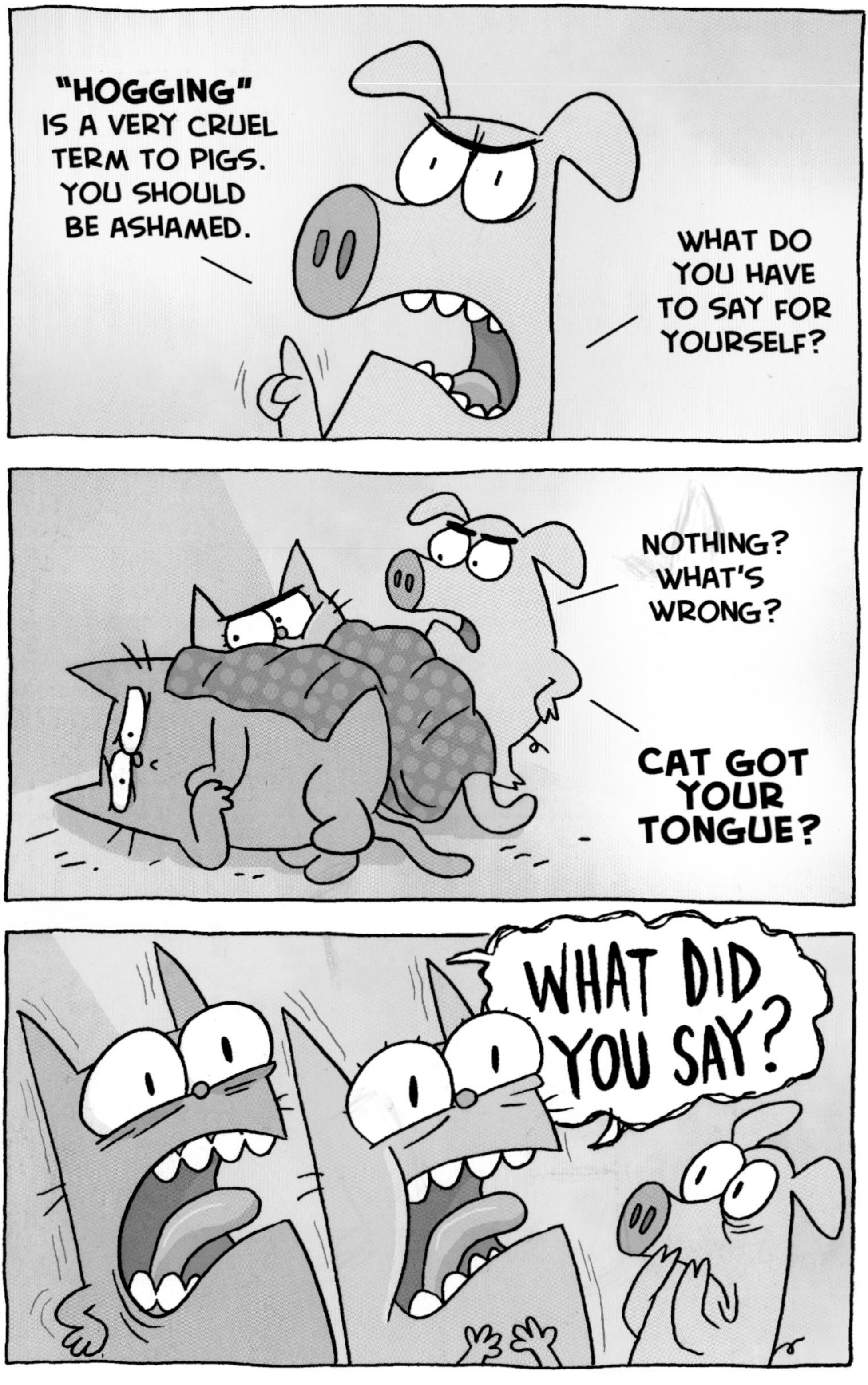
"HOGGING" IS A VERY CRUEL TERM TO PIGS. YOU SHOULD BE ASHAMED.
WHAT DO YOU HAVE TO SAY FOR YOURSELF?
NOTHING? WHAT'S WRONG?
CAT GOT YOUR TONGUE?
WHAT DID YOU SAY?

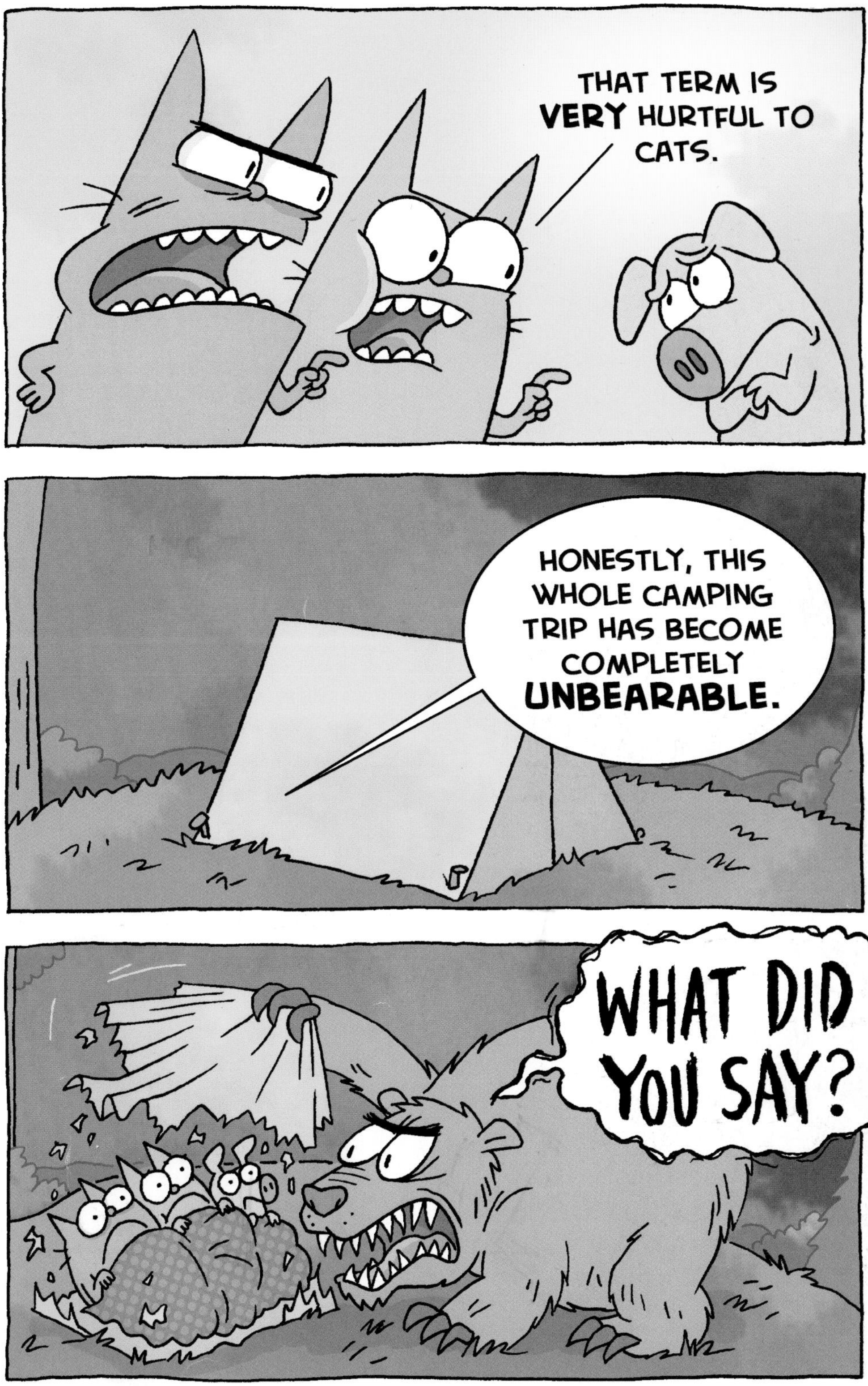
THAT TERM IS **VERY** HURTFUL TO CATS.
HONESTLY, THIS WHOLE CAMPING TRIP HAS BECOME COMPLETELY **UNBEARABLE.**
WHAT DID YOU SAY?

THE PERFECT DAY

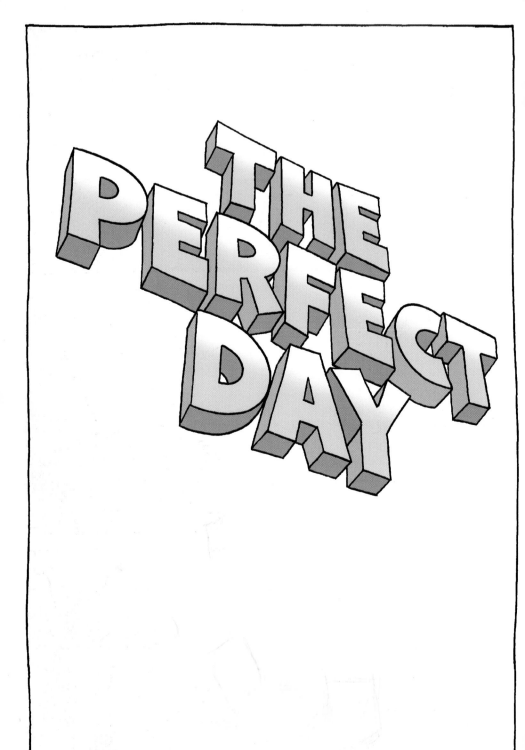

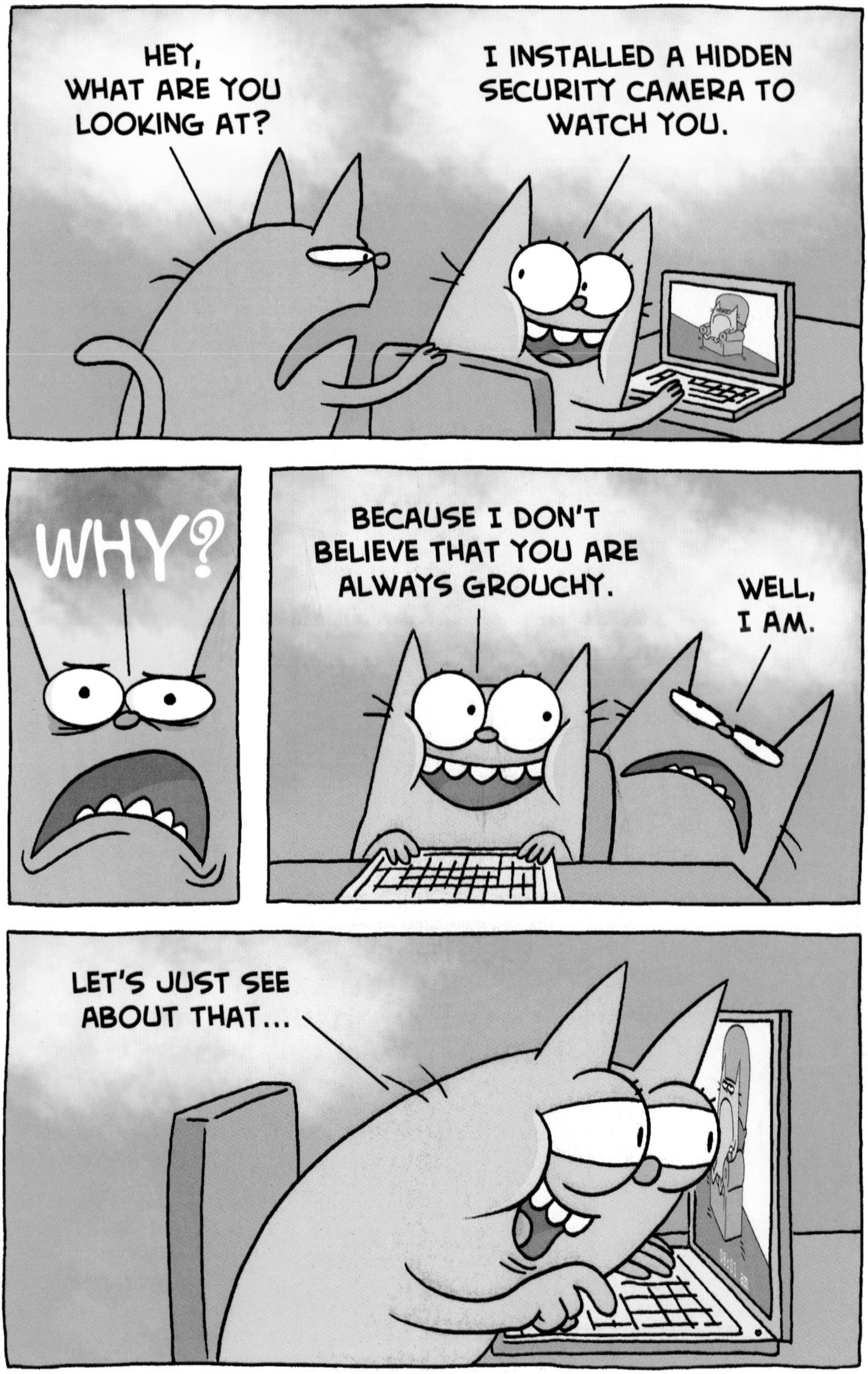
HEY, WHAT ARE YOU LOOKING AT?
I INSTALLED A HIDDEN SECURITY CAMERA TO WATCH YOU.
WHY?
BECAUSE I DON'T BELIEVE THAT YOU ARE ALWAYS GROUCHY.
WELL, I AM.
LET'S JUST SEE ABOUT THAT...

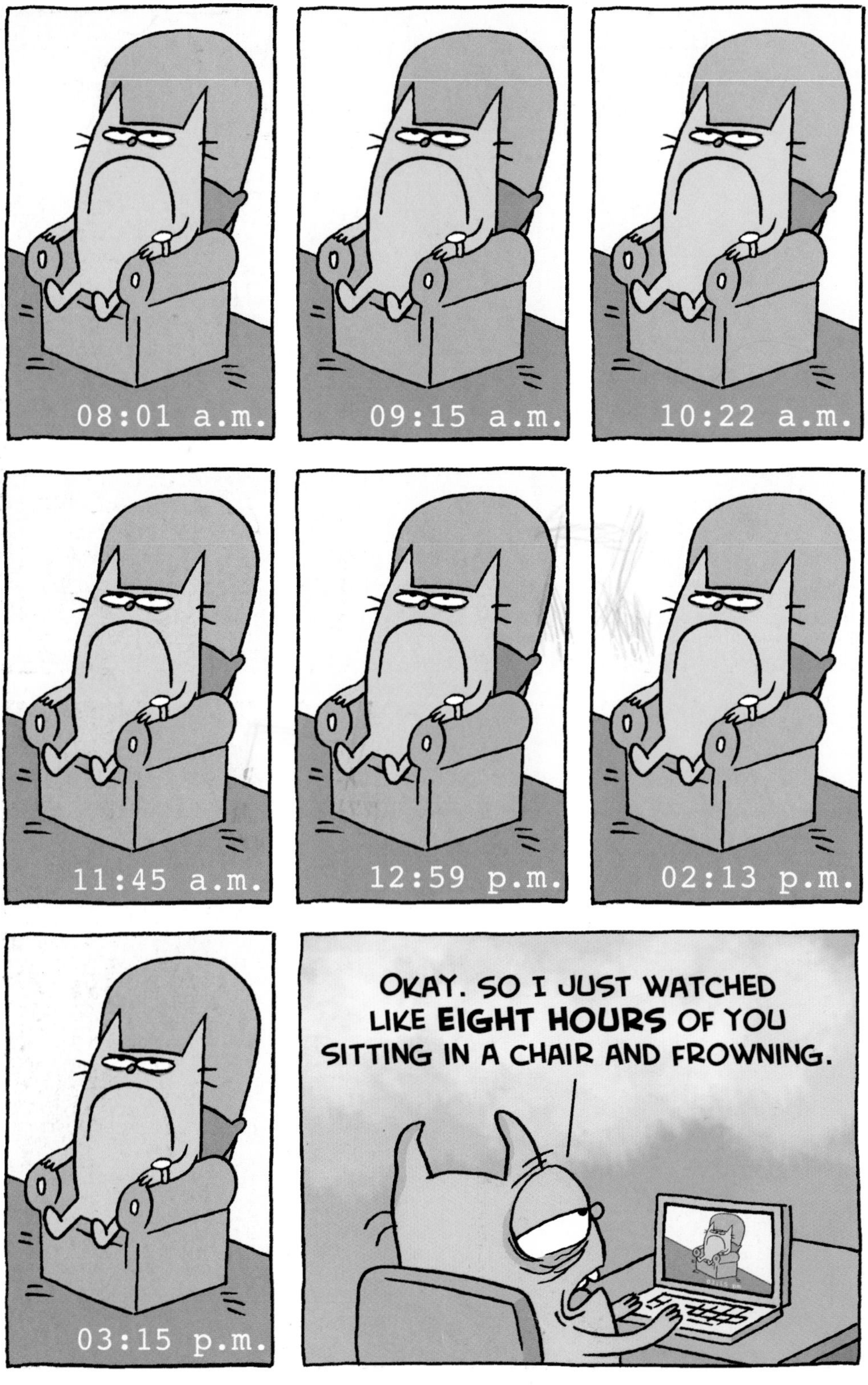
08:01 a.m.
09:15 a.m.
10:22 a.m.
11:45 a.m.
12:59 p.m.
02:13 p.m.
03:15 p.m.
OKAY. SO I JUST WATCHED LIKE **EIGHT HOURS** OF YOU SITTING IN A CHAIR AND FROWNING.

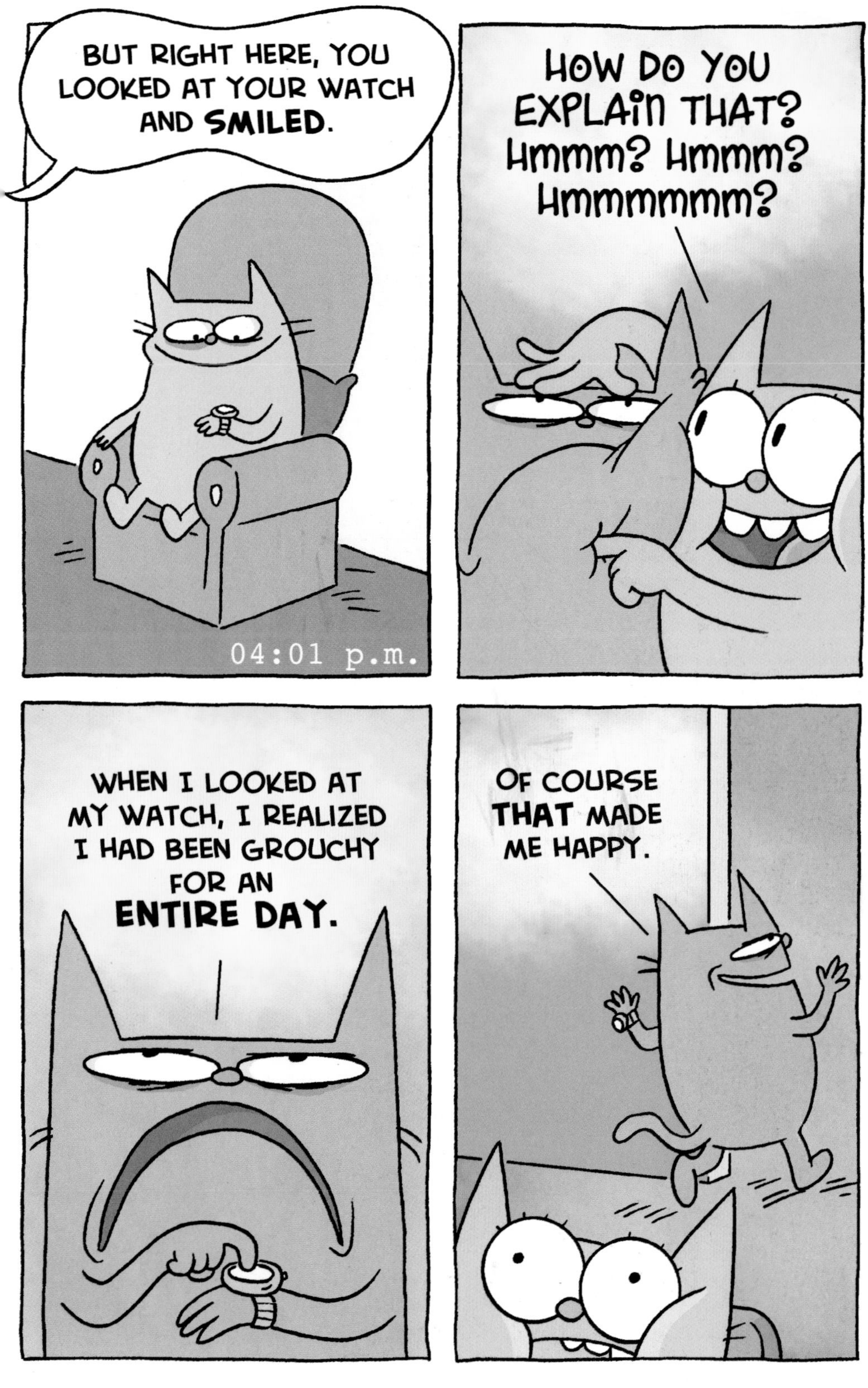

BUT RIGHT HERE, YOU LOOKED AT YOUR WATCH AND **SMILED**.
04:01 p.m.
HOW DO YOU EXPLAIN THAT? Hmmm? Hmmm? Hmmmmmm?
WHEN I LOOKED AT MY WATCH, I REALIZED I HAD BEEN GROUCHY FOR AN **ENTIRE DAY**.
OF COURSE **THAT** MADE ME HAPPY.

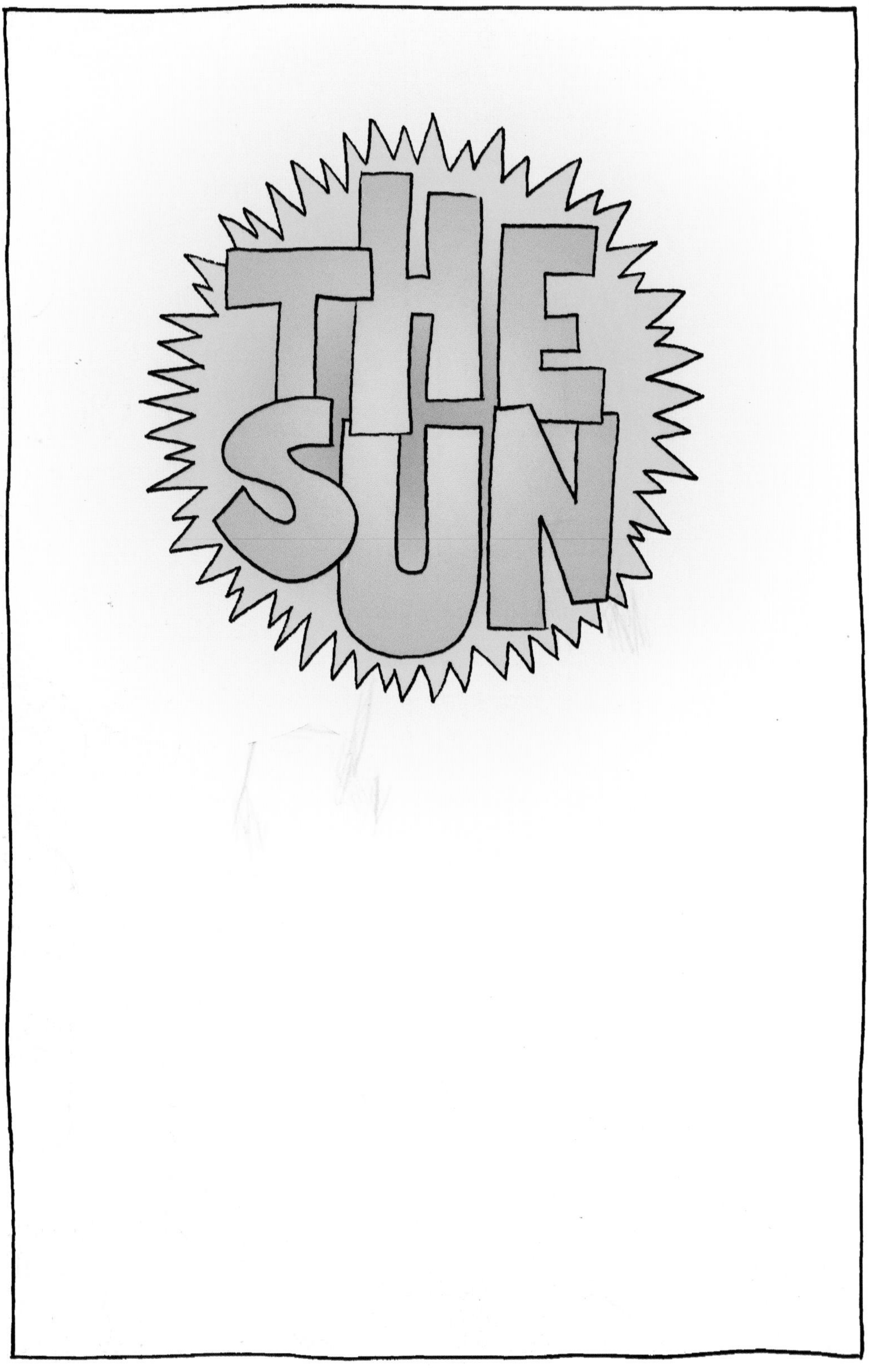
THE SUN

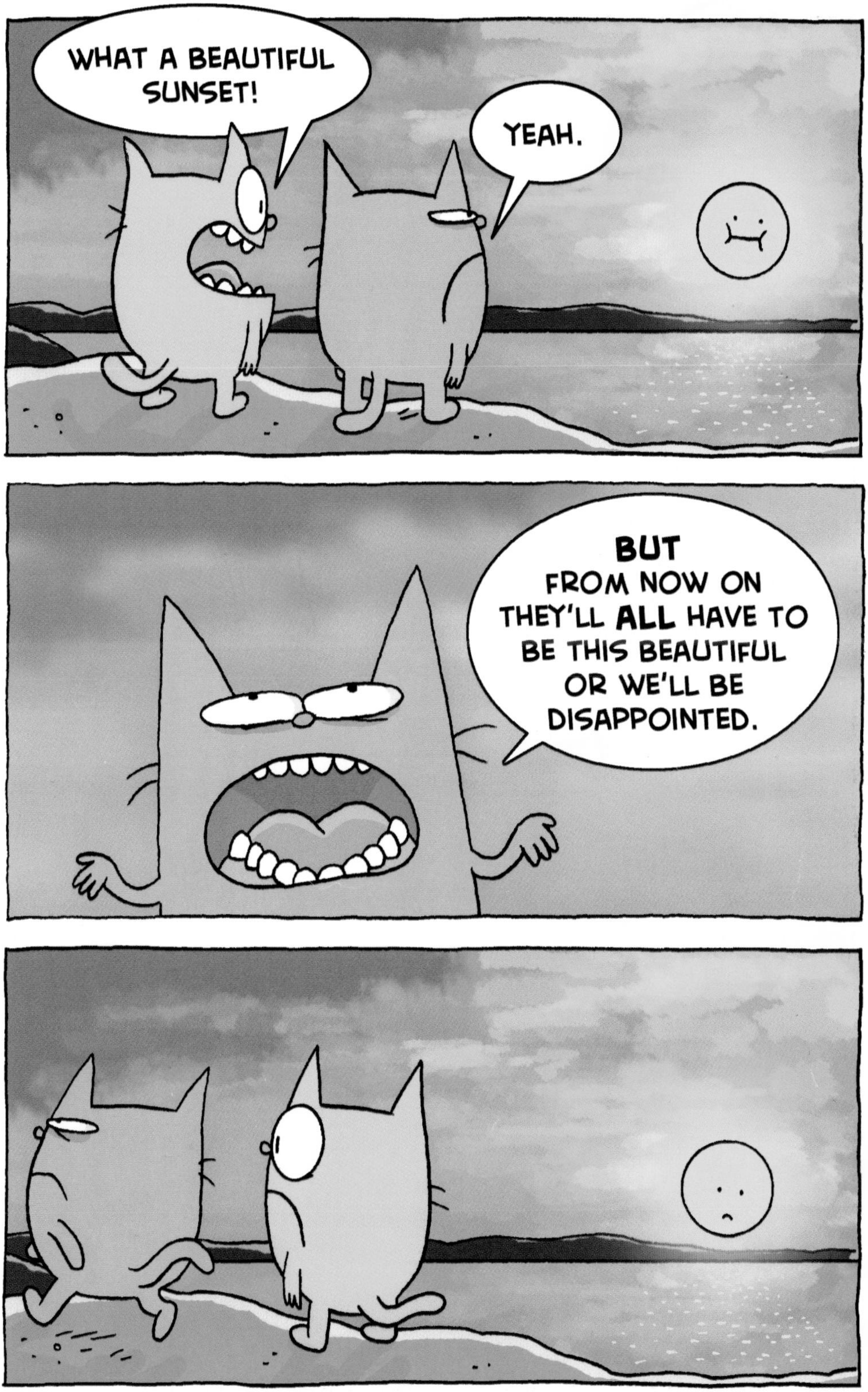
WHAT A BEAUTIFUL SUNSET!
YEAH.
BUT FROM NOW ON THEY'LL ALL HAVE TO BE THIS BEAUTIFUL OR WE'LL BE DISAPPOINTED.

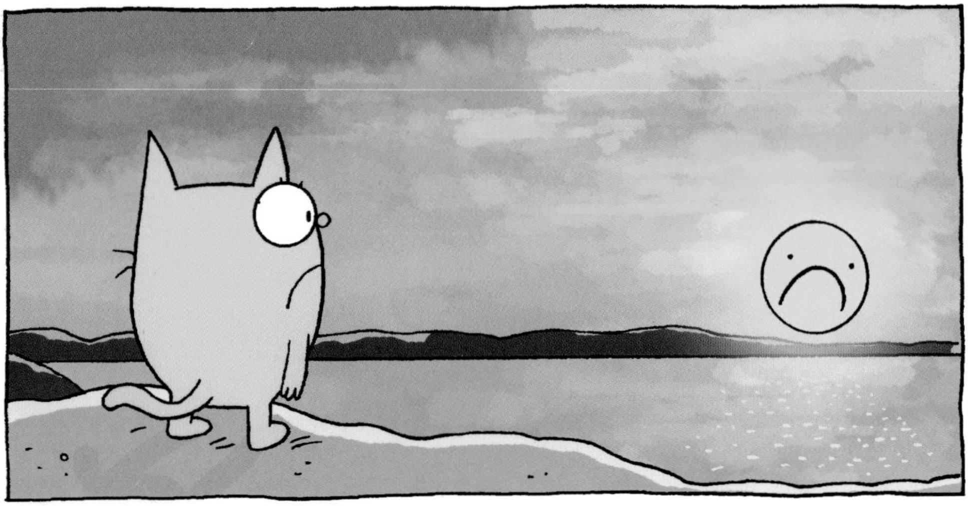

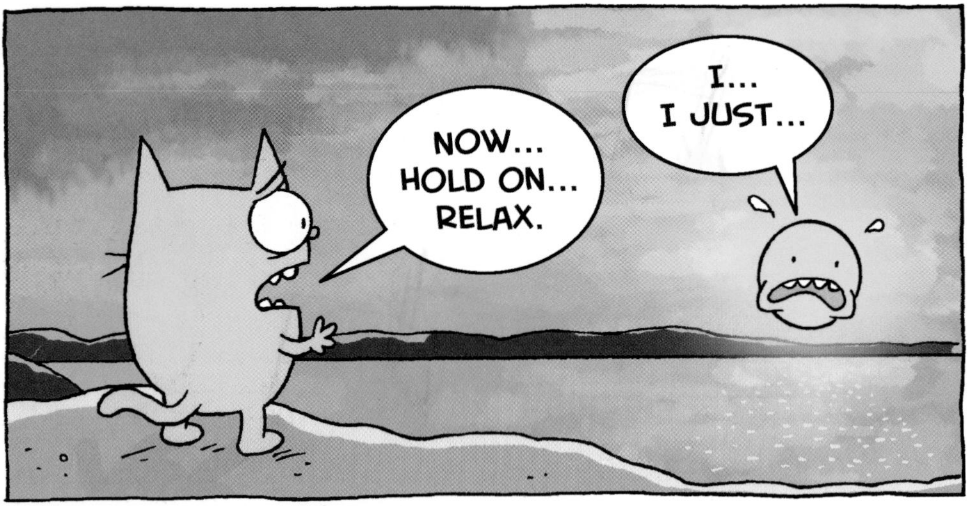
NOW...
HOLD ON...
RELAX.
I...
I JUST...

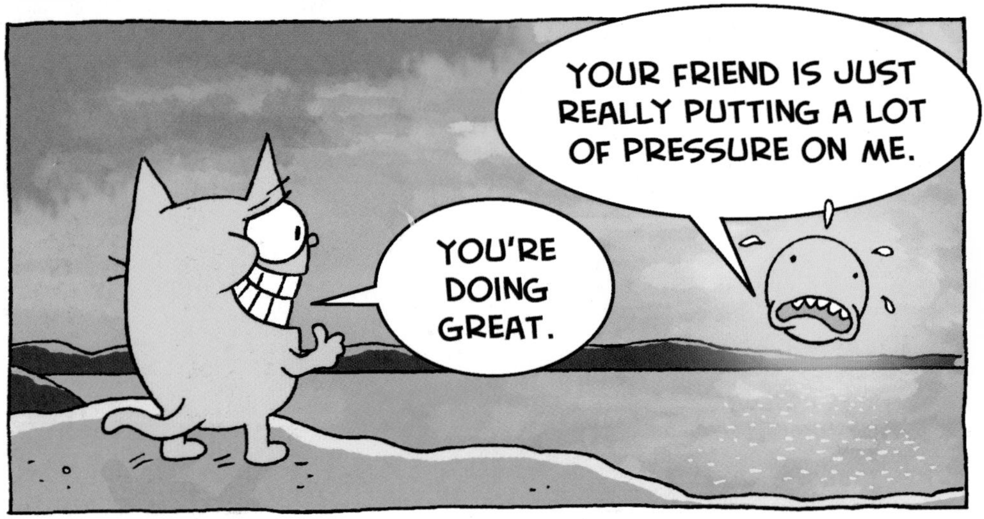
YOUR FRIEND IS JUST REALLY PUTTING A LOT OF PRESSURE ON ME.
YOU'RE DOING GREAT.

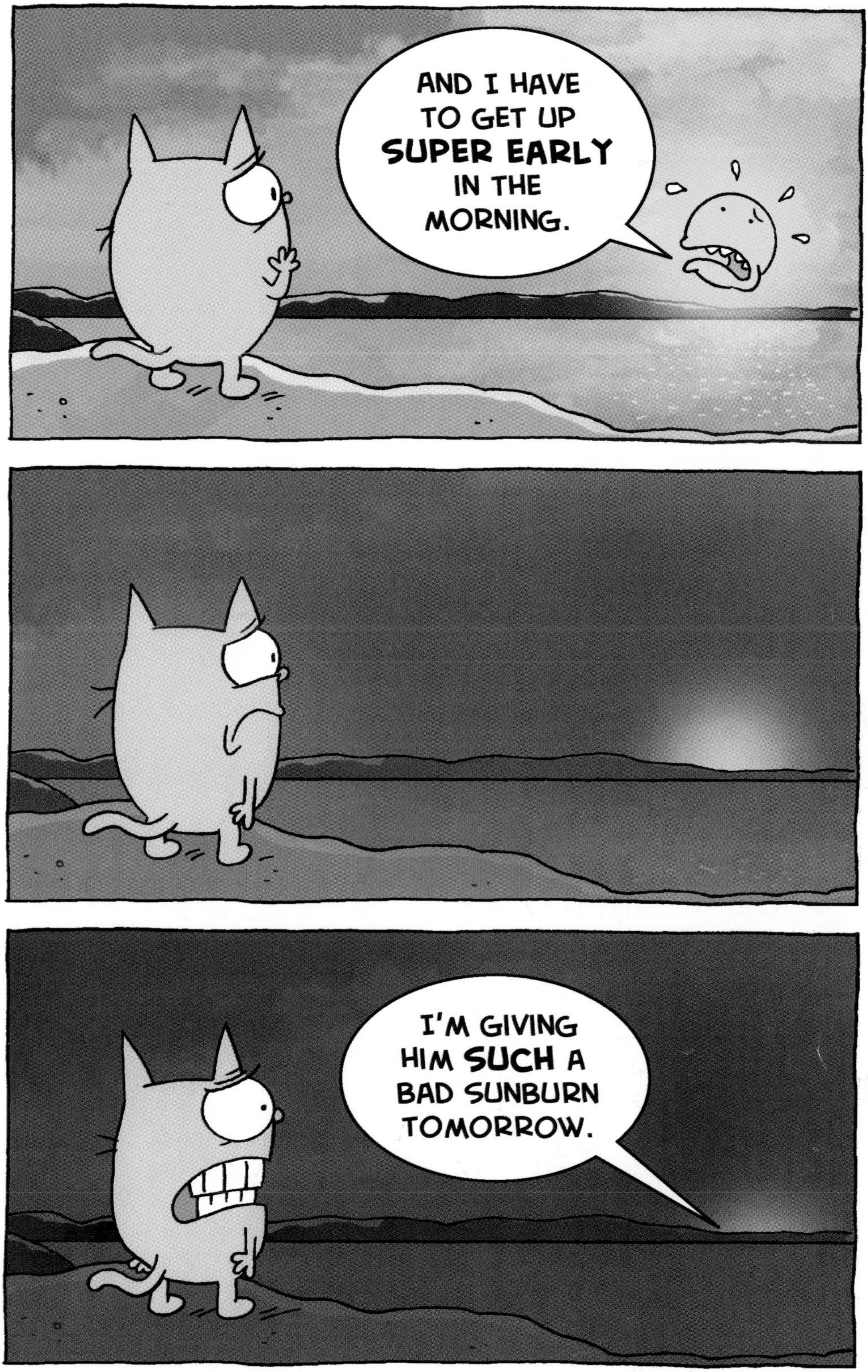
AND I HAVE TO GET UP SUPER EARLY IN THE MORNING.
I'M GIVING HIM SUCH A BAD SUNBURN TOMORROW.

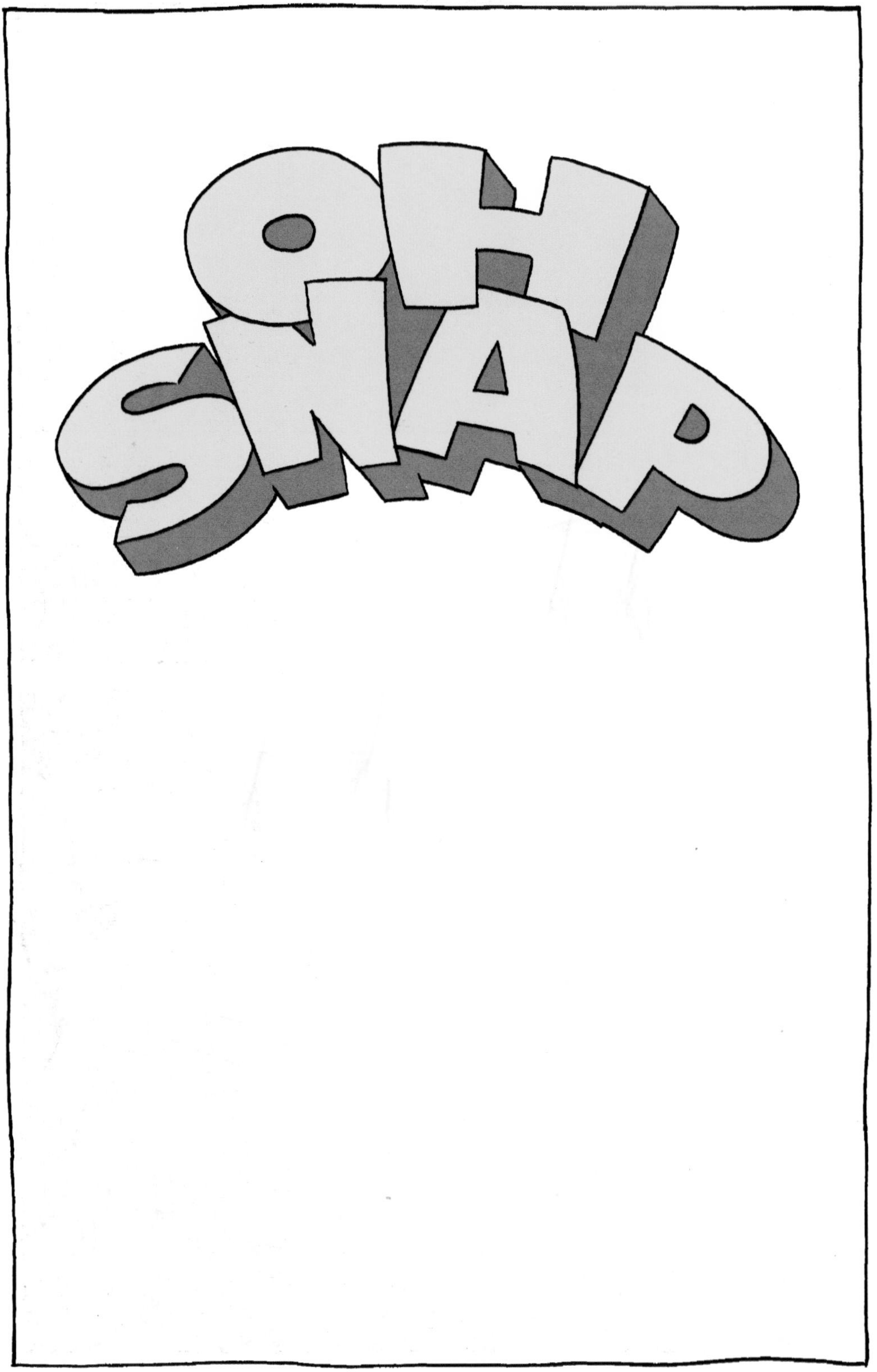
OH SNAP

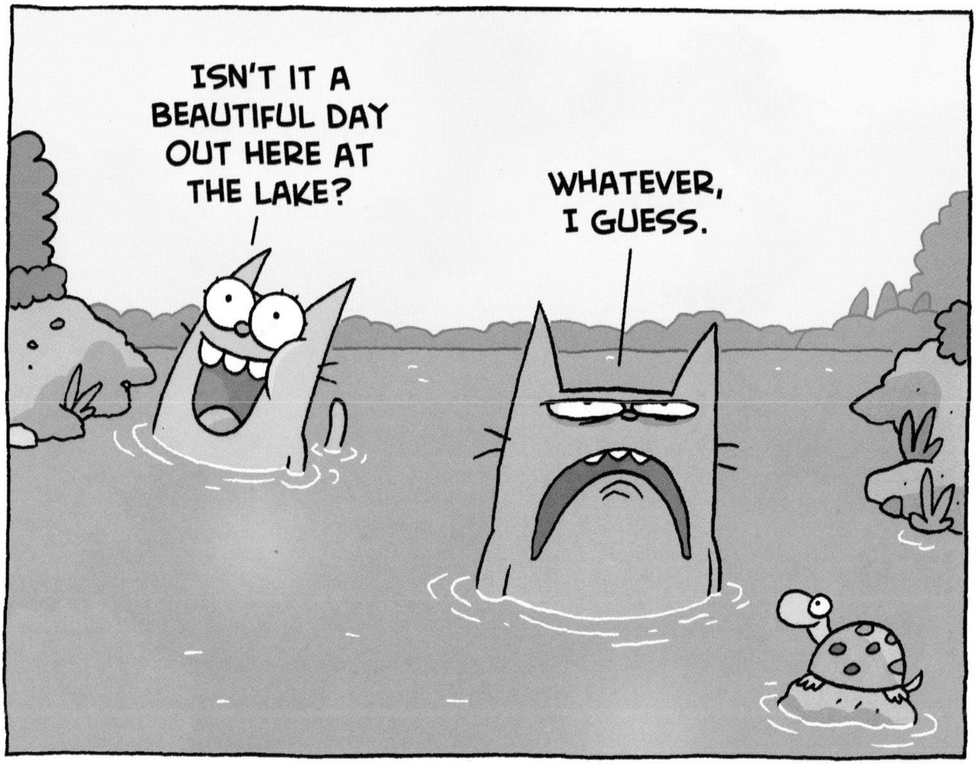
ISN'T IT A BEAUTIFUL DAY OUT HERE AT THE LAKE?
WHATEVER, I GUESS.

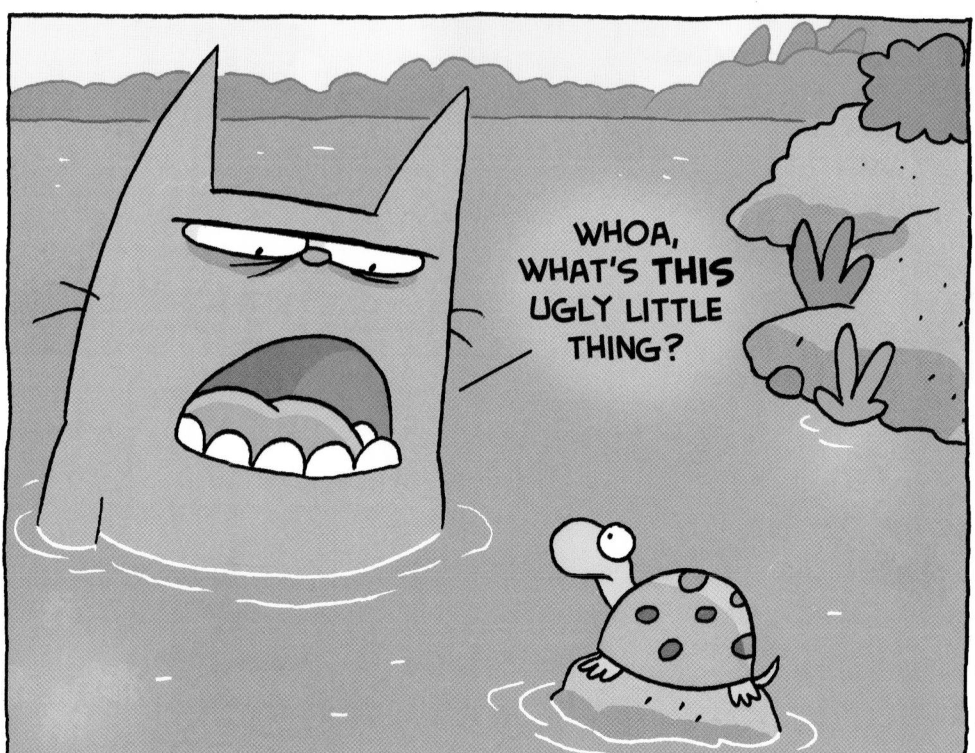
WHOA, WHAT'S **THIS** UGLY LITTLE THING?

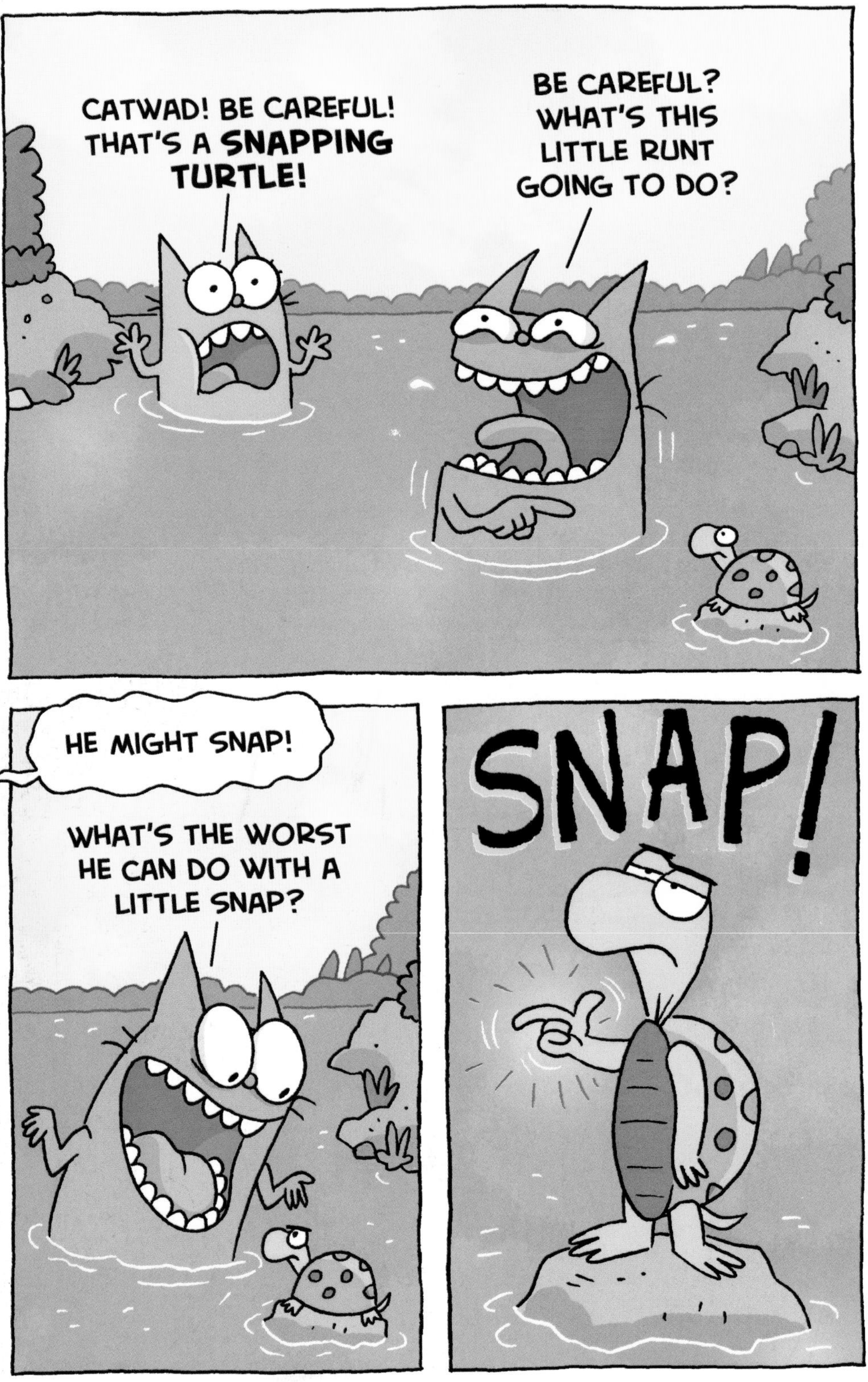
CATWAD! BE CAREFUL! THAT'S A SNAPPING TURTLE!
BE CAREFUL? WHAT'S THIS LITTLE RUNT GOING TO DO?
HE MIGHT SNAP!
WHAT'S THE WORST HE CAN DO WITH A LITTLE SNAP?
SNAP!

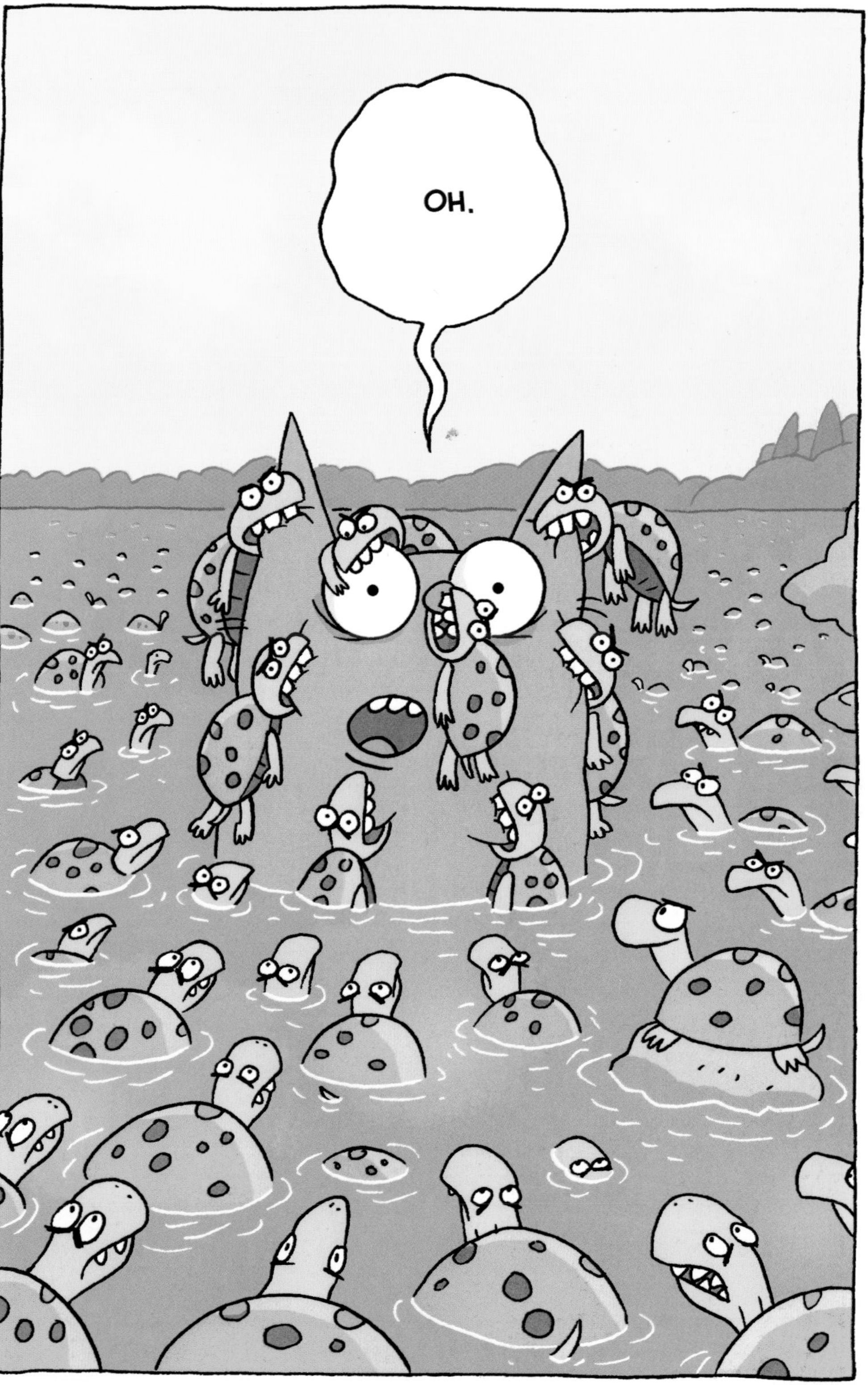
OH.

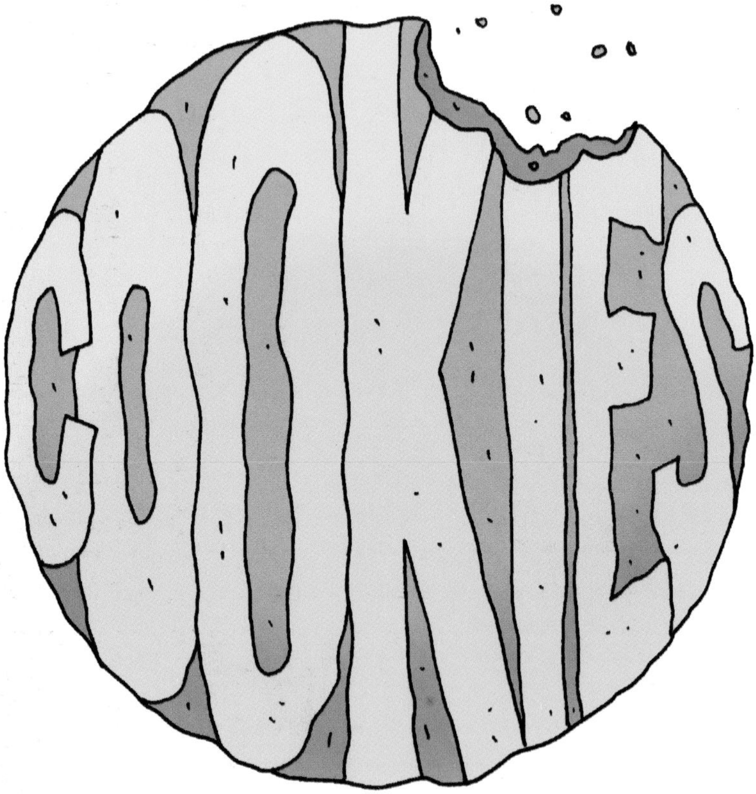
COOKIES

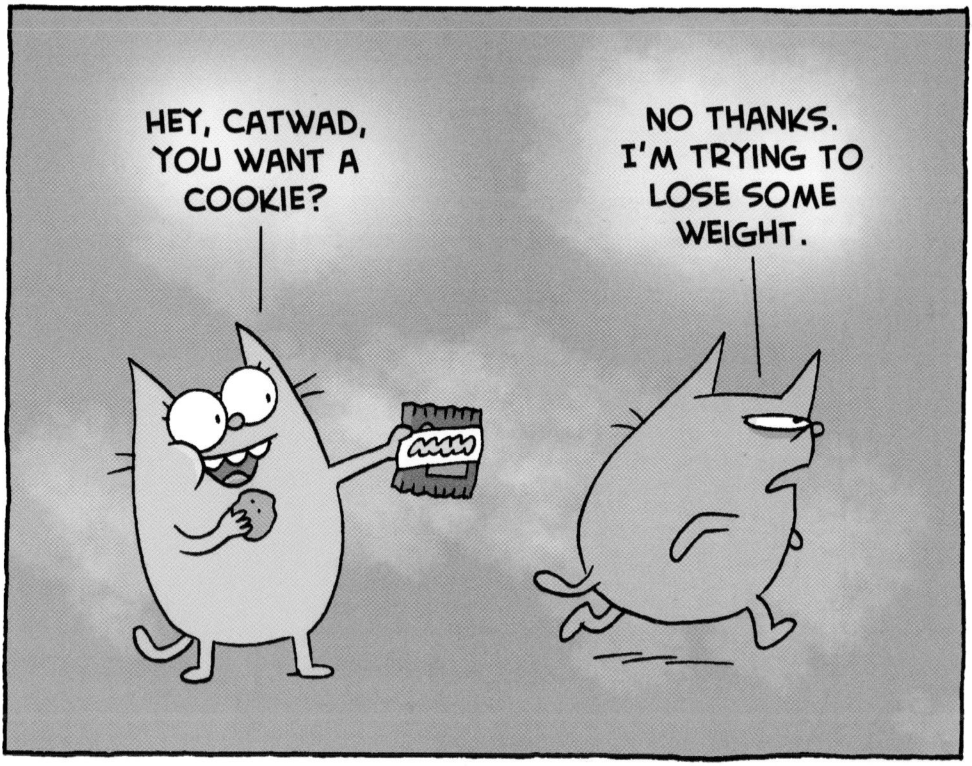
HEY, CATWAD,
YOU WANT A
COOKIE?
NO THANKS.
I'M TRYING TO
LOSE SOME
WEIGHT.

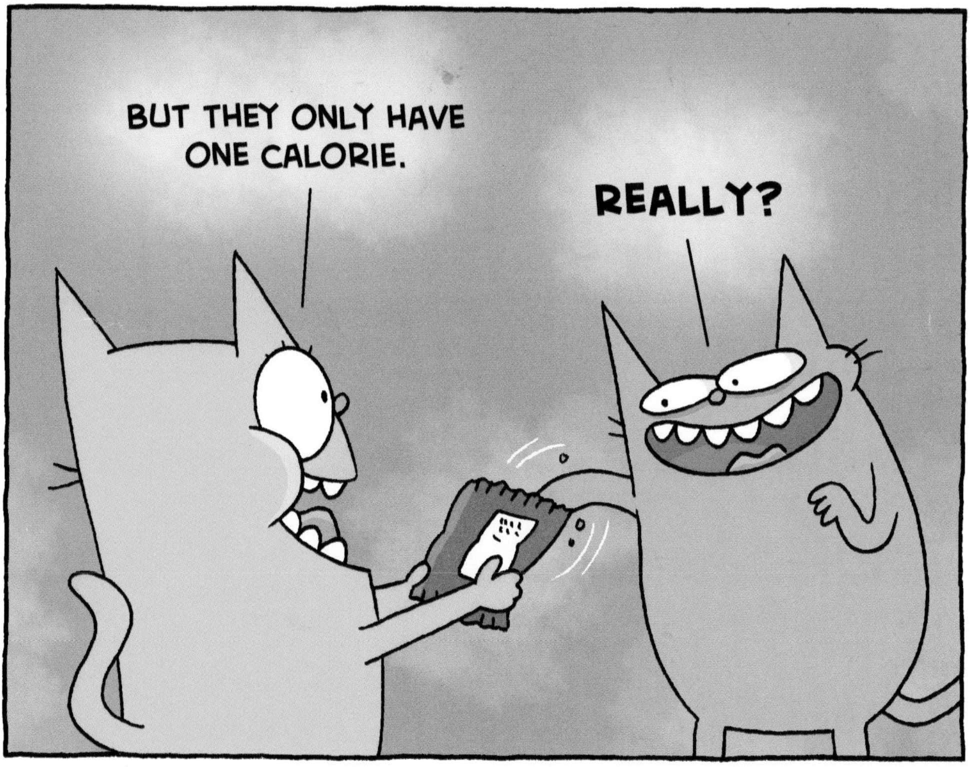
BUT THEY ONLY HAVE
ONE CALORIE.
REALLY?

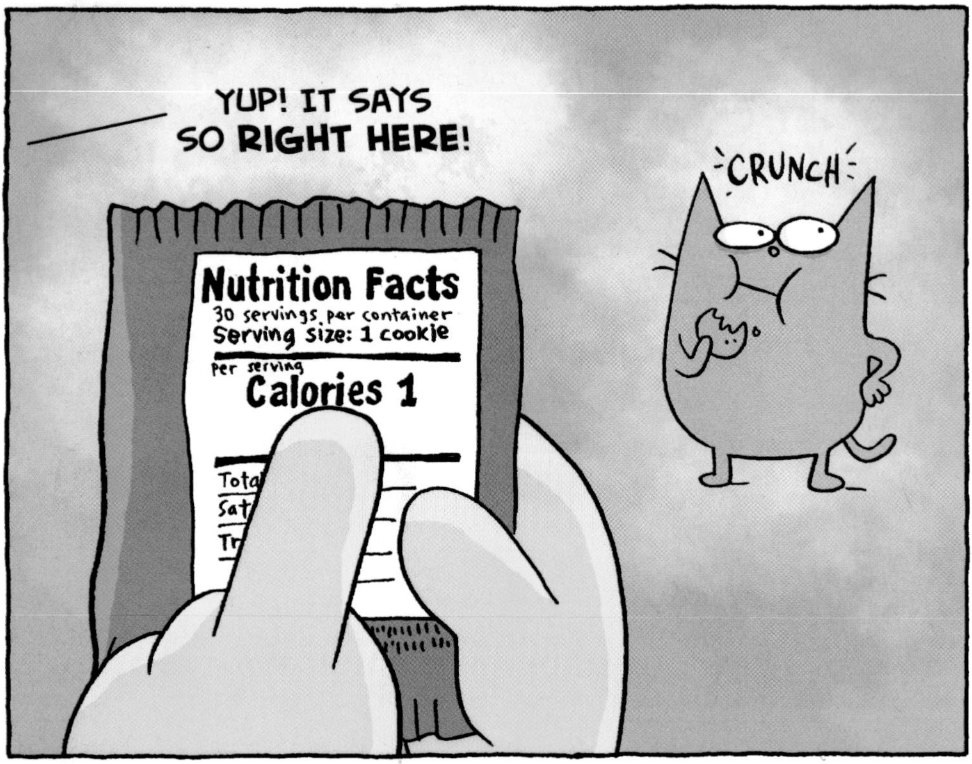
YUP! IT SAYS SO RIGHT HERE!
CRUNCH
Nutrition Facts
30 servings per container
Serving size: 1 cookie
per serving
Calories 1

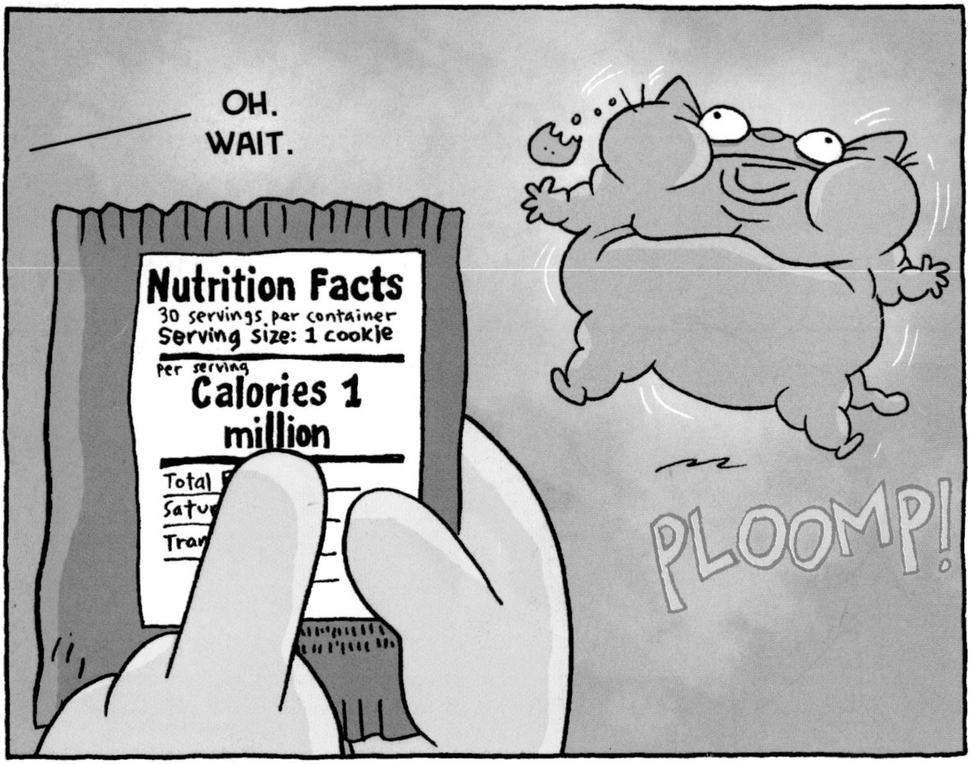
OH. WAIT.
Nutrition Facts
30 servings per container
Serving size: 1 cookie
per serving
Calories 1 million
PLOOMP!

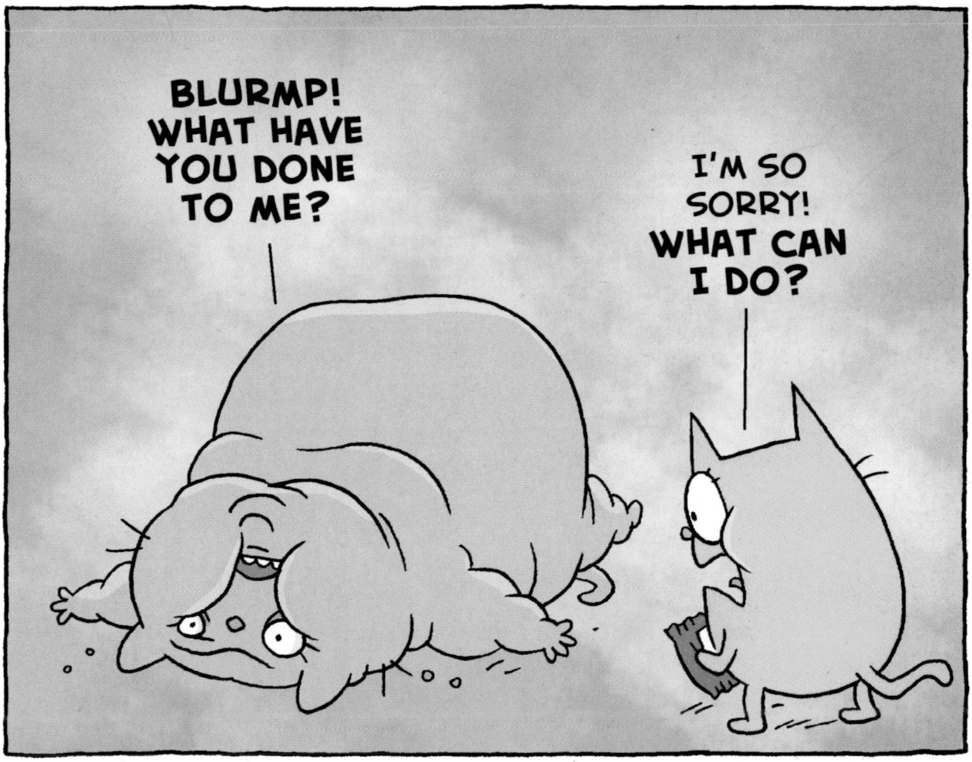
BLURMP! WHAT HAVE YOU DONE TO ME?
I'M SO SORRY! WHAT CAN I DO?

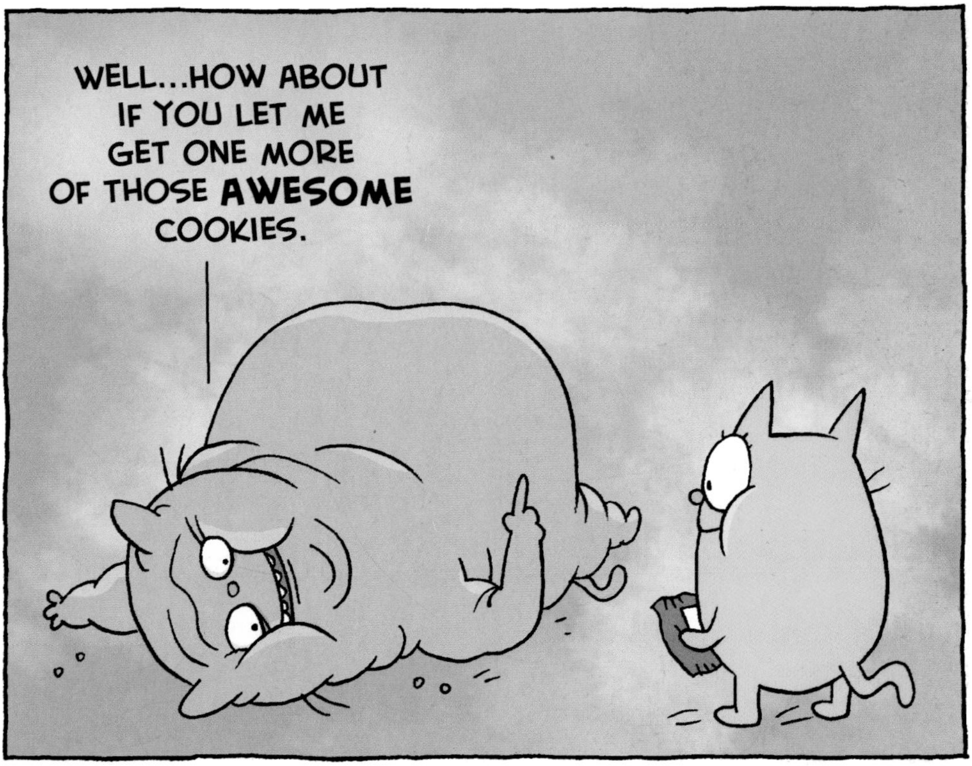
WELL...HOW ABOUT IF YOU LET ME GET ONE MORE OF THOSE AWESOME COOKIES.

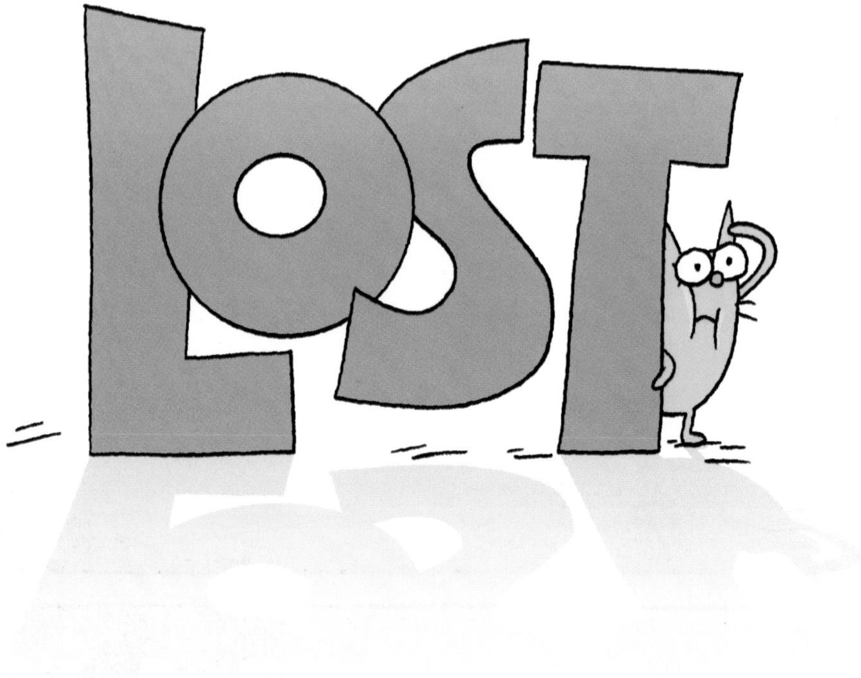
LOST

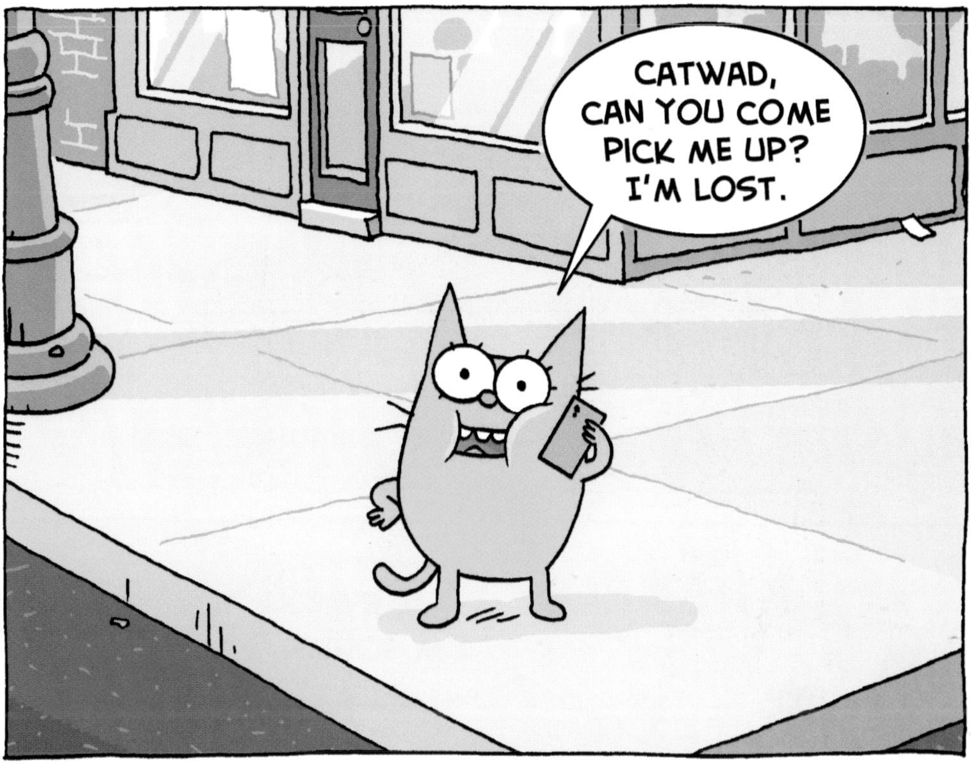
CATWAD, CAN YOU COME PICK ME UP? I'M LOST.

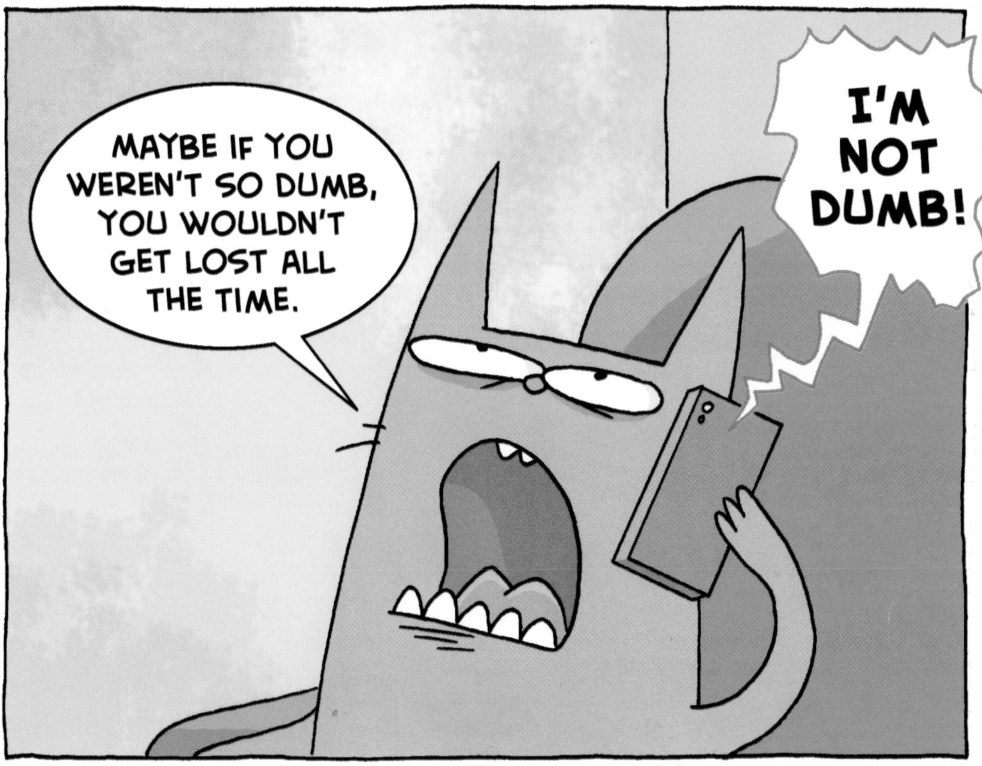
MAYBE IF YOU WEREN'T SO DUMB, YOU WOULDN'T GET LOST ALL THE TIME.
I'M NOT DUMB!

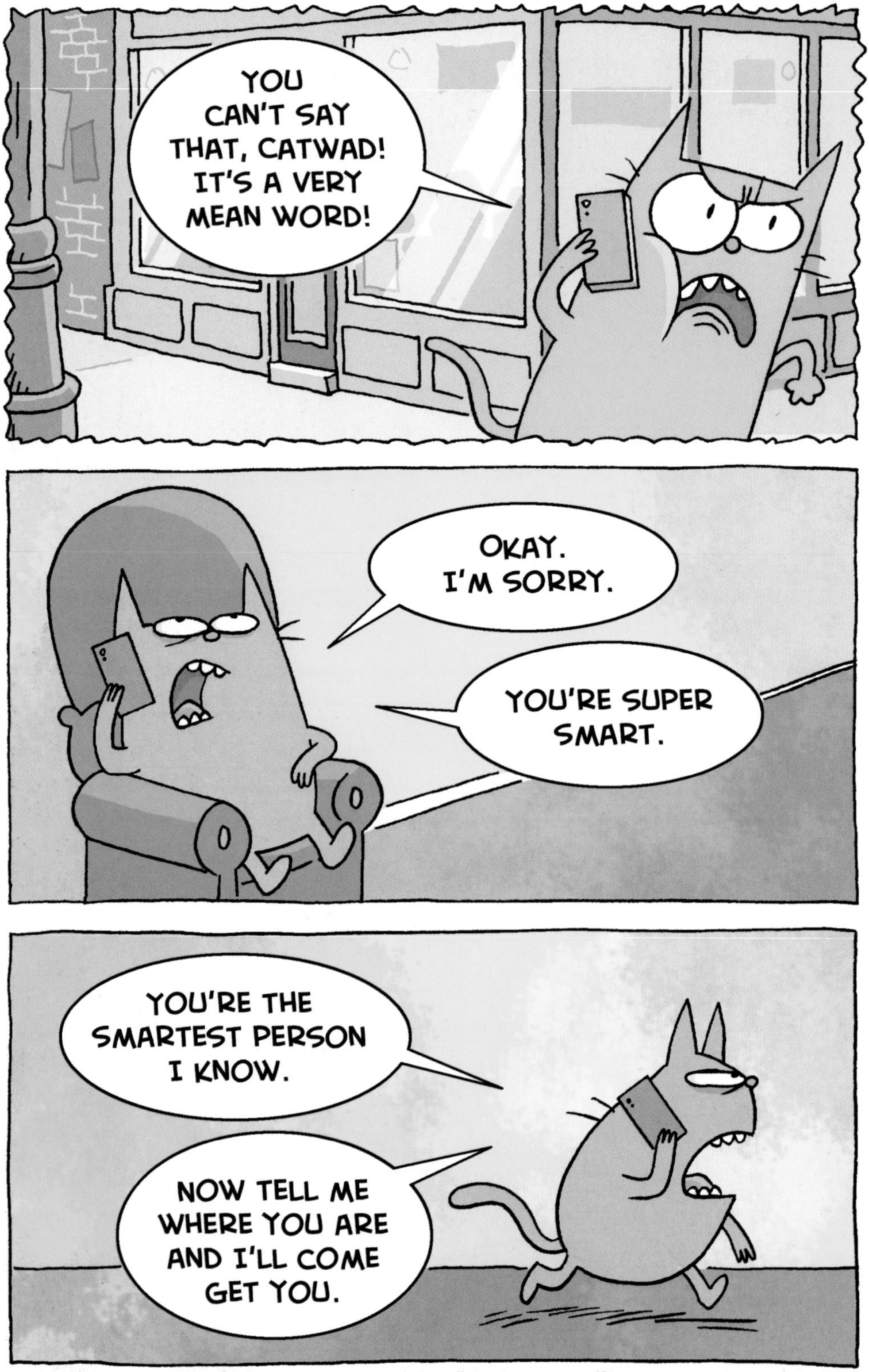
YOU CAN'T SAY THAT, CATWAD! IT'S A VERY MEAN WORD!
OKAY. I'M SORRY.
YOU'RE SUPER SMART.
YOU'RE THE SMARTEST PERSON I KNOW.
NOW TELL ME WHERE YOU ARE AND I'LL COME GET YOU.

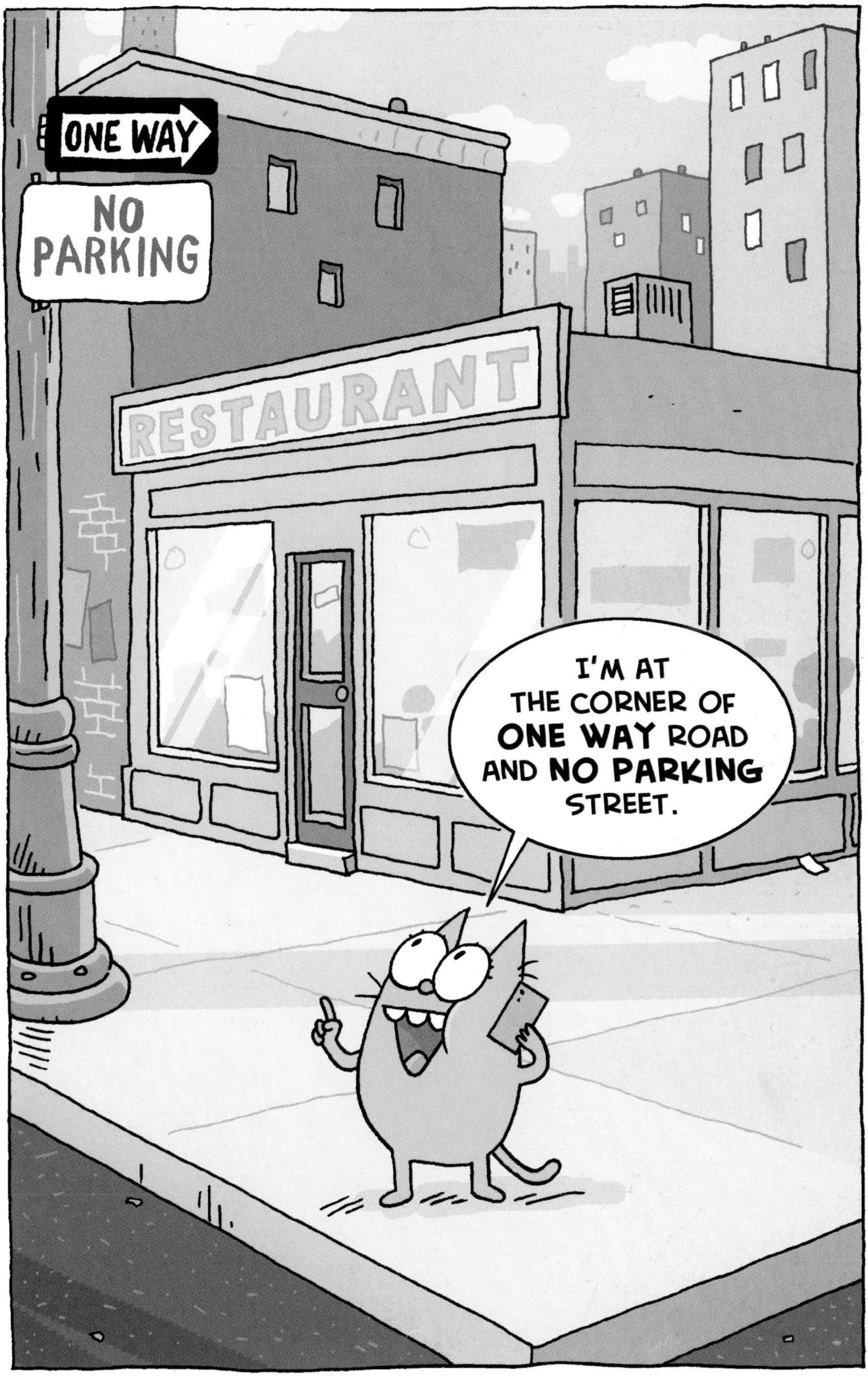
ONE WAY
NO PARKING
RESTAURANT
I'M AT THE CORNER OF ONE WAY ROAD AND NO PARKING STREET.

LAUNDRY

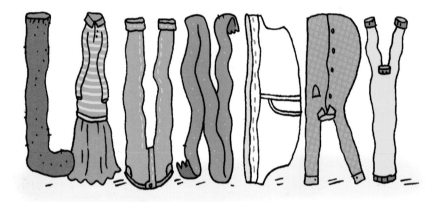

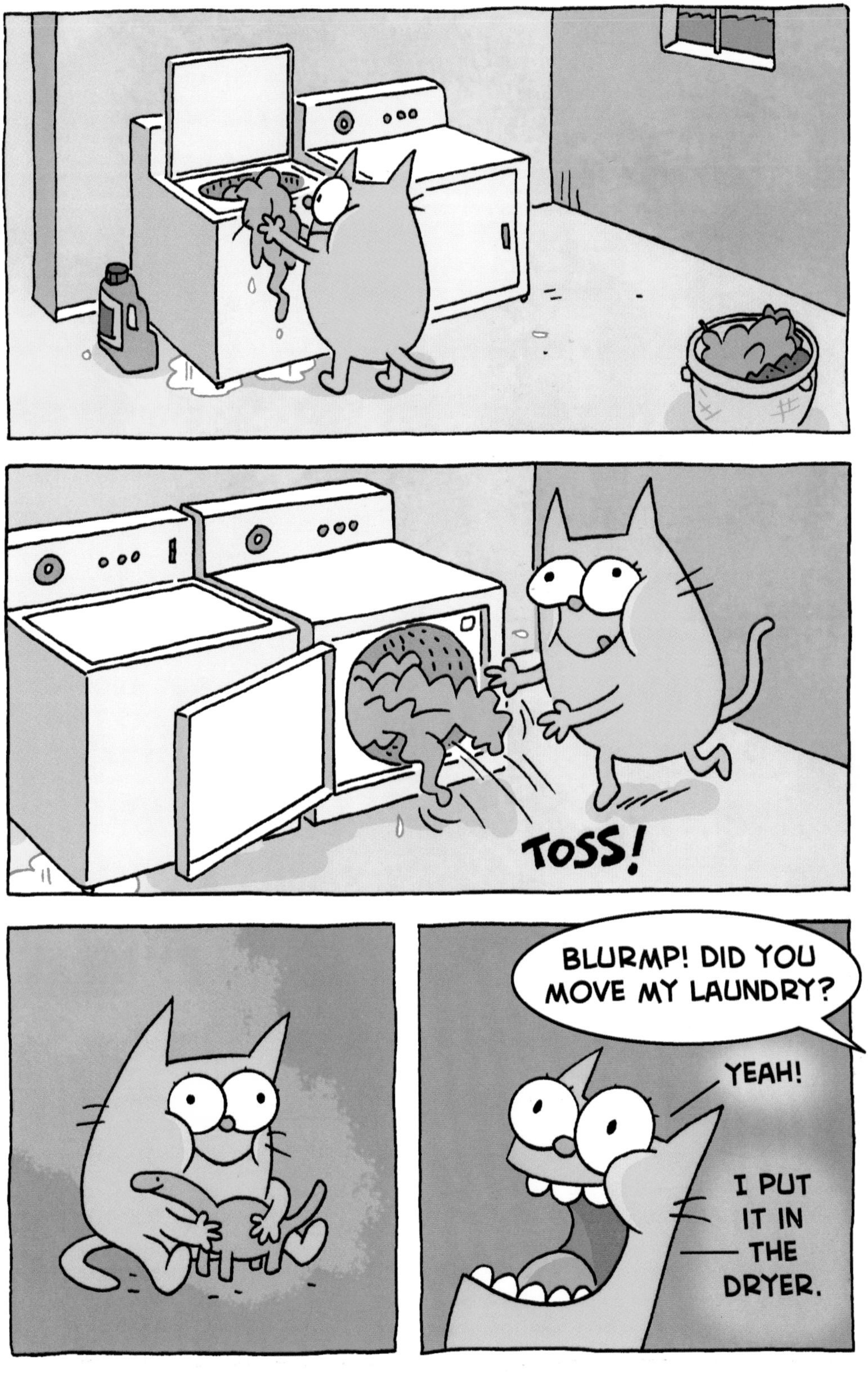
TOSS!
BLURMP! DID YOU MOVE MY LAUNDRY?
YEAH!
I PUT IT IN THE DRYER.

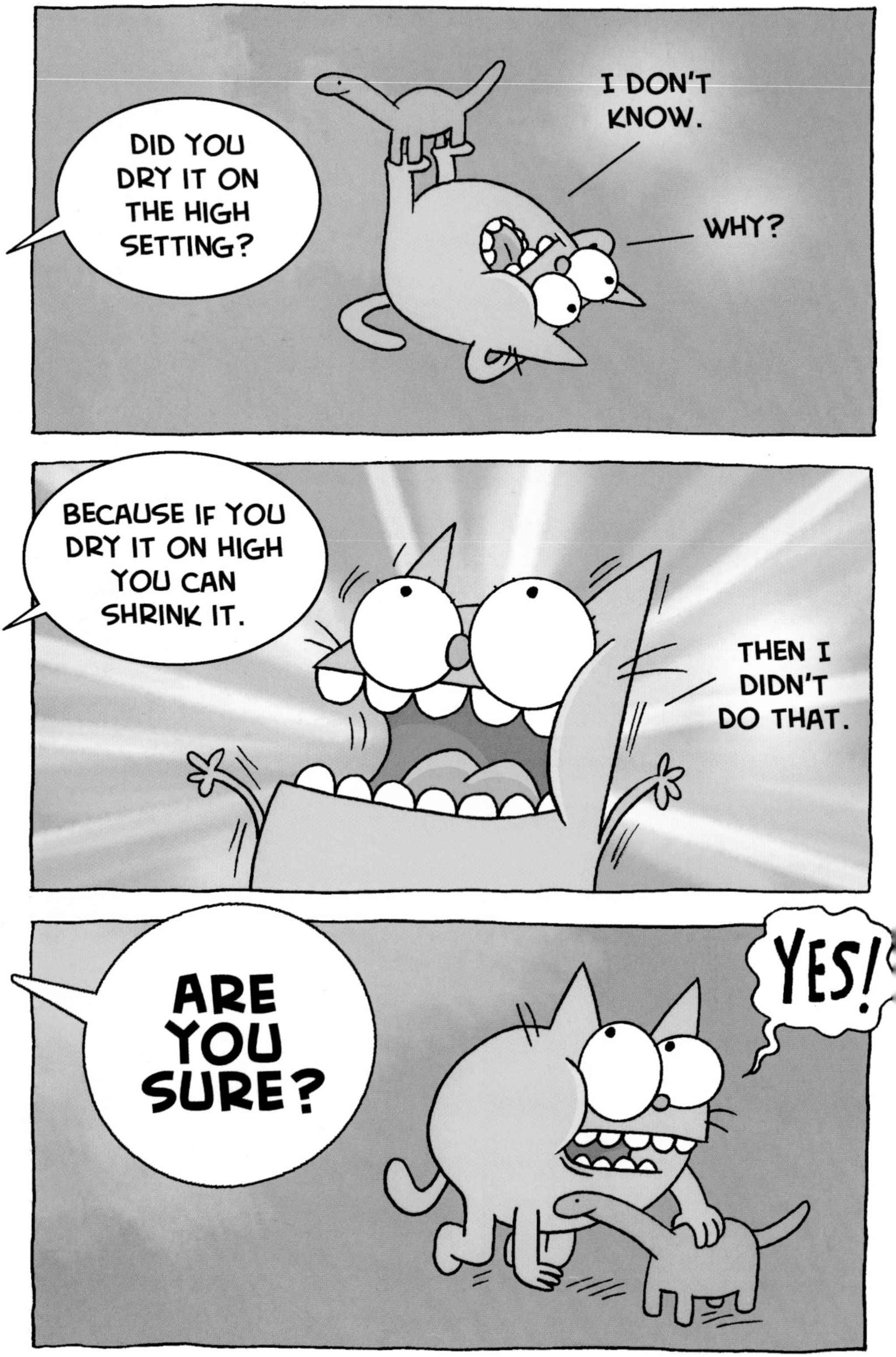
DID YOU DRY IT ON THE HIGH SETTING?
I DON'T KNOW.
WHY?
BECAUSE IF YOU DRY IT ON HIGH YOU CAN SHRINK IT.
THEN I DIDN'T DO THAT.
ARE YOU SURE?
YES!

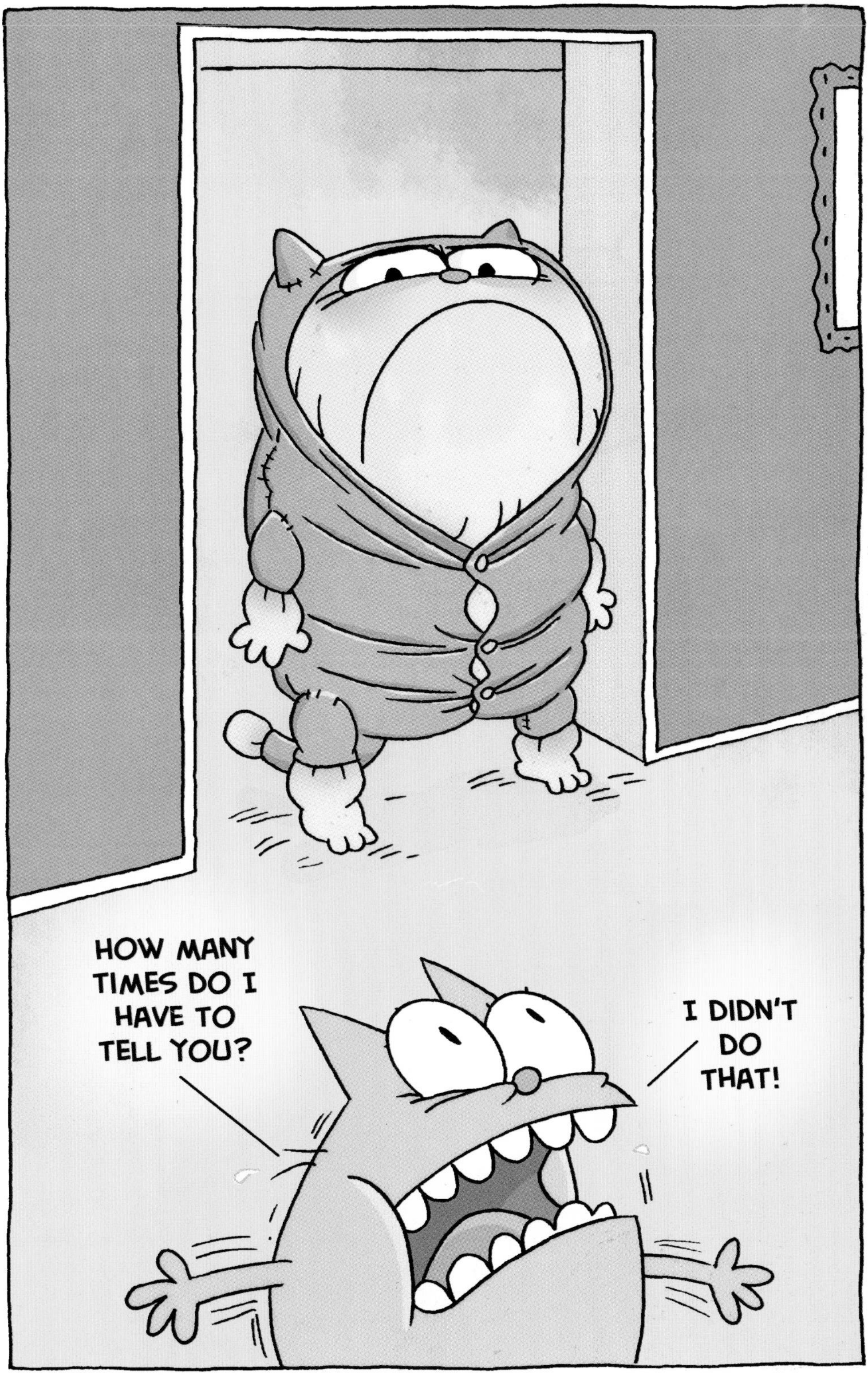
HOW MANY TIMES DO I HAVE TO TELL YOU?
I DIDN'T DO THAT!

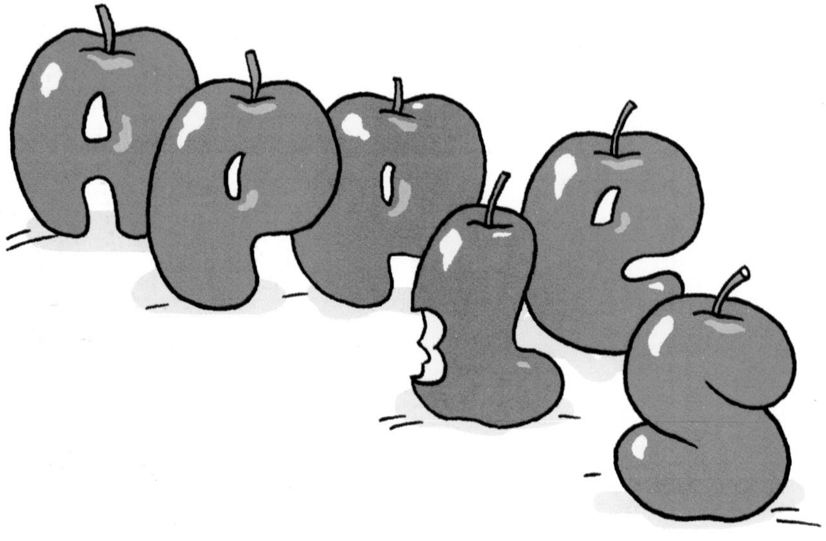
APPLES

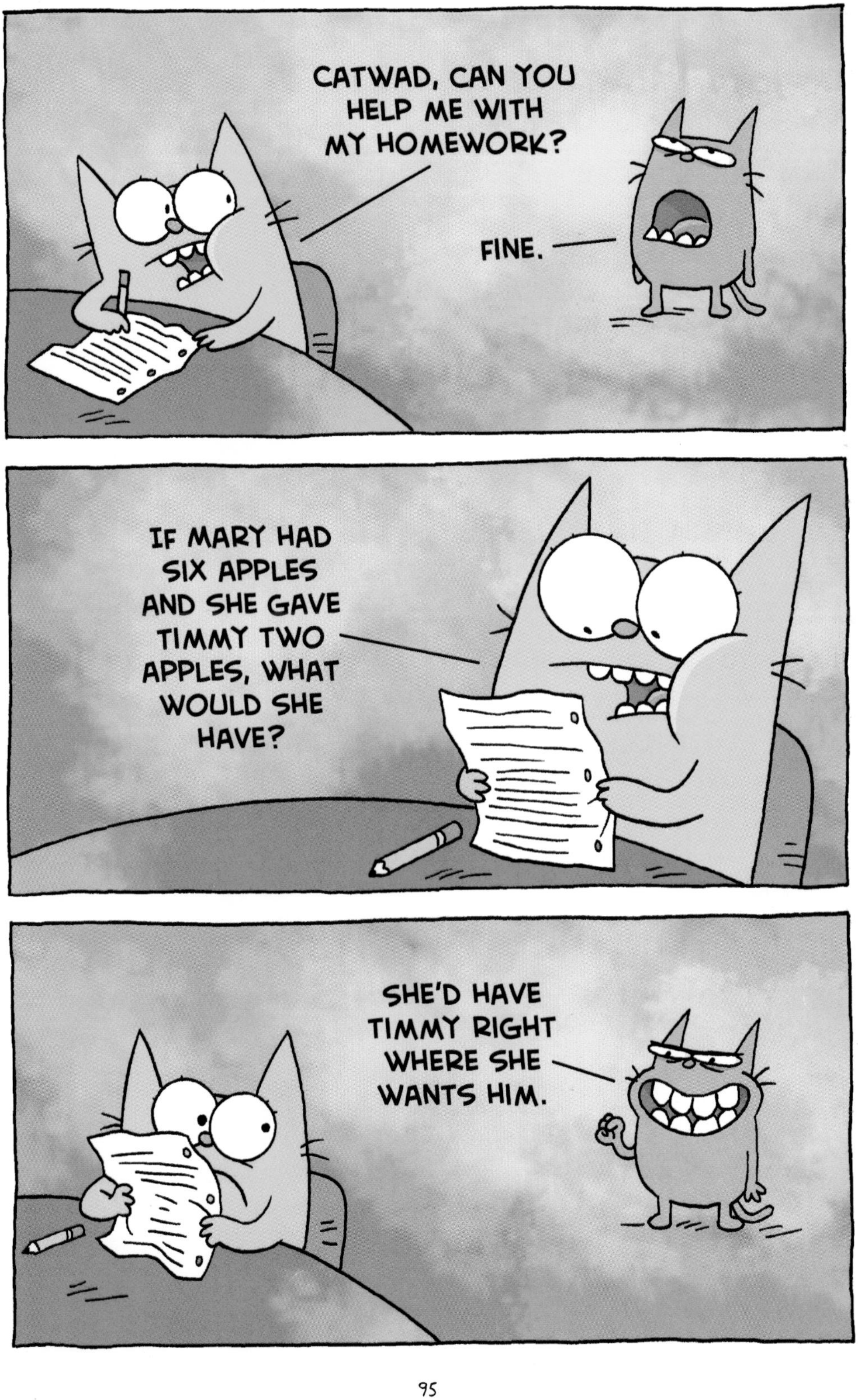
CATWAD, CAN YOU HELP ME WITH MY HOMEWORK?
FINE.
IF MARY HAD SIX APPLES AND SHE GAVE TIMMY TWO APPLES, WHAT WOULD SHE HAVE?
SHE'D HAVE TIMMY RIGHT WHERE SHE WANTS HIM.

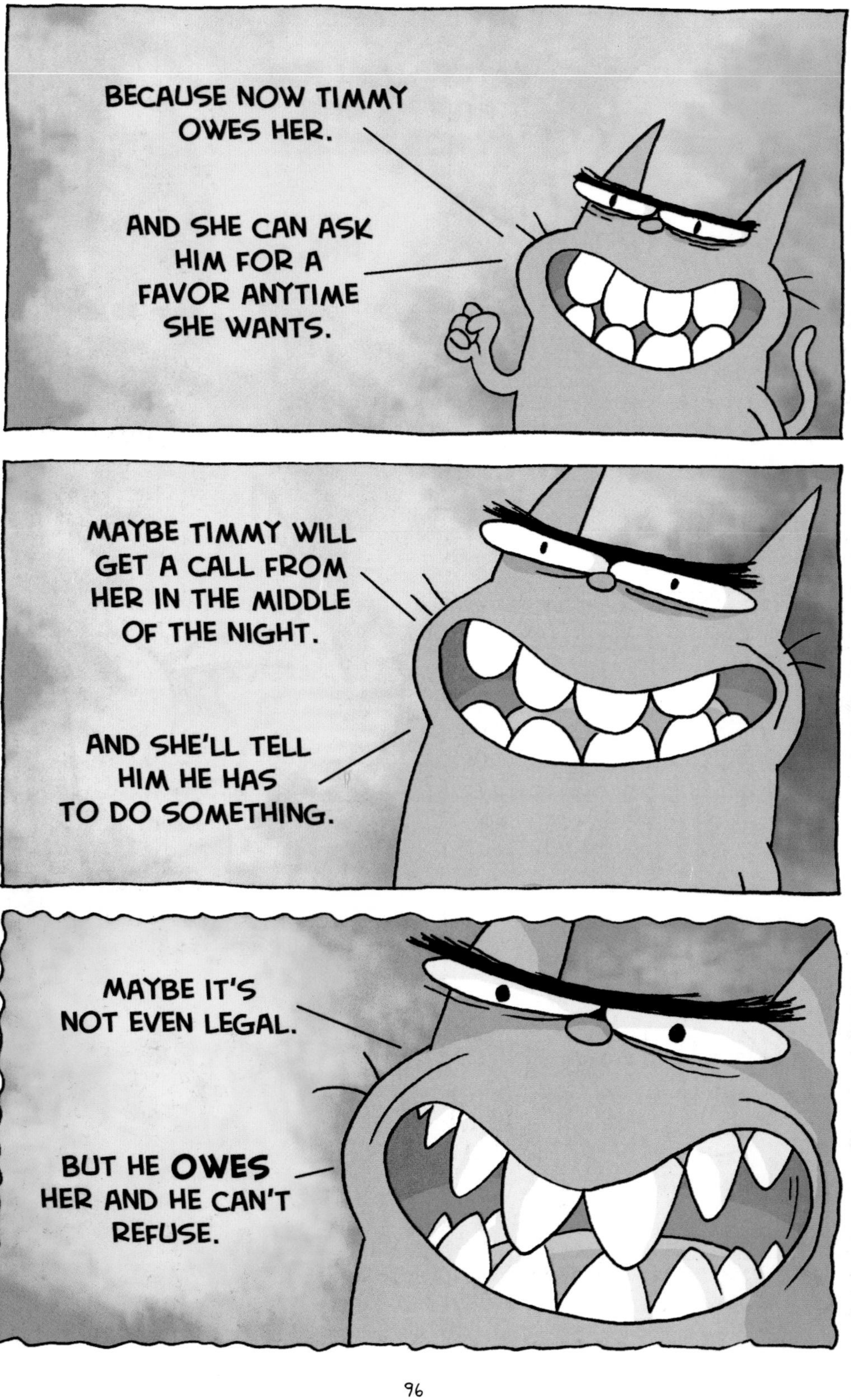

BECAUSE NOW TIMMY OWES HER.
AND SHE CAN ASK HIM FOR A FAVOR ANYTIME SHE WANTS.
MAYBE TIMMY WILL GET A CALL FROM HER IN THE MIDDLE OF THE NIGHT.
AND SHE'LL TELL HIM HE HAS TO DO SOMETHING.
MAYBE IT'S NOT EVEN LEGAL.
BUT HE **OWES** HER AND HE CAN'T REFUSE.

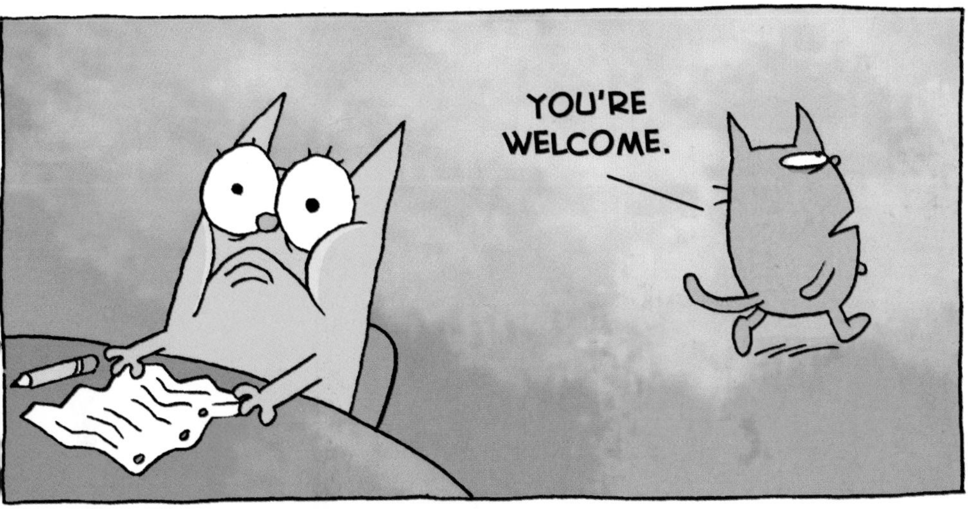
YOU'RE WELCOME.

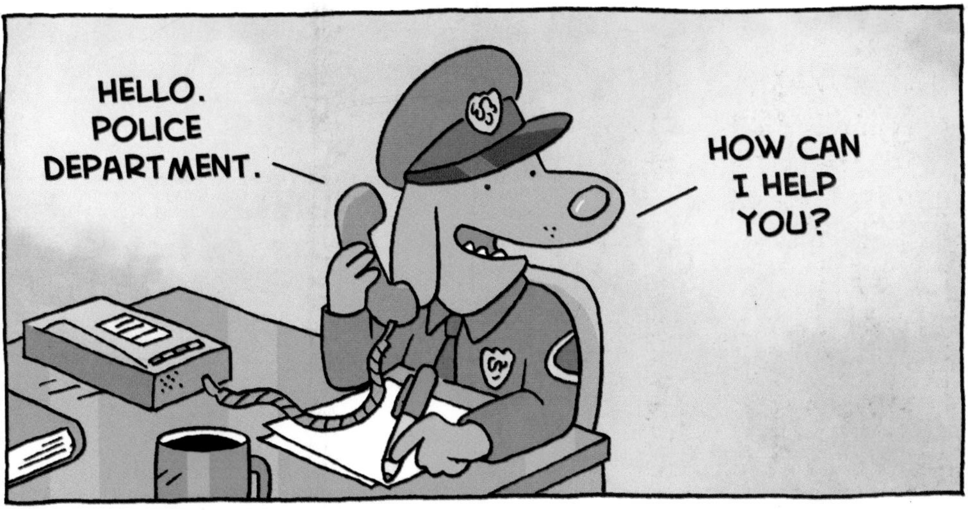
HELLO. POLICE DEPARTMENT.
HOW CAN I HELP YOU?

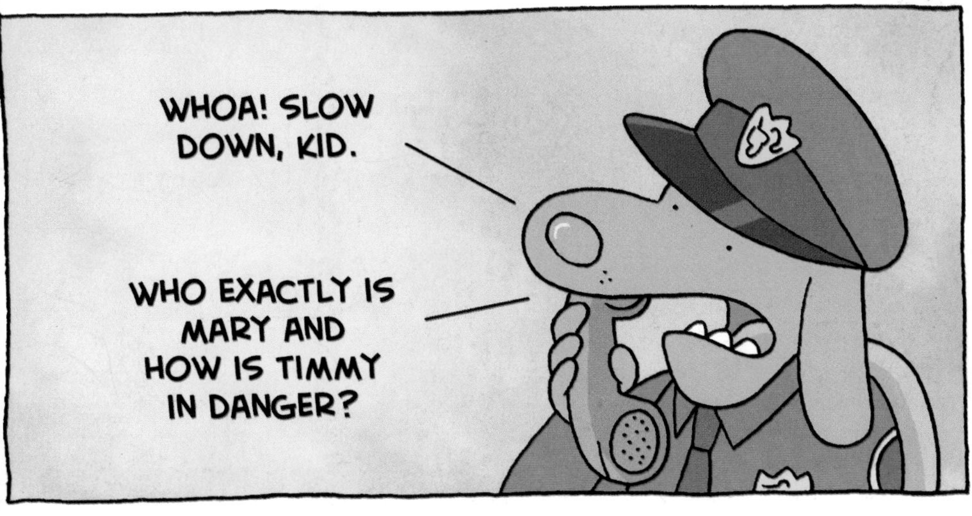
WHOA! SLOW DOWN, KID.
WHO EXACTLY IS MARY AND HOW IS TIMMY IN DANGER?

highlighter

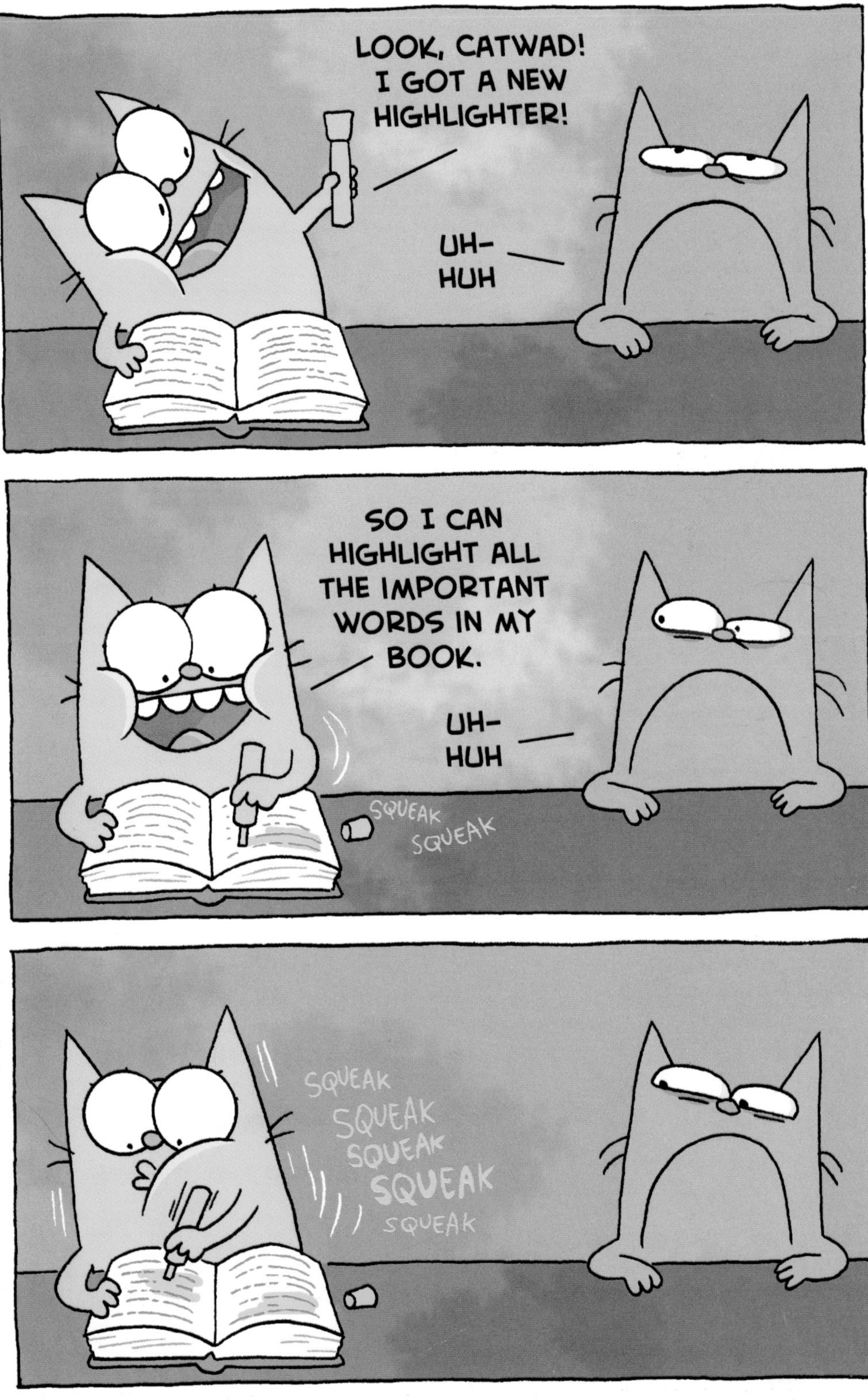
LOOK, CATWAD! I GOT A NEW HIGHLIGHTER!
UH-HUH
SO I CAN HIGHLIGHT ALL THE IMPORTANT WORDS IN MY BOOK.
UH-HUH
SQUEAK
SQUEAK
SQUEAK
SQUEAK
SQUEAK
SQUEAK
SQUEAK

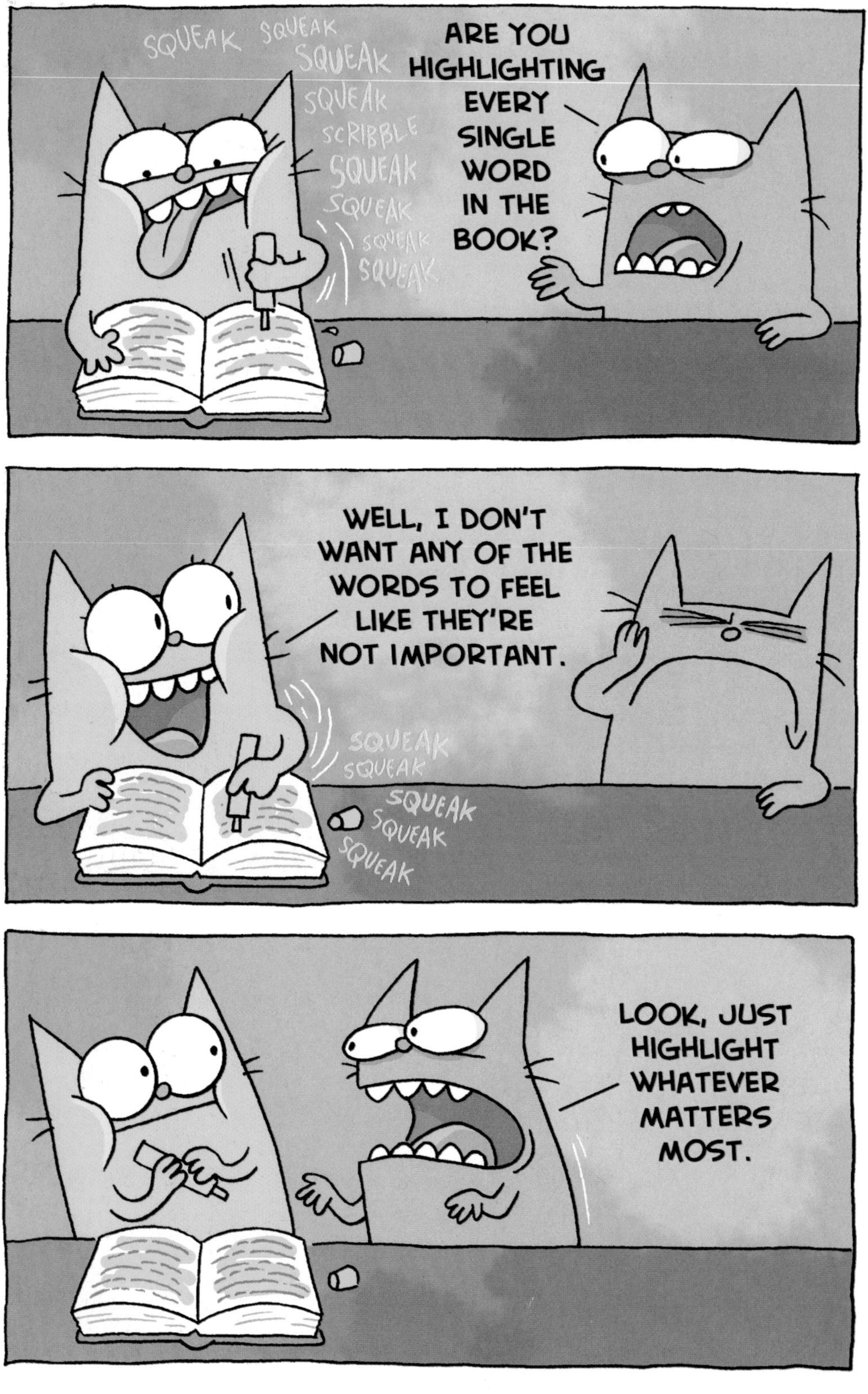
SQUEAK SQUEAK SQUEAK SQUEAK SCRIBBLE SQUEAK SQUEAK SQUEAK SQUEAK
ARE YOU HIGHLIGHTING EVERY SINGLE WORD IN THE BOOK?
WELL, I DON'T WANT ANY OF THE WORDS TO FEEL LIKE THEY'RE NOT IMPORTANT.
SQUEAK SQUEAK SQUEAK SQUEAK SQUEAK
LOOK, JUST HIGHLIGHT WHATEVER MATTERS MOST.

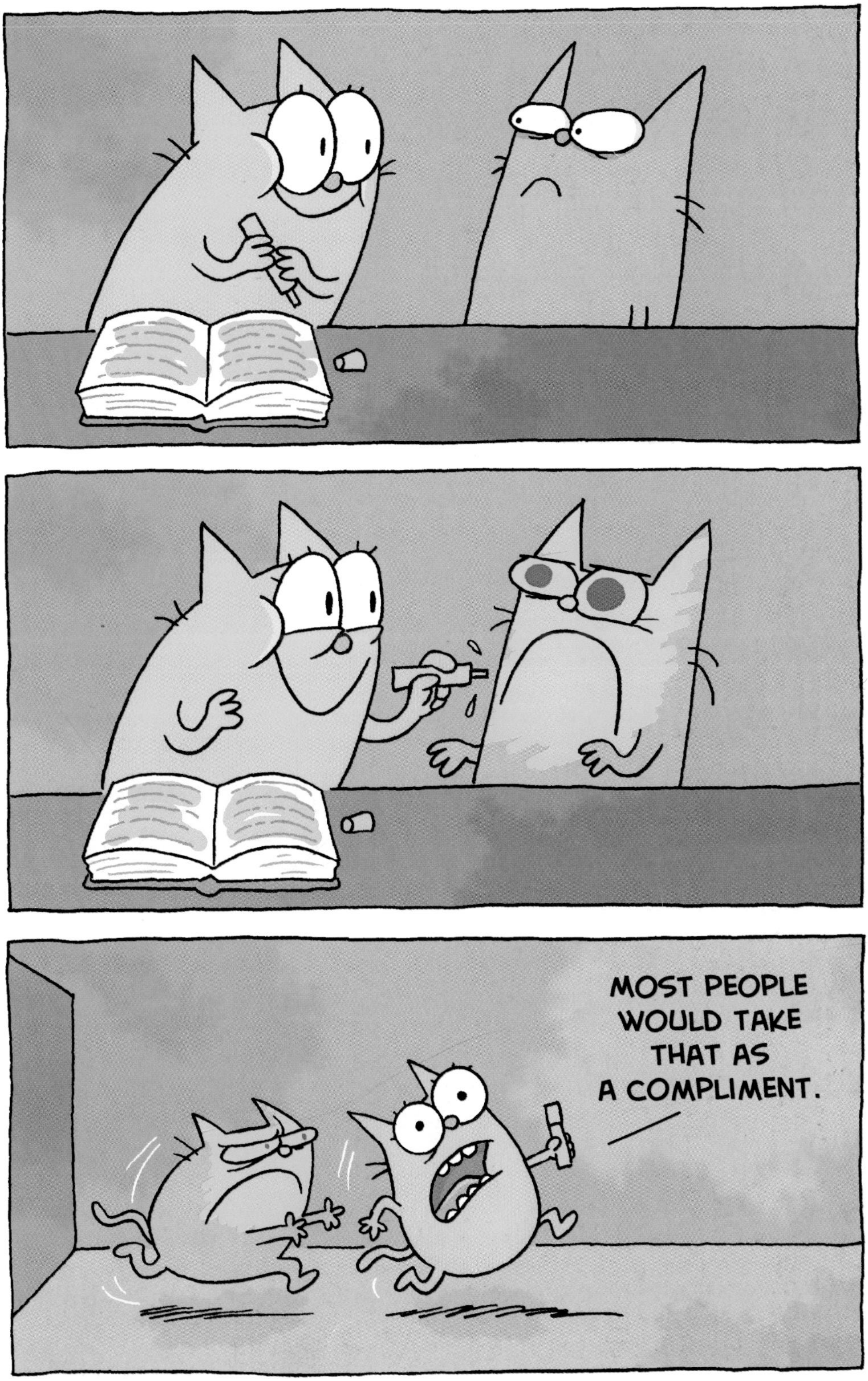
MOST PEOPLE WOULD TAKE THAT AS A COMPLIMENT.

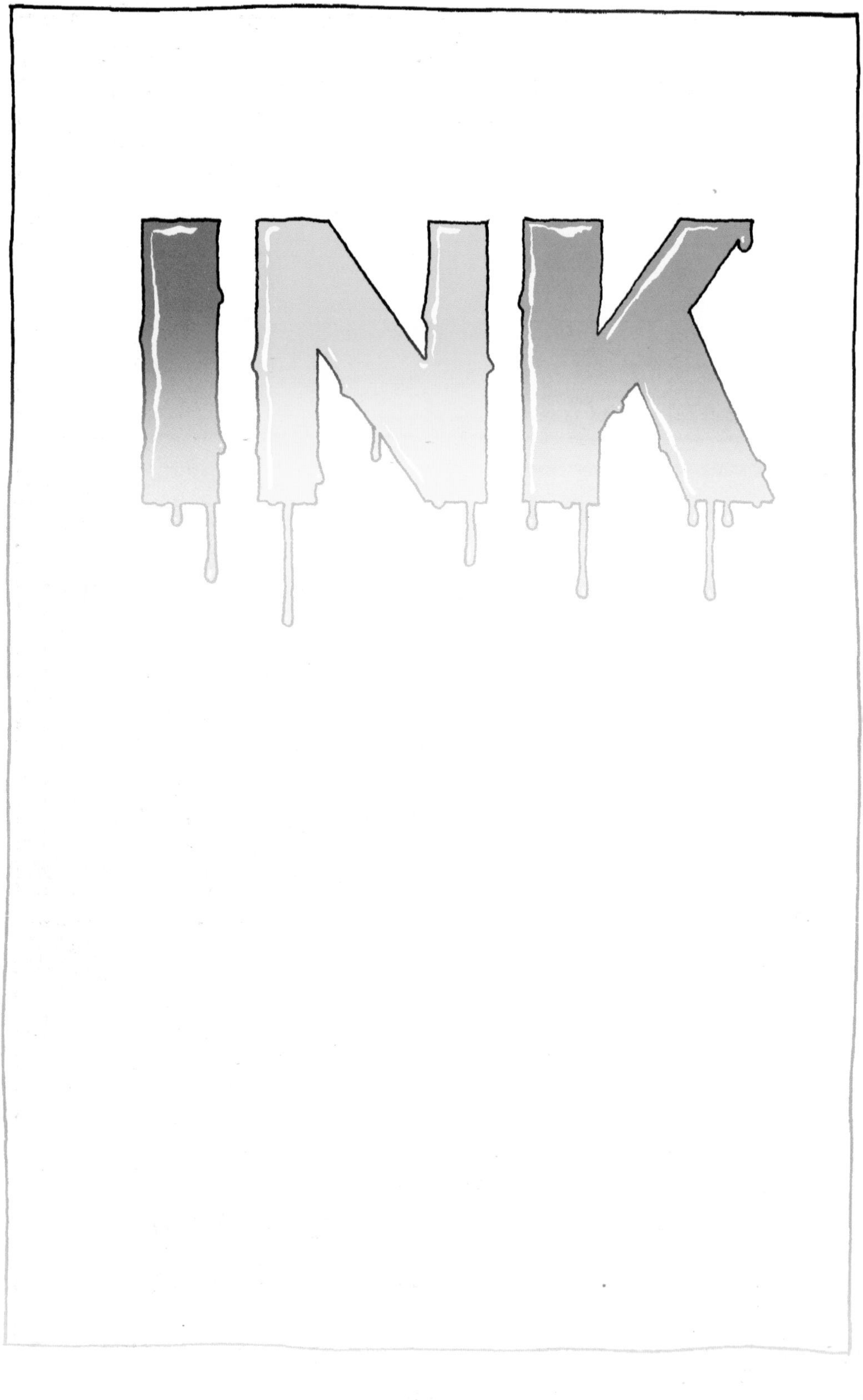
INK

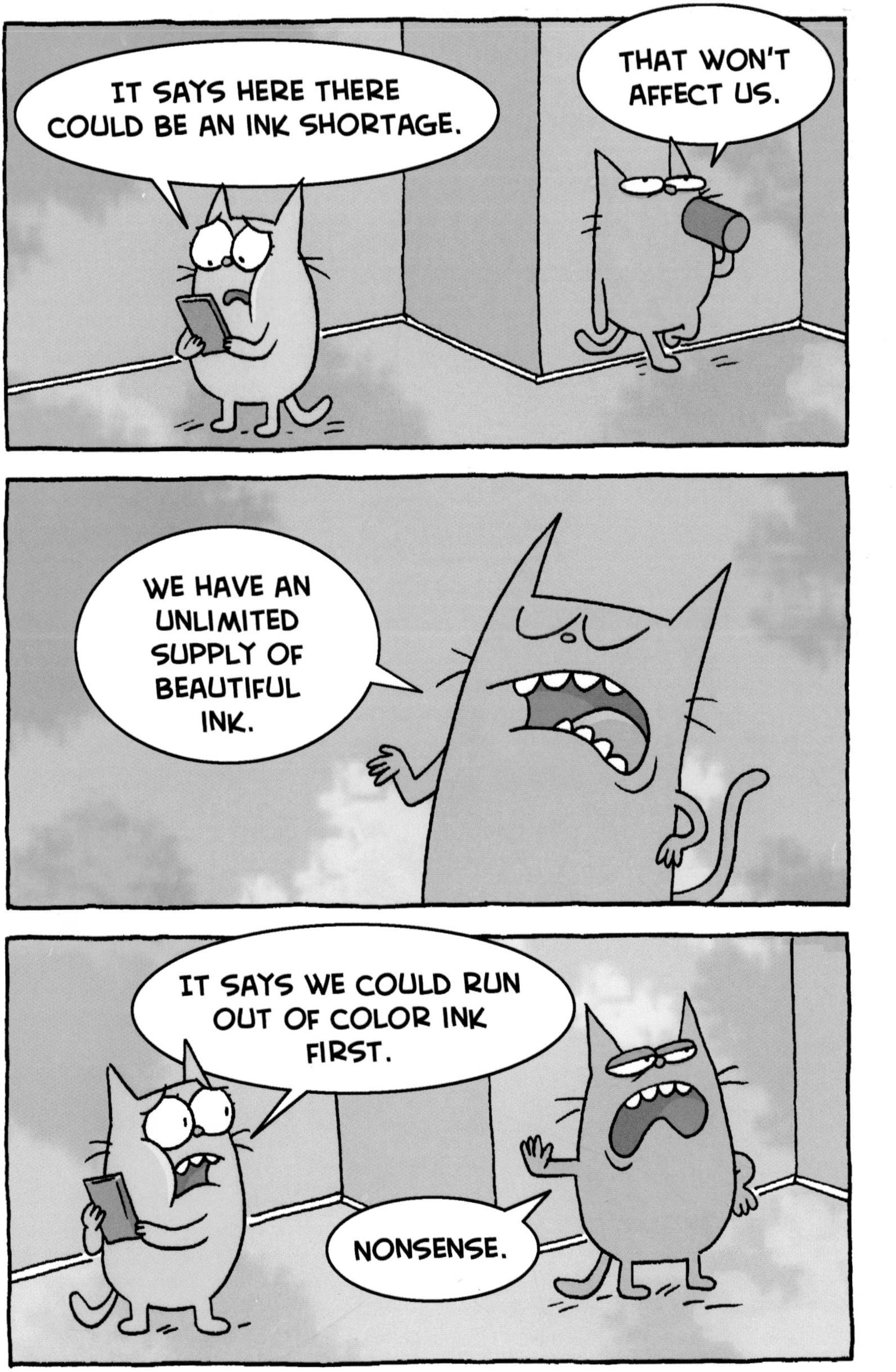
IT SAYS HERE THERE COULD BE AN INK SHORTAGE.
THAT WON'T AFFECT US.
WE HAVE AN UNLIMITED SUPPLY OF BEAUTIFUL INK.
IT SAYS WE COULD RUN OUT OF COLOR INK FIRST.
NONSENSE.

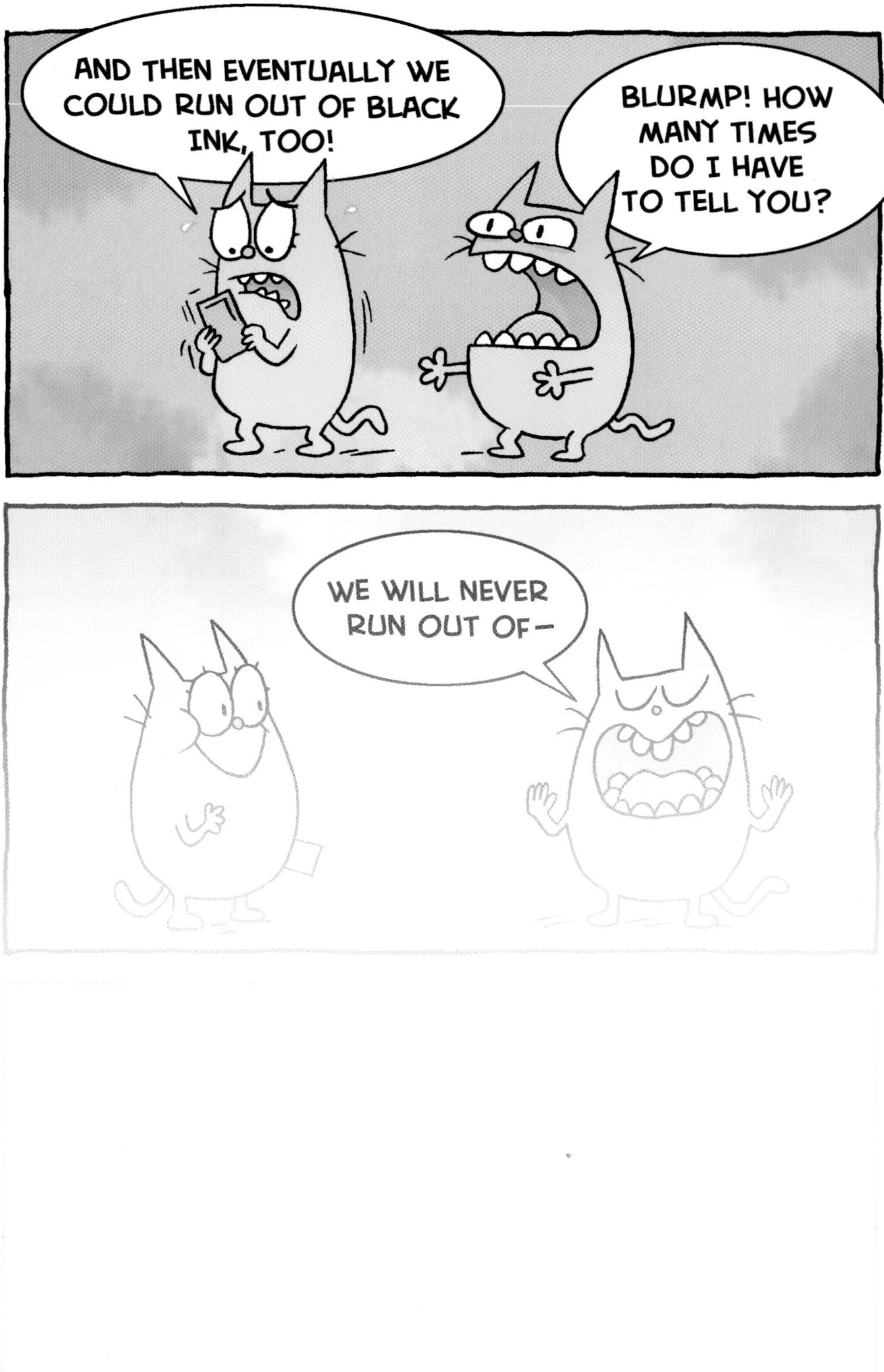
AND THEN EVENTUALLY WE COULD RUN OUT OF BLACK INK, TOO!
BLURMP! HOW MANY TIMES DO I HAVE TO TELL YOU?
WE WILL NEVER RUN OUT OF—

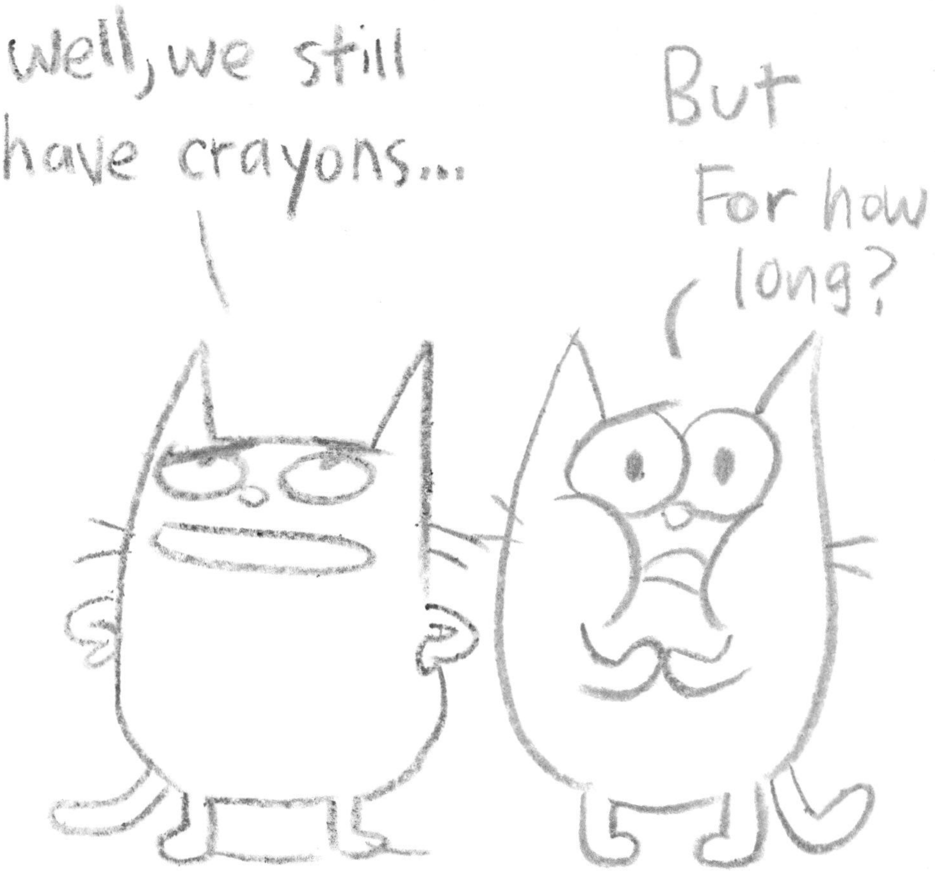
Well, we still have crayons...
But For how long?

Poetry

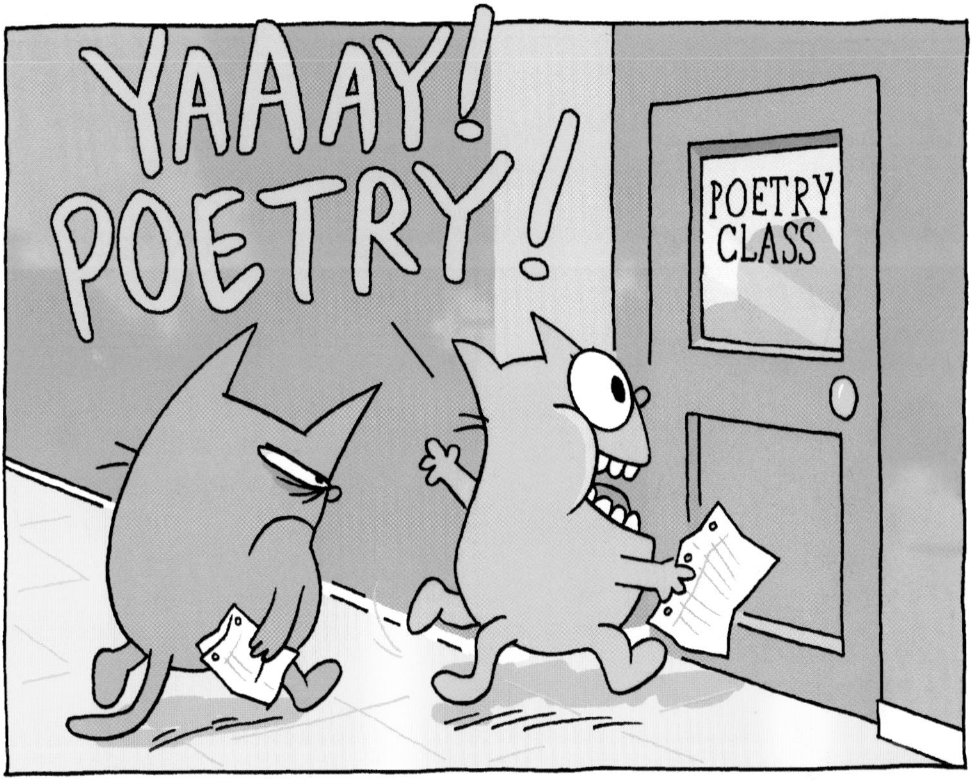
YAAAY! POETRY!
POETRY CLASS

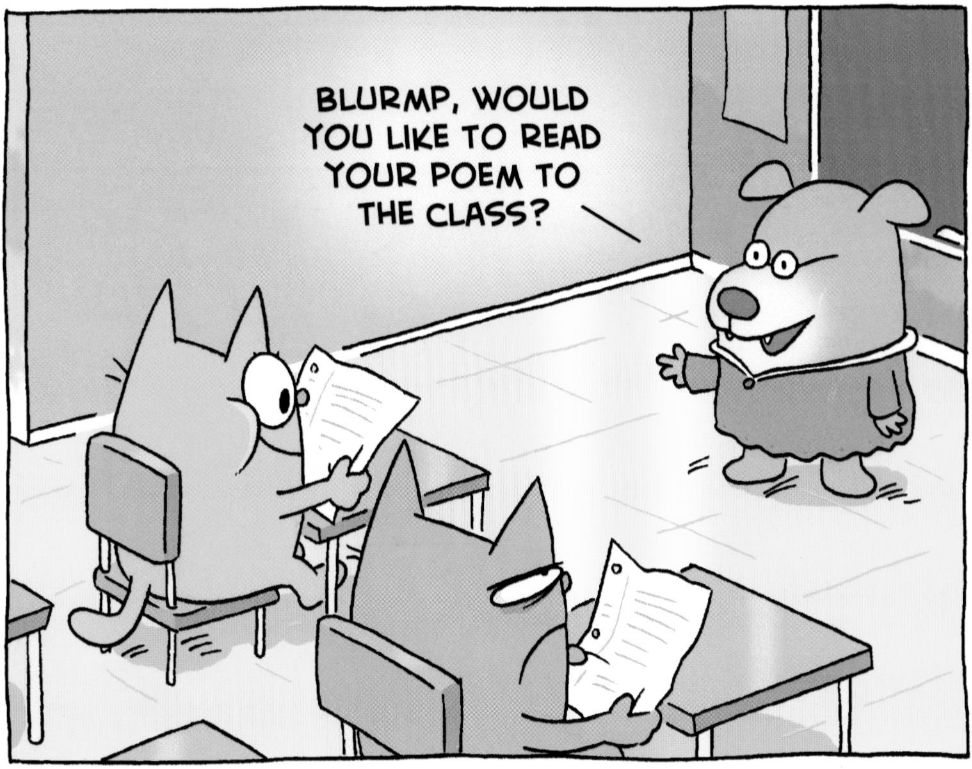
BLURMP, WOULD YOU LIKE TO READ YOUR POEM TO THE CLASS?

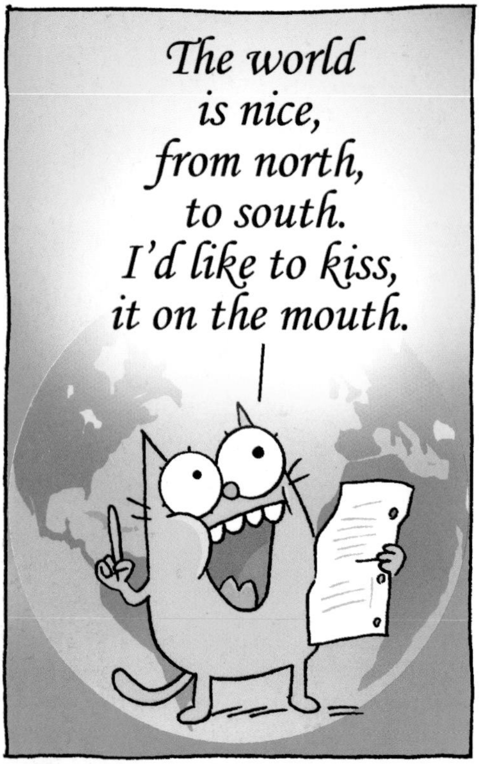
The world is nice, from north, to south. I'd like to kiss, it on the mouth.

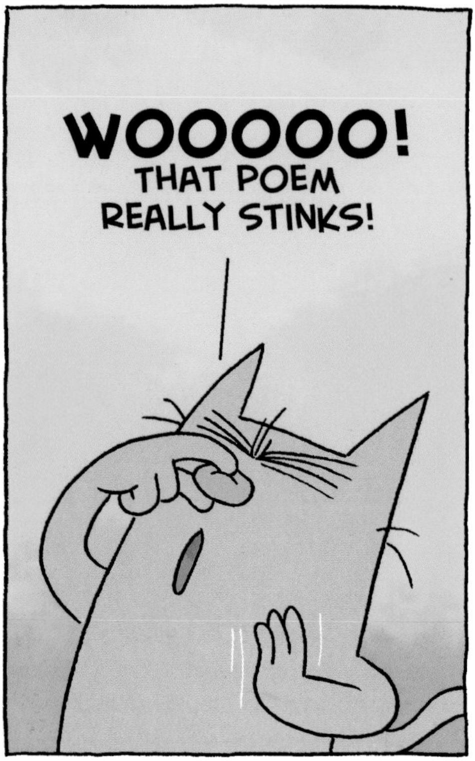
WOOOOO!
THAT POEM REALLY STINKS!

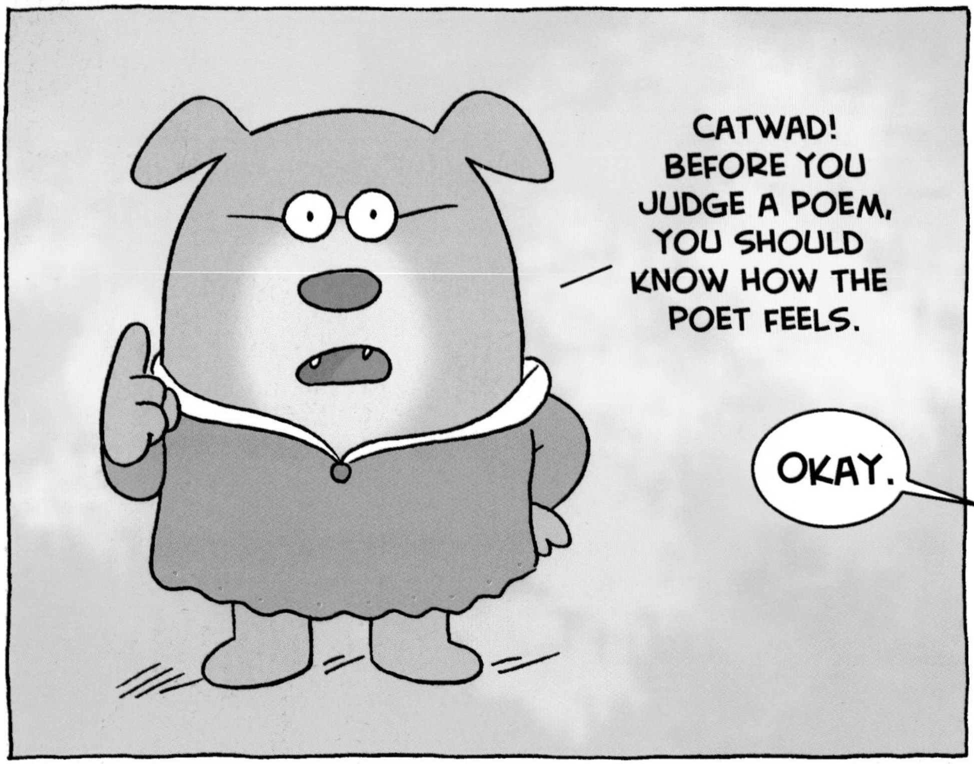
CATWAD! BEFORE YOU JUDGE A POEM, YOU SHOULD KNOW HOW THE POET FEELS.
OKAY.

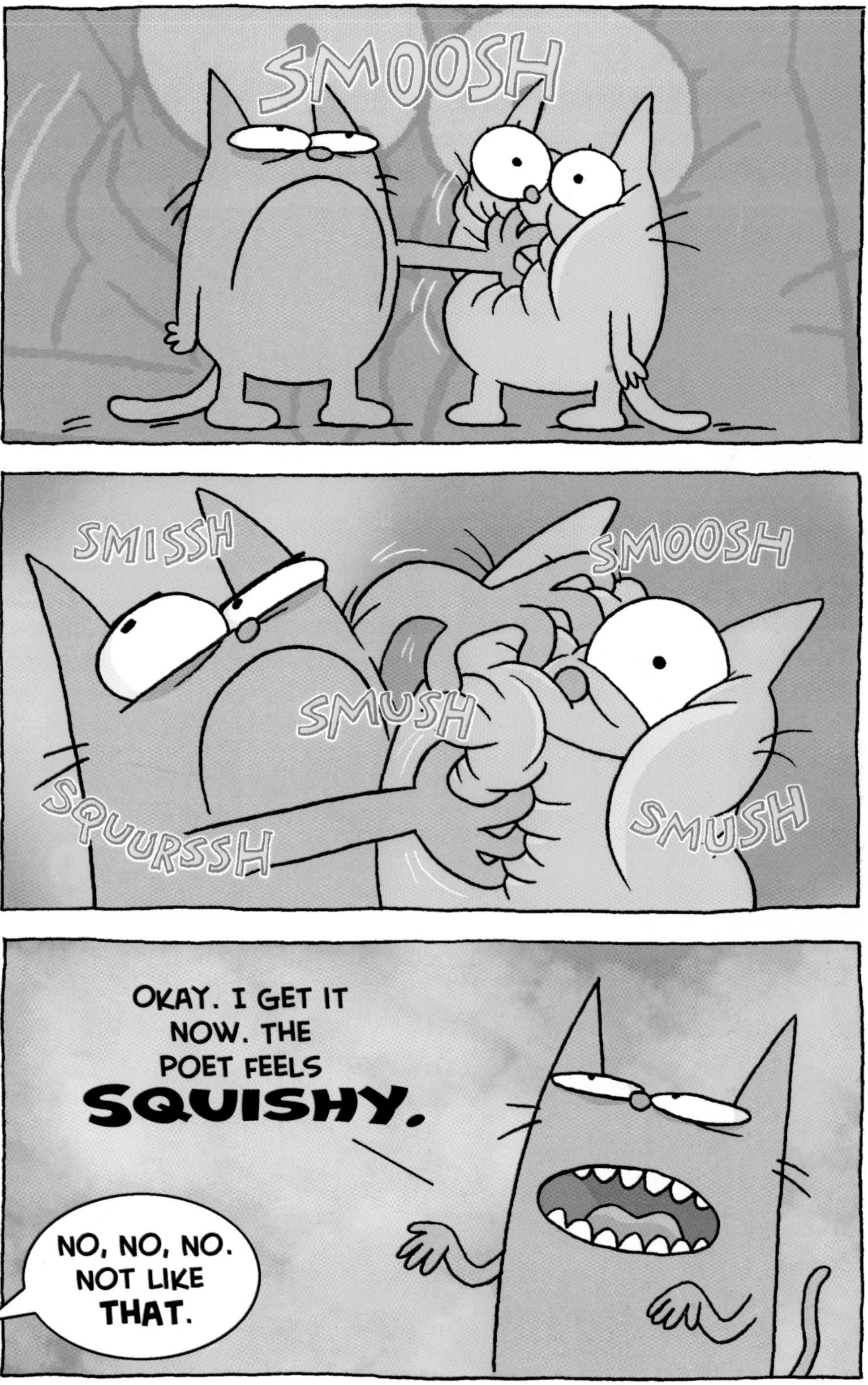
SMOOSH
SMISSH
SMOOSH
SMUSH
SQUURSSH
SMUSH
OKAY. I GET IT NOW. THE POET FEELS **SQUISHY.**
NO, NO, NO. NOT LIKE **THAT.**

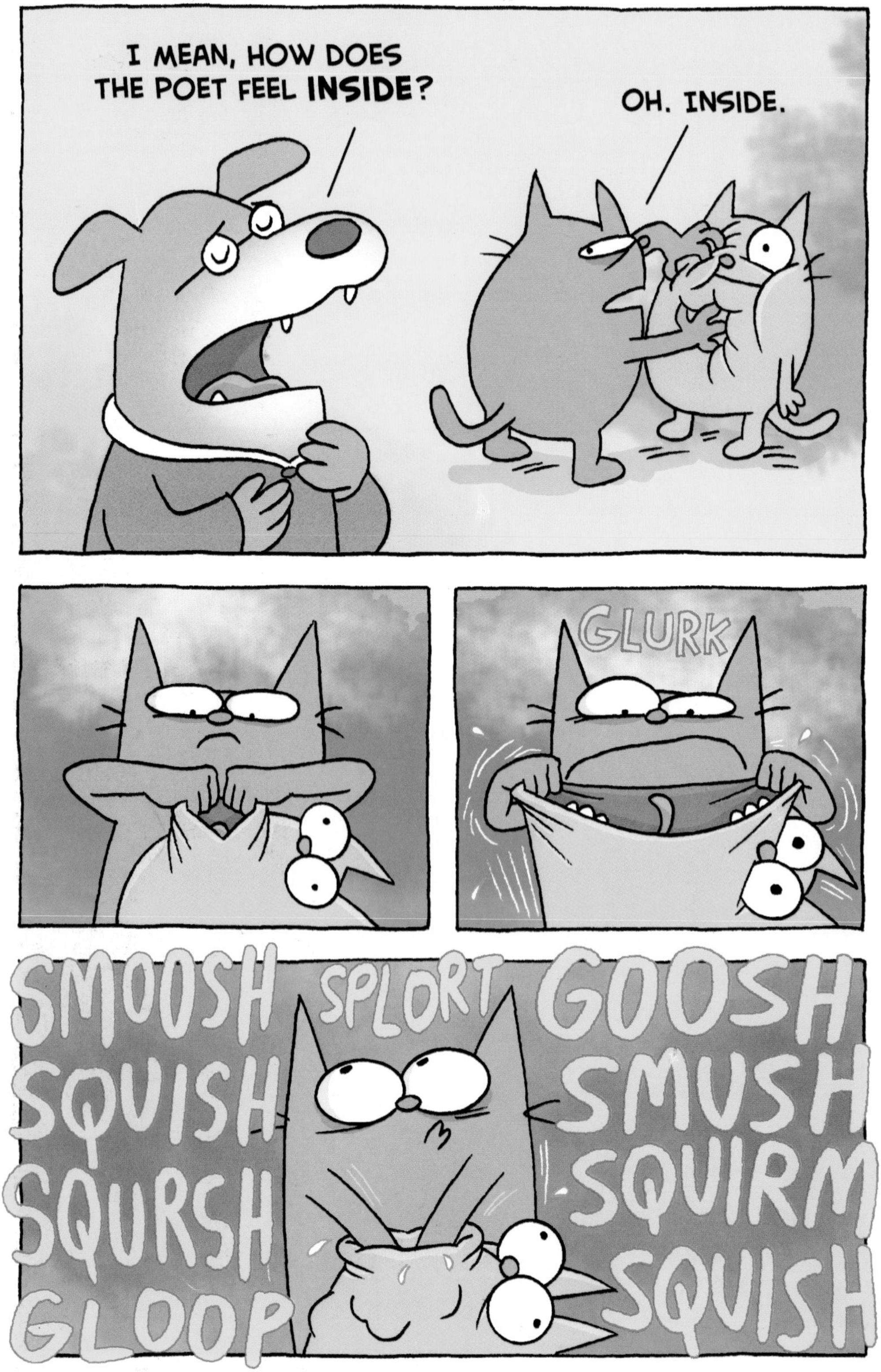
I MEAN, HOW DOES THE POET FEEL INSIDE?
OH. INSIDE.
GLURK
SMOOSH
SPLORT
GOOSH
SQUISH
SMUSH
SQURSH
SQUIRM
GLOOP
SQUISH

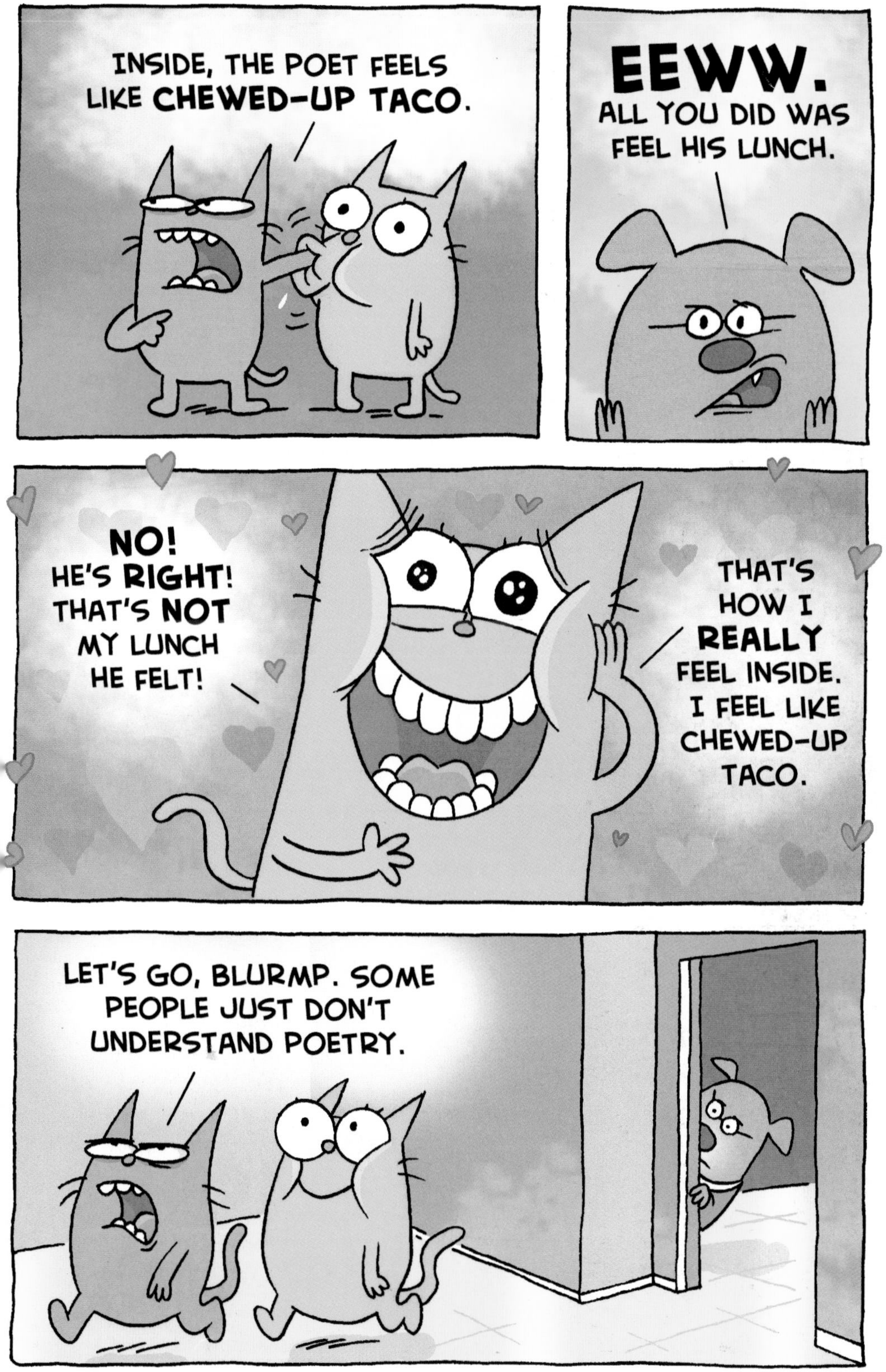
INSIDE, THE POET FEELS LIKE **CHEWED-UP TACO**.
EEWW.
ALL YOU DID WAS FEEL HIS LUNCH.
NO! HE'S **RIGHT**! THAT'S **NOT** MY LUNCH HE FELT!
THAT'S HOW I **REALLY** FEEL INSIDE. I FEEL LIKE CHEWED-UP TACO.
LET'S GO, BLURMP. SOME PEOPLE JUST DON'T UNDERSTAND POETRY.

TRASH

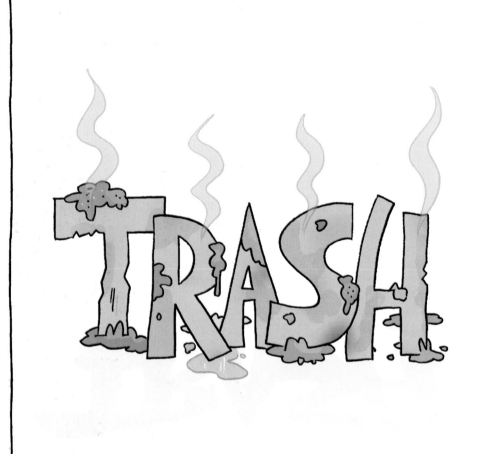

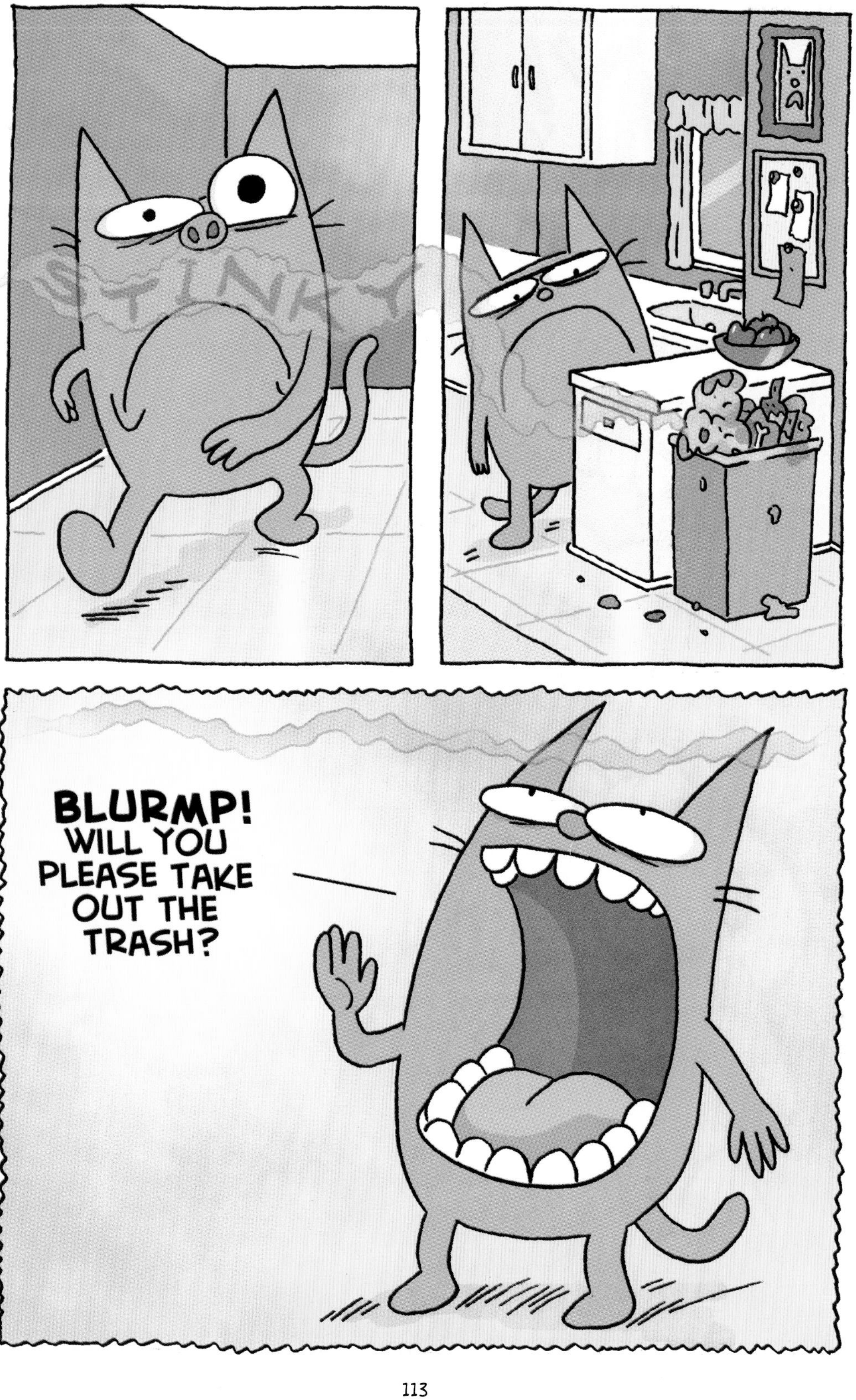
STINKY
BLURMP! WILL YOU PLEASE TAKE OUT THE TRASH?

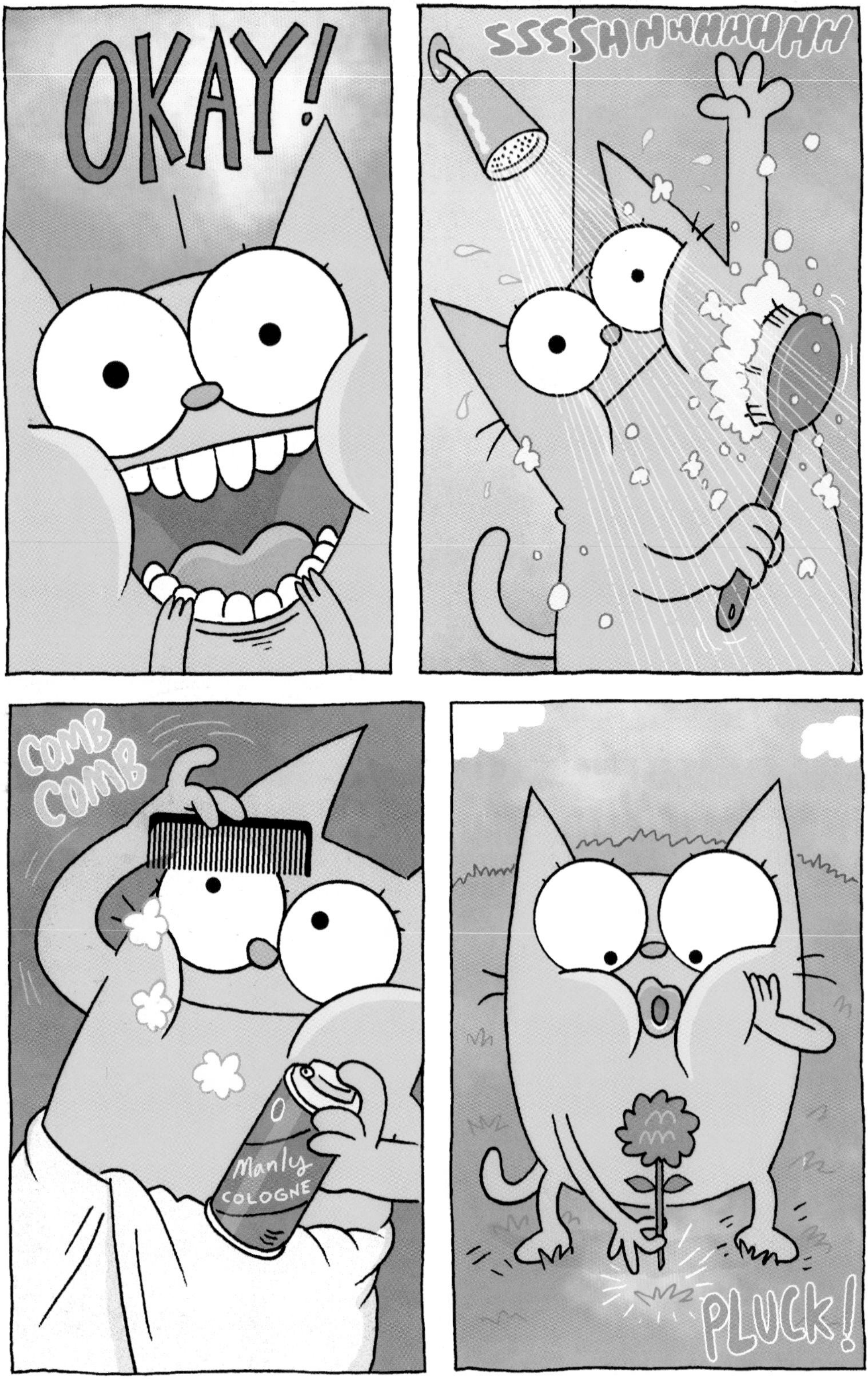
OKAY!
SSSSHHHHHHHH
COMB
COMB
Manly
COLOGNE
PLUCK!

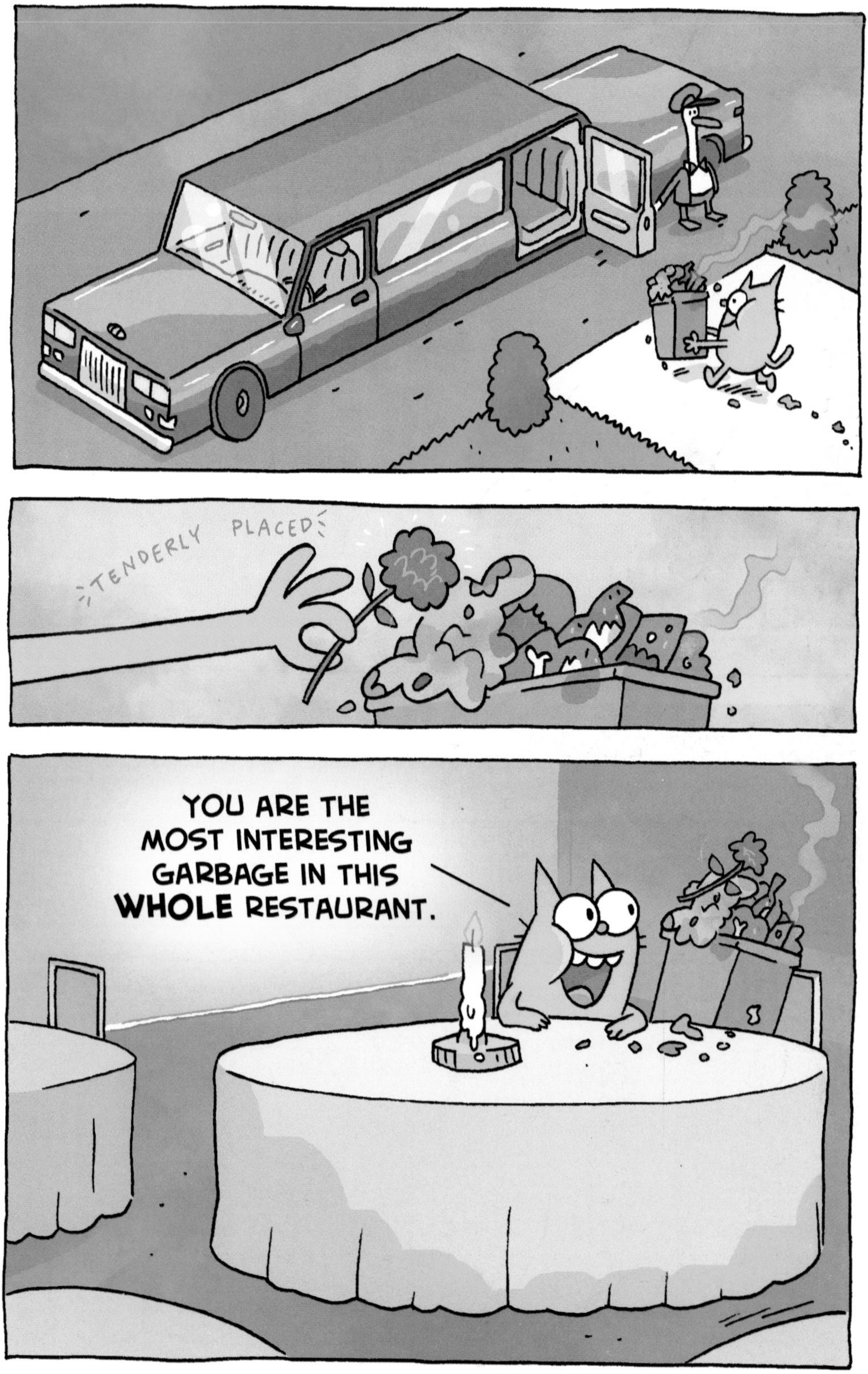
TENDERLY PLACED
YOU ARE THE MOST INTERESTING GARBAGE IN THIS WHOLE RESTAURANT.

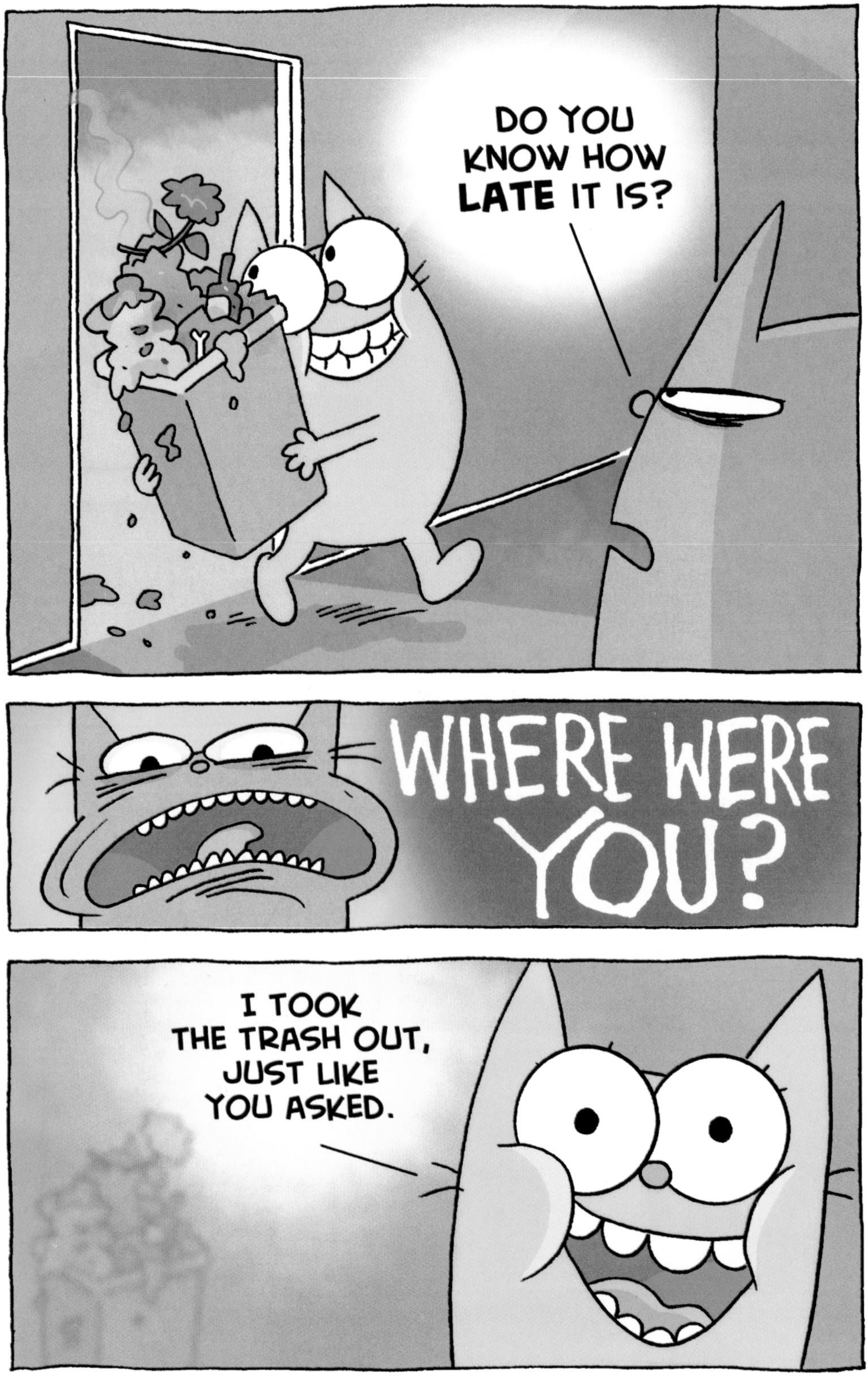
DO YOU KNOW HOW LATE IT IS?
WHERE WERE YOU?
I TOOK THE TRASH OUT, JUST LIKE YOU ASKED.

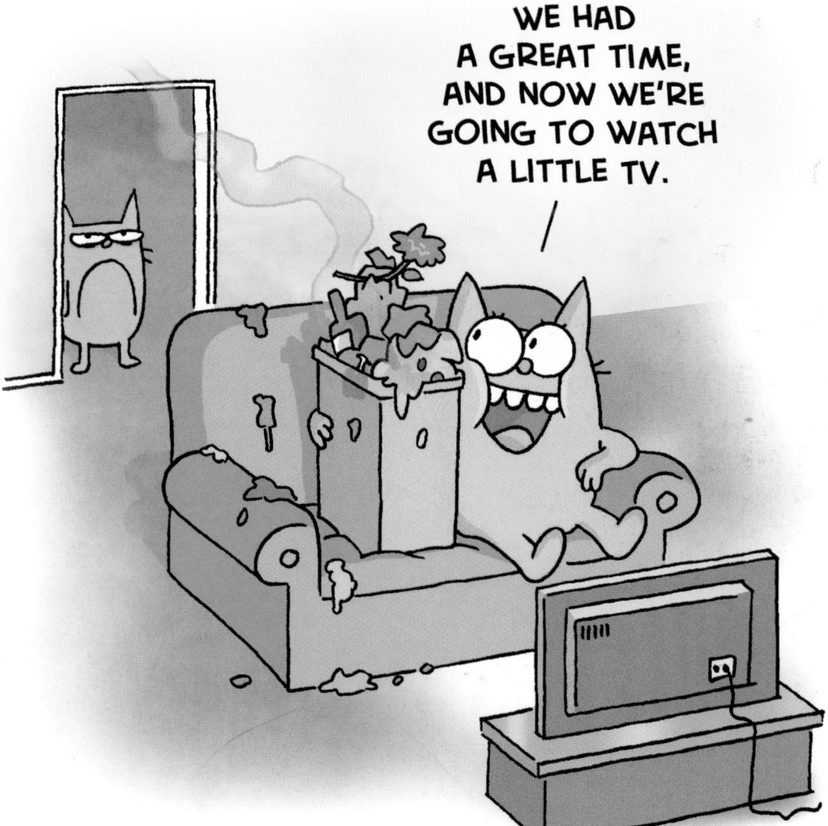
WE HAD
A GREAT TIME,
AND NOW WE'RE
GOING TO WATCH
A LITTLE TV.

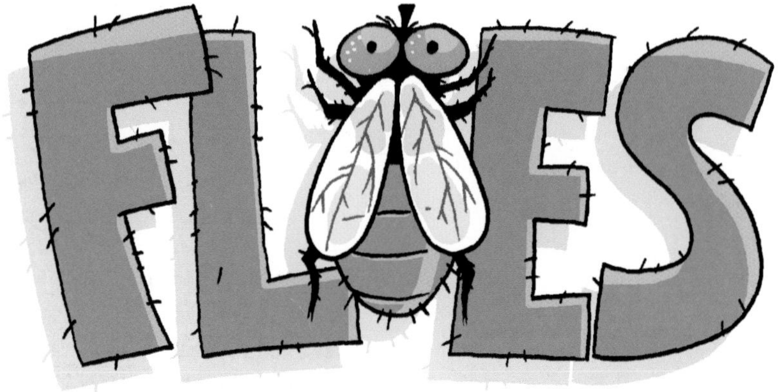FLIES

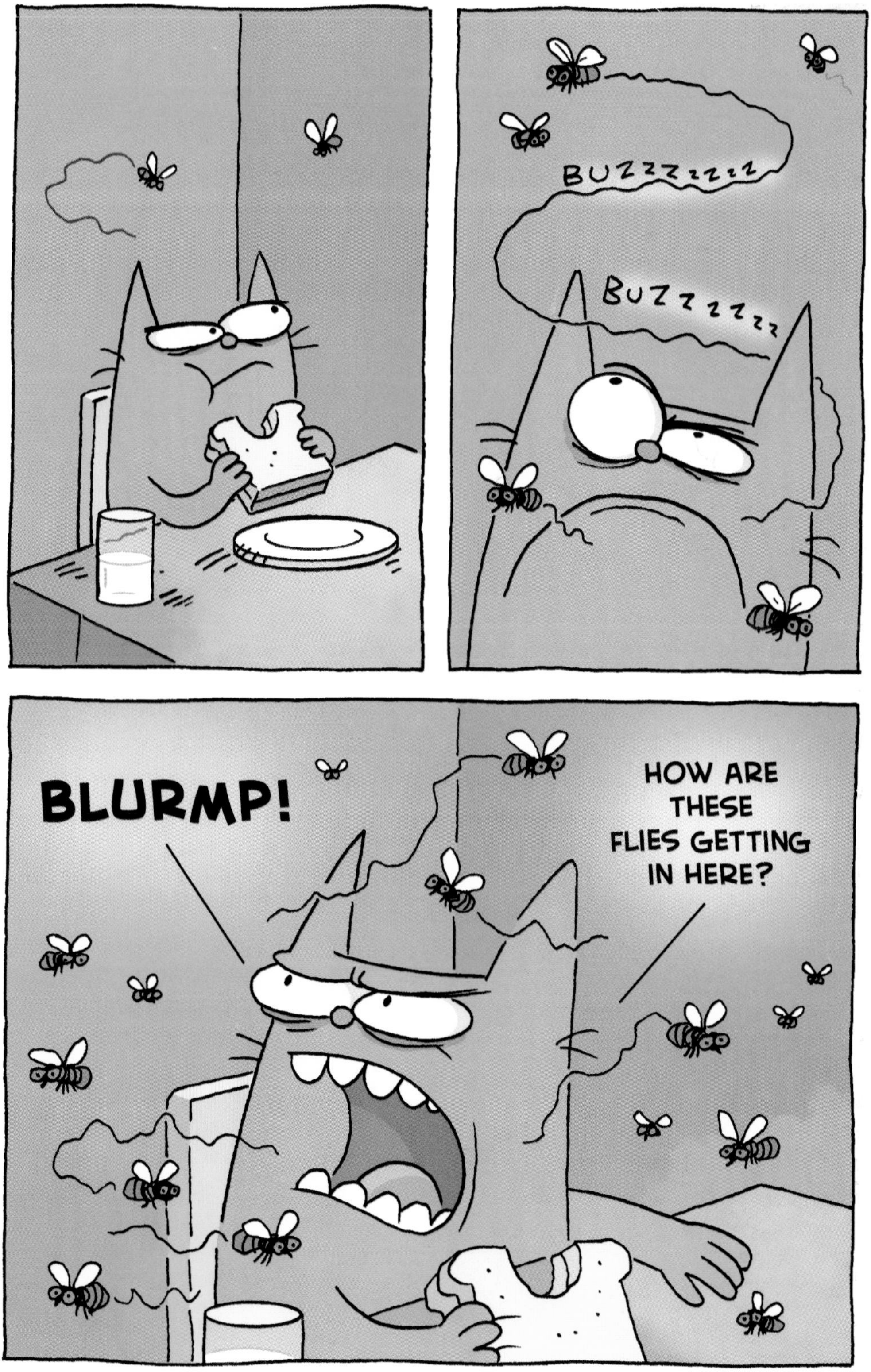
BUZZZzzzz
BUZZzzzzz
BLURMP!
HOW ARE THESE FLIES GETTING IN HERE?

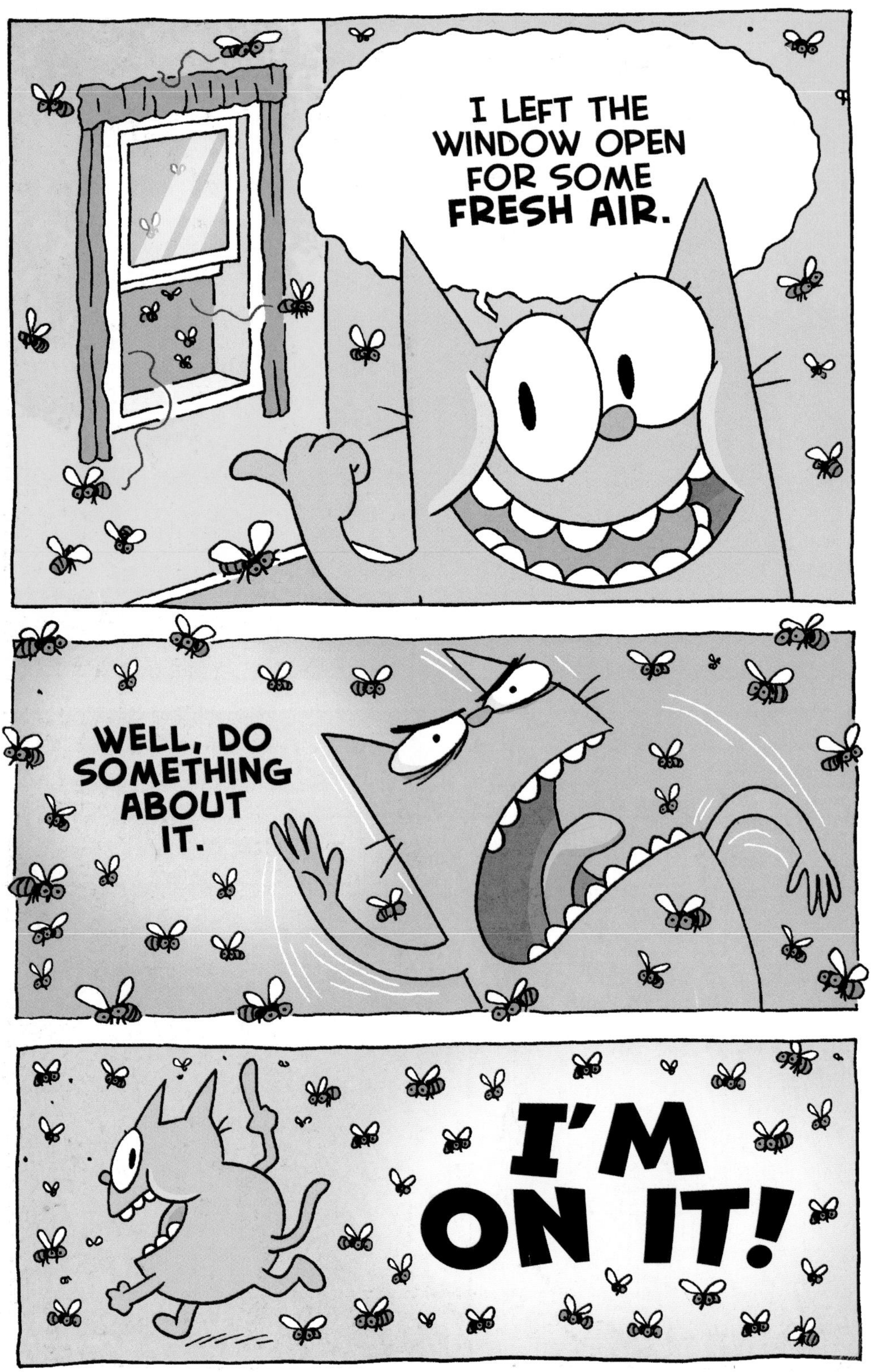
I LEFT THE WINDOW OPEN FOR SOME FRESH AIR.
WELL, DO SOMETHING ABOUT IT.
I'M ON IT!

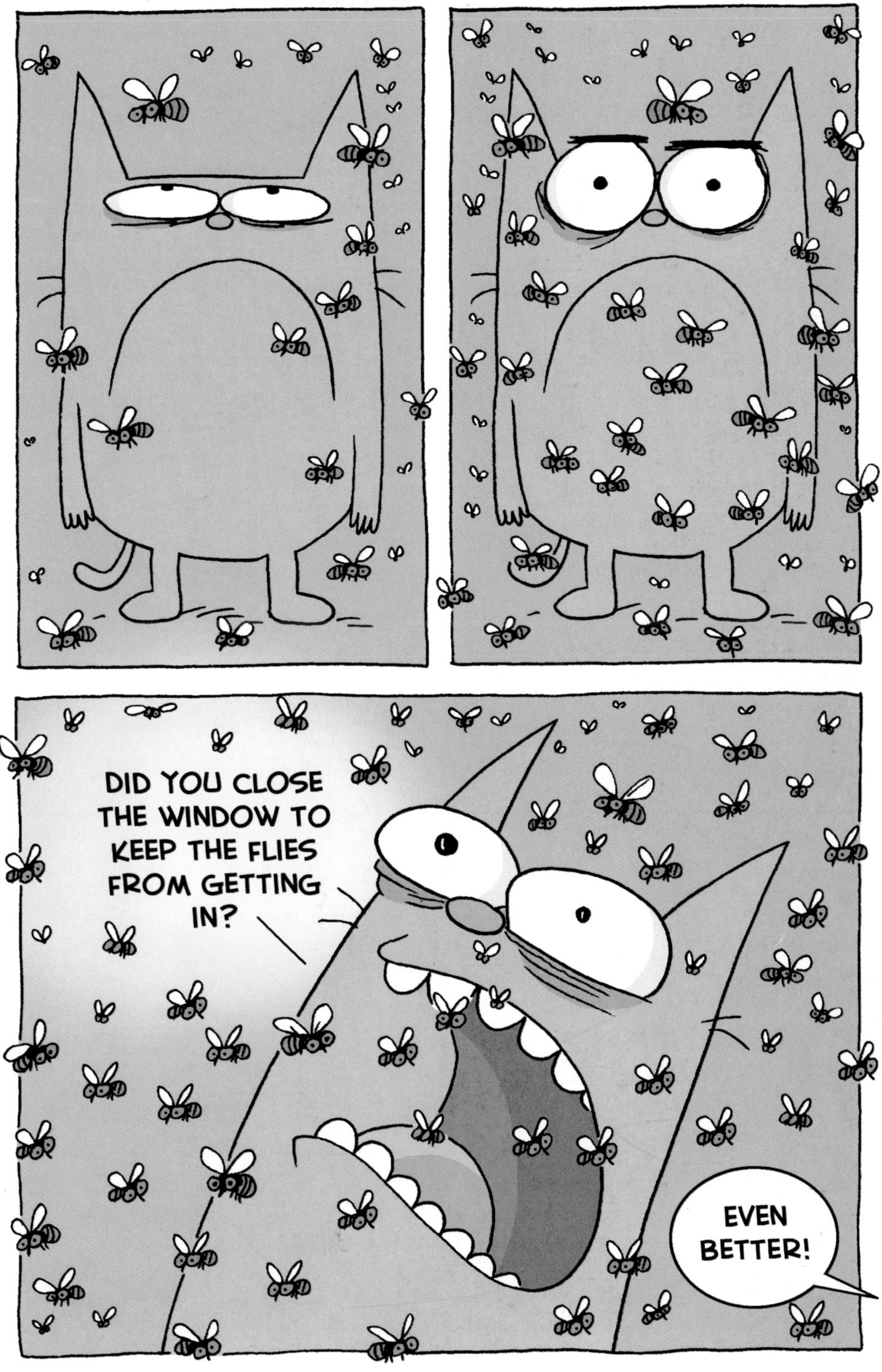
DID YOU CLOSE THE WINDOW TO KEEP THE FLIES FROM GETTING IN?
EVEN BETTER!

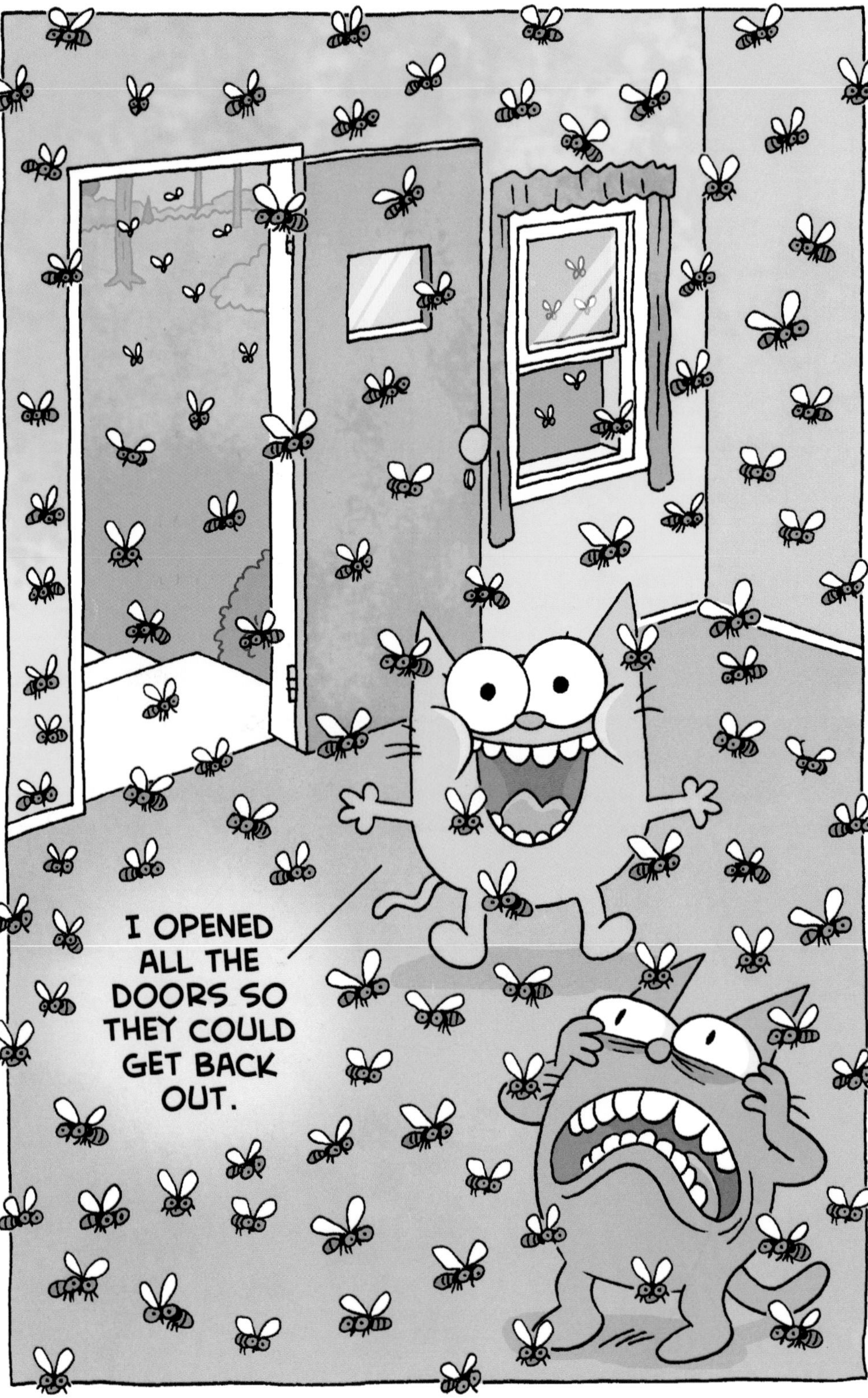
I OPENED ALL THE DOORS SO THEY COULD GET BACK OUT.

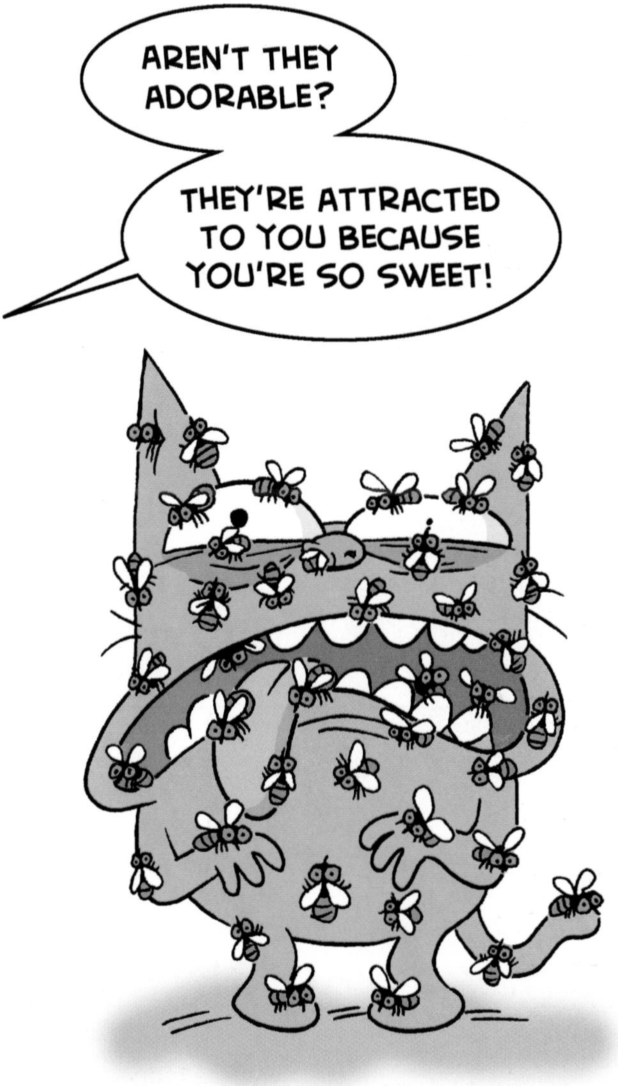
AREN'T THEY ADORABLE?
THEY'RE ATTRACTED TO YOU BECAUSE YOU'RE SO SWEET!

EVERYBODY KNOWS

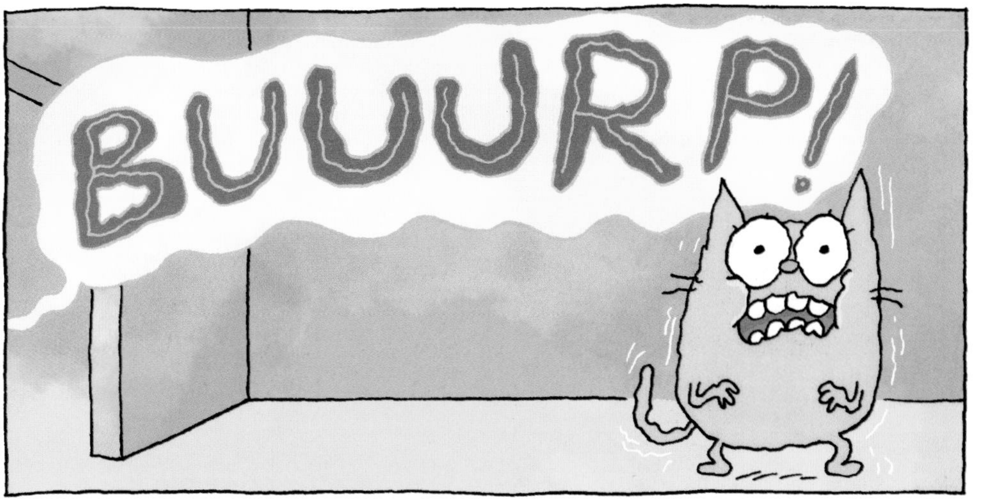
BUUURP!

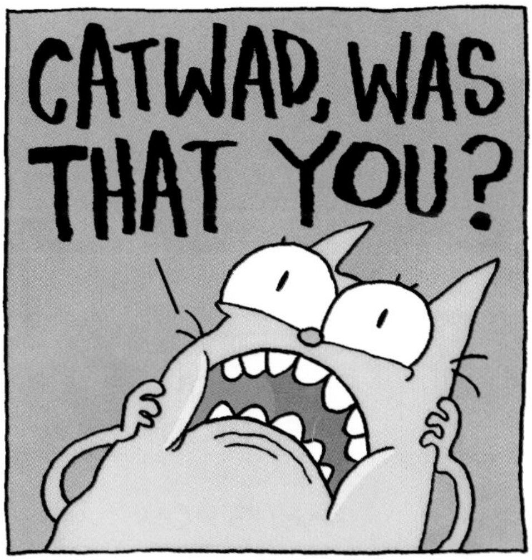
CATWAD, WAS THAT YOU?

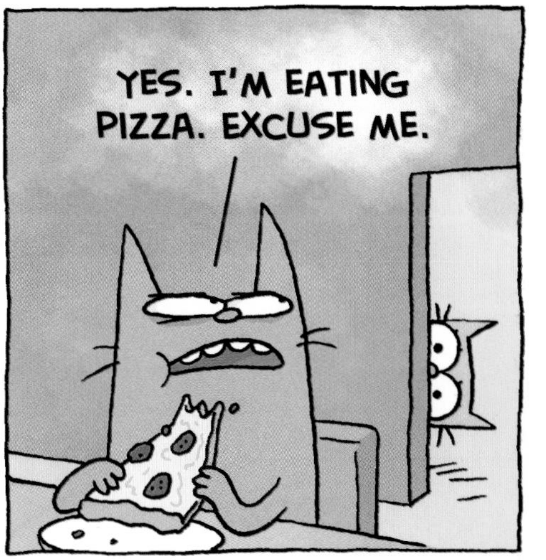
YES. I'M EATING PIZZA. EXCUSE ME.

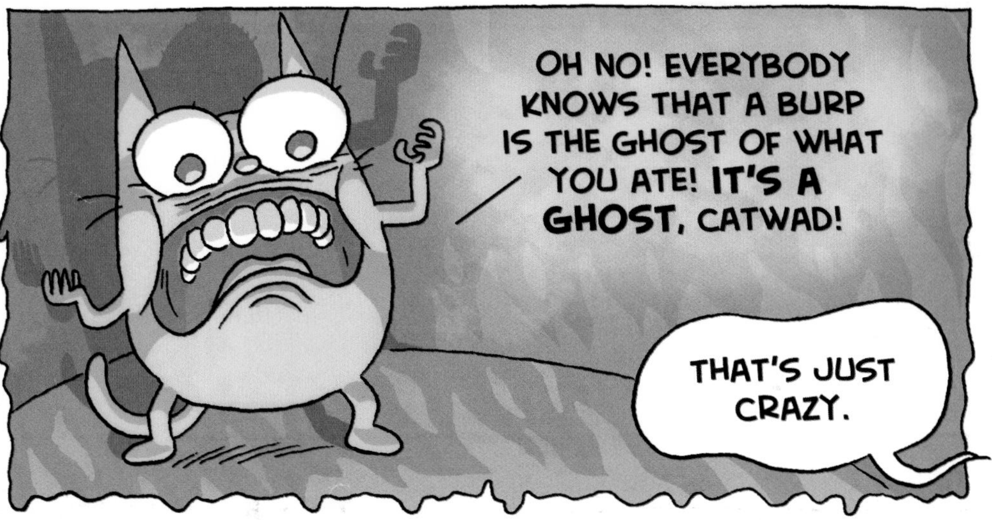
OH NO! EVERYBODY KNOWS THAT A BURP IS THE GHOST OF WHAT YOU ATE! **IT'S A GHOST**, CATWAD!
THAT'S JUST CRAZY.

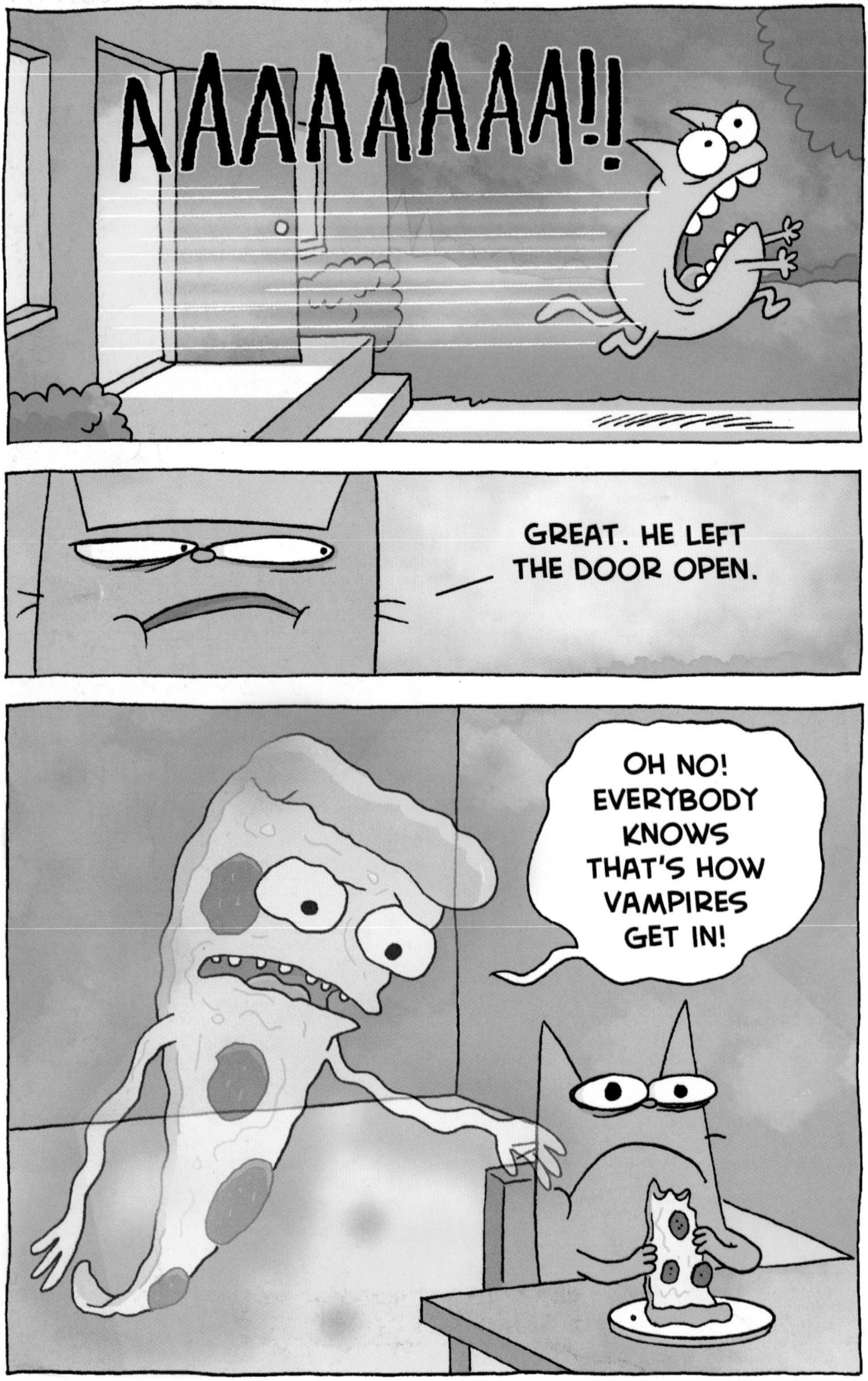
AAAAAAAA!!
GREAT. HE LEFT THE DOOR OPEN.
OH NO! EVERYBODY KNOWS THAT'S HOW VAMPIRES GET IN!

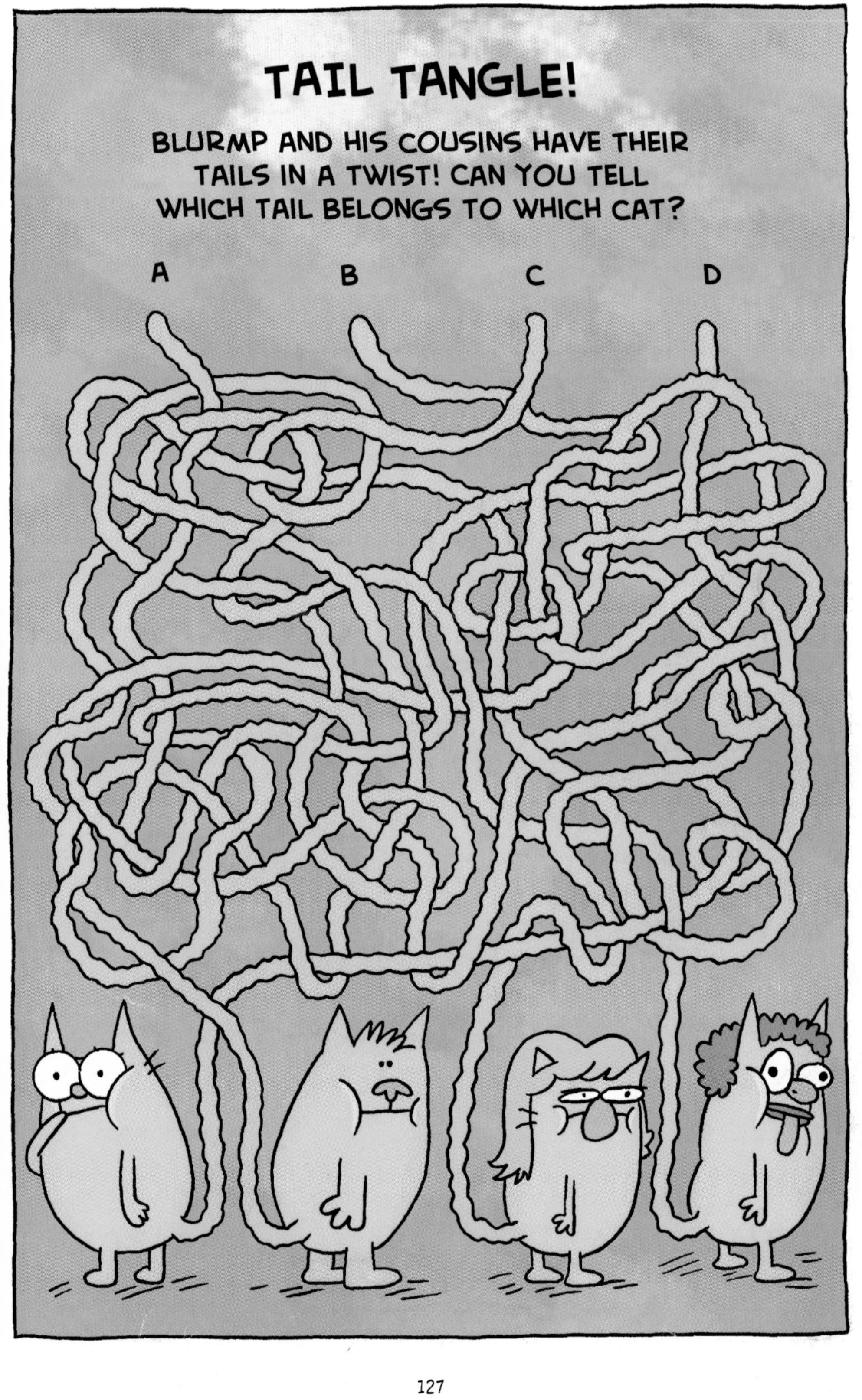
TAIL TANGLE!
BLURMP AND HIS COUSINS HAVE THEIR TAILS IN A TWIST! CAN YOU TELL WHICH TAIL BELONGS TO WHICH CAT?
A
B
C
D

WORD SEARCH!

CATWAD AND BLURMP HAVE HIDDEN SOME OF THEIR FAVORITE WORDS IN THE PUZZLE FOR YOU TO FIND! THEY CAN BE FRONTWARD OR BACKWARD, STRAIGHT, UP AND DOWN, OR DIAGONAL!

U	L	R	I	W	V	H	G	C	H	U	R	K	Y	M
G	N	U	S	A	D	N	E	S	S	P	F	L	F	I
P	S	H	F	S	D	Y	N	J	R	E	G	N	A	S
S	S	Q	A	W	P	W	F	E	O	B	X	S	W	E
S	O	P	D	P	A	Z	T	S	Q	Y	T	C	W	R
E	R	X	A	T	P	T	U	S	W	W	Y	G	S	Y
N	G	H	Q	R	Y	Y	L	G	F	I	P	R	M	S
D	L	O	A	F	Z	C	A	K	U	R	E	T	A	Y
N	R	R	W	U	W	X	W	Z	H	W	C	O	R	C
I	B	N	H	A	I	R	D	U	O	K	W	S	U	K
K	W	W	I	G	J	K	P	L	R	N	B	N	R	N
I	F	I	L	Z	F	S	F	L	P	P	B	E	J	P
F	J	F	J	K	R	A	X	B	Z	J	L	G	Q	E
U	V	N	I	C	E	D	A	I	K	D	E	V	E	I
L	U	C	B	V	B	L	Y	R	J	K	R	Y	N	D

ANGER
AWFUL
FLOWERS
GROSS
HAPPY
JOY

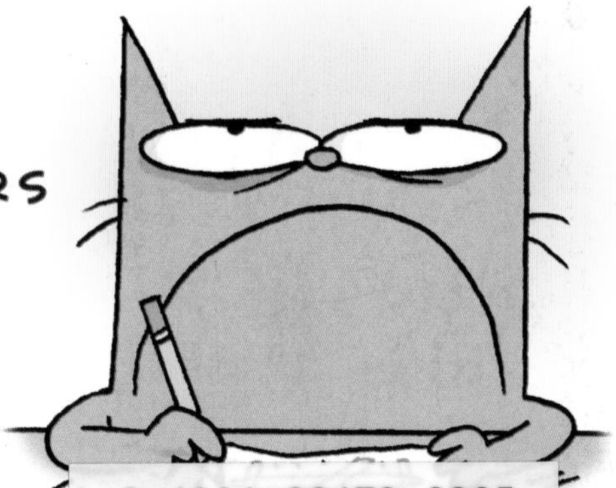

KINDNESS
MISERY
NICE
PRETTY
SADNESS
UNHAPPY